also by Daniel Vilmure
Life in the Land of the Living

DANIEL VILMURE

A NOVEL

TOBY'S LIE

SIMON & SCHUSTER
New York London Toronto
Sydney Tokyo Singapore

SIMON & SCHUSTER
Rockefeller Center
1230 Avenue of the Americas
New York, NY 10020

SIMON & SCHUSTER and colophon are registered
trademarks of Simon & Schuster Inc.

Designed by Levavi & Levavi

Manufactured in the United States of America

1 2 3 4 5 6 7 8 9 10

Library of Congress Cataloging-in-Publication Data
Vilmure, Daniel.
Toby's lie : a novel / Daniel Vilmure.
p. cm.   I. Title.
PS3572.I39T63 1995
813'.54—dc20   94-45602
CIP

ISBN 0-684-80204-X

Acknowledgments

To Marie-Joele Ingalls, my accomplice in sangría;
To Mary, my sister, five-snowballs-to-one;
To Marcus and Jean, two angels in New Orleans;
To Moshe and Bruce, roommates deluxe;
To Venkatalakshmi Bakshi, for the palmreading;
To Eric Steel, editor, overdue in Mexico;
To Mary Evans, midwife, who likes a good plot;
And finally to someone who doesn't have a name.
Thanks from my heart for your love and support.

To my mother and father, with love

There is a Smile of Love,
And there is a Smile of Deceit,
And there is a Smile of Smiles
In which these two Smiles meet.

WILLIAM BLAKE

I have never lied—except for maybe once. That lie is my own. And this is its story. . . .

MY MOTHER WAS moving out of the house, and she took me out of school that afternoon to help her.

"Family emergency," she told the principal's receptionist.

Family emergency . . .

It was no exaggeration.

Mom had decided—for reasons unknown to everybody but her—to take an efficiency apartment across town. It consisted of a little bed, in a little bedroom, with a little kitchenette and a black-and-white TV. It was the sort of thing Lucy and Ricky Ricardo would have hidden out in if Ricky had gotten in trouble with the mob. Out back was a yard with an old junked car. On top of it were lizards doing push-ups in the sun. Inside there were roaches, and a faucet keeping time. There was drummer boy wallpaper. My mother loved it.

"Bet you'll never guess how much I'm paying for this place."

"*You're* paying? I thought maybe *they* were paying *you.*"

They referred to students at the local university. My mother used to make pin money allowing them to perform strange experiments on her. One month, for the med school, she walked around with a plastic tube inserted down her throat. Mom lost twenty pounds, made $1,200 ("That's a lot of fucking pins," my father observed), and wore a special T-shirt that read: I'M WITH ALIEN.

"It's a steal," Mom said. "I got it for a song."

"But you can't sing."

Mom touched her nose: "Exactly."

Everything Mom owned, and then some, had been packed with anal-compulsive care into six cardboard boxes in the back-seat of her car. Only the unruly hem of her wedding gown man-aged to announce itself in a yellow swell of silk. When Mom tried to tamp it down, it only bulged more—until at last she wrestled it out and slung it round her shoulders like a predator's kill.

"Ridiculous things, wedding dresses," she proclaimed. The gown responded in hisses of lace. "Awkward as a parachute, ugly as a circus tent, impossible to move in—"

"Isn't that the idea?"

Mom snorted once and plumped the dress down on the porch. It stood, then it sank like a swooning girl at mass. I plucked the veil up and draped it round my forehead.

"The neighbors'll think you're *gay*," my mother scolded, and brushed the brown hair from my straw-colored eyes.

I didn't say a word. There were other veils around me. For one: I *was* gay. Not that it really mattered. And what neighbors there were were nowhere to be seen. The apartment was con-cealed behind a tangle of palmettos at the end of a dirt road bor-dered by a fence. It was creepy. There were used car parts everywhere. And bits of broken mirror. And mosquitoes. Great big ones.

"Mom, are you a drug dealer?"

"No, I'm not a drug dealer."

"This is the sort of place that a dealer would live in."

"How would you know?"

"I've seen a lot of movies."

"You've seen too many movies. Come help me with this box."

If my mother was a dealer, she was dealing heavy drugs. Her boxes bore the weight of seventeen years of marriage. There were books, and eight-tracks, and clothes, and tarnished silver. There were seventeen years of canceled checks and tax receipts. There were old sewing patterns, and shoes, and journal entries. There was crystal wrapped in bubble-pack and chintzy jewelry.

"What's in this one?" I asked.

It was light as I lifted.

"Open it and see," she told me. "Open it and see."

I set the box down on a bruise-colored stain that spread like a Rorschach across my mother's carpet. From the silence that sanctified the air as I knelt, I expected something more than what the box contained. I felt like a kid promised something at Christmas, a kid denied a promise: I felt ripped off. Still, I tried, but couldn't stifle a laugh when the box opened up on my father's dirty laundry.

"He's helpless, he is," my mother explained, squatting down beside me and rifling through the pile. She fondled a pair of skidmarked underwear like a buyer for a Saks Fifth Ave. for fetishists.

"Mom, that's disgusting!"

"These are your father's!"

"I don't care if they belong to Mother Teresa! They're filthy, Ma! Jesus! Put 'em down, will ya?"

She strolled about the kitchenette, twirling them around her finger.

"Can't imagine what your poor dad'll ever do without me. Can't cook. Can't sew. Can't even tie a tie. Every morning, you know, I tie his tie for him."

"He ties my tie for me, Ma."

"Ha! That's what *you* think!"

With a flick of the wrist she pitched the undies in the sink and ran water on them, and stared out the window. I came up behind her and put my arms around her. Everything felt like an Afterschool Special.

"Mom, why are you leaving?"

"I don't know," she said. Her voice was in splinters. She was trying not to cry.

"Are you having an affair?"

"I should be so lucky!"

"Is Dad?"

"Who knows? Who cares!"

She was bawling.

"What's going on, Ma? This is weird. I can't handle it."

"You'll just have to handle it," she said, and stiffened up.

"Are you getting a divorce?"

She sniffed. "We're too Catholic."

"I know."

"Little heathen."

"Would you like to?"

"I don't know."

"Do you love Dad?"

"Yes."

"Did he hurt you?"

"*To*-by!"

"You can tell me! I'm here! I'm right here!"

"*My pre-cious boy!*"

Mom hugged me then. Her tits squished against me. It was sort of incestuous, but kinda nice, too. I held her for a while, and she clenched her arms around me, and then we started waltzing, very slowly, on the tile. Mom had taught me to waltz the week before, in the garage, for the prom, which I had to take a fat girl to. I wanted to take my boyfriend, a swimmer. We even talked about it. We would make the evening news. As I danced with my mother I shut my eyes tight and pretended I was dancing with my boyfriend, the swimmer. I imagined it was his body I was holding, not hers. Mom didn't notice. It was all very sexy. I didn't even register the roaches on the walls. At some point our waltzing unwound into a boxstep and I started humming "Red River

Valley." I pretended I was Henry Fonda in *The Grapes of Wrath*, and I cupped my mother's chin in my hands, like Ma Joad's, and I crooned like Tommy does toward the end of the movie:

> *Come and sit by my side if you love me,*
> *Do not has-ten to bid me adieu,*
> *Just re-mem-ber the Red Ri-ver Valley,*
> *And the cowboy that loves you so true. . . .*

Then we started laughing. Everything would be all right.

 "PROMISE YOU WON'T tell your father where I am?" Mom said as she abandoned me at our abandoned home.
"Uh-huh, I promise."
She touched her nose: "Our secret!"

 "WHERE'S YOUR MOTHER, Toby?"
I was playing dumb. I was sitting on the frontporch, on the porchswing, swinging. I was reading *The Idiot*. Dad had finished work.
"Don't know, Pop. Didn't pick me up from school. Had to catch a ride with—"
"That's damned funny." Dad scratched his head and did Freudian things with his tie. He made a jingling noise with his shiny metal car keys. "Probably at the store. Whatcha reading?"
"Dostoev—"
"Don't forget to cut the grass."
The door shut behind him.

THAT NIGHT, AT four in the morning, Dad woke me. "Toby?" he said, slugging my shoulder. "Toby? Tobias? Are you awake?" Pop kept slugging me, harder and harder. My shoulder was swelling. "You up, boy? You up?"

At last I sat up in my bed and looked at him.

"Yes, I am up." I rubbed my shoulder. "What *is* it?"

"Can't sleep," Dad said, and wiped his nose with his forearm. The hall light was on. It made a halo around him. "Your mother's not home."

"She isn't?"

"She isn't. And hell if I know where my baby girl could be." Dad ran his fingers through his hair like a model. He sneezed and he hiccuped. "Excuse us," he said.

"Why don't you have another Bud Light or something?"

"We're out."

"But we had two sixes in the box!"

"Uh-huh." Dad's eyes, in the darkness, went glassy. "I drank them," he said. "I blew chunks, Tobe."

"I'm sorry."

Dad sat on the edge of my bed in his misery. He was staring at his hands. He was shivering a little.

"I think that she left us."

"What makes you say that, Dad?"

"I got these antennae."

Dad pointed at his head.

"What antennae?" I asked.

His hands grabbed for my hands. He pressed my fingers to his skull. I was Phrank the Phrenologist.

"Don't feel any antennae."

"A husband's got antennae. Like radar. Like bats."

I flapped the sheets and started squeaking.

"Toby, this is serious. Should we call the police?"

"You've come home lots of times this late before."

"That's different."

"Why's it different?"

"I'm a *guy.*"

"I don't get it."

"*Guys,* you know," Dad began, and then spluttered. "*It's a guy thing.*"

"Oh."

"Like *Monday Night Football.*"

I turned on the bedside lamp and he shouted. His hand shot out and he slapped the lamp over.

"Too bright," he told me.

" 'That's coming out of your allowance.' "

"Don't be a smartass."

We sat there in the darkness.

"Are you drunk, Dad?"

"Yes."

"Are you very drunk?"

He nodded.

"If I ask you something, Dad, will you tell me the truth?"

"Turn the lamp on."

"But—but you just knocked it over!"

"I hate being honest in the dark. Turn it on."

I picked up the lamp and switched it on on the table. Dad's face swam into focus like a scruffy sea monster's.

"Are you having an affair?"

"Am I having a *what?*"

"An affair. Are you boinking some gorgeous young woman?"

"May God strike me dead if I so much as ever breathed at any woman other than your lovely blessed mother."

"Can I take that as a no?"

"You can take that as a no."

I let the silence settle, then I focused on him harder.

"Is Mom having an affair?"

"She wouldn't do that to me."

"Does she love you?"

"She's a liar if she says that she don't. Have you talked to her?"

"No."

"Do you know where she is?"

I said that I didn't.

"Are you lying to me, Tobe?"

"Would I lie to you?"

"Tobe, we dads . . . have antennae."

"Like bats?"

Dad squeaked. "I wanna show you something."

We stumbled from my bedroom across the hall into their bedroom, which was lit up and gaudy as a Las Vegas lounge.

"Got school in the morning."

"Fuck school," Dad grumbled. "Your mother's gone AWOL. This is fam'ly. It's important."

Strewn about the white disheveled sheet atop their mattress were a thousand different Kodak Instamatic shots of them. Mom and Dad at the beach at Daytona. Mom and Dad at Disney World. Mom and Dad smooching. Mom and Dad hiding in a Kmart photo booth.

"Where'd you get these pictures, Dad?"

"In the closet. They're the only things your mother didn't steal."

Dad grabbed my shoulders and wheeled me around until I was facing two gutted closets. There, in the space where Mom's things used to be, hung hangers and dusty, denuded wooden shelves.

"She's gone all right," I said, turning to him.

Dad was looking at the Kodak Instamatics on the bed.

"See this one?" he asked, bending wretchedly over. It was Mom in a little red choo-choo, at a fairground. Dad sat behind her, leering like a letch. They were young and horny. They were beautiful and handsome. It was the sort of picture that made you wonder what their hands were doing. "That was at the Florida State Fair," Dad confided. "An hour after we took that picture, we made love in somebody's Chevrolet. I remember the way the upholstery smelled. And Jimi Hendrix was on—'Crosstown

Traffic,' I think. You were conceived then. I knew it when we came. It was like we'd won the lotto. You'd better go to bed now."

I squeezed Dad's arm and left him staring at the pictures. I went back to my room, and I put some Hendrix on, and stared up at the ceiling. But I couldn't sleep. I lay there listening to Dad shift about, thinking of him and Mom fucking in a Chevy. *Who was better in bed, Mom or Dad? I wondered.* I was sure Mom was. She had the bigger soul. But Dad loved her more, and she was all he had, so probably he was better: he was more appreciative. I knew they still fucked. Sometimes I could hear them. They were into each other. They were constantly flirting. And I believed Dad when he swore that he hadn't been cheating, and I knew he wasn't lying when he said Mom hadn't either. So what *was* it? Should I tell him where she was? All I had to do was march into his bedroom. I'd tell him, he'd hug me, he'd fetch the car keys, we'd drive rakishly and recklessly to Mom's drug dealer pad, he'd plead with her a little, and then we'd bring her home. It was easy. It was cinchy. It was cake on a plate. So what was I waiting for? Why'd I hesitate?

"Dad?"

I was standing before him in their bedroom. He lay wrecked amid a troubled sea of Instamatic snapshots.

"What is it, Tobe?"

"I've got something to say."

"Well then, spill it."

"Sleep tight."

I kissed him.

"Sleep tight, kiddaroono."

I left. I felt like shit.

 DAD WOKE ME up at six in the morning so I could go to mass with him at St. Patrick's Catholic Church. It wasn't enough that I went to a Jesuit school—which was systematically undermining whatever faith I might have had to begin with— Dad insisted I accompany him to morning mass. I would kneel with him. I would sing with him. I would get the words to the Apostle's Creed wrong with him. It was a Catholic sort of bonding. I liked shaking hands at the Sign of the Cross. It was whack. "Hello there, Dad, peace be with you!" "Well, howdy there, son, and also with *you!*" When we shook, I'd do funky things with my grip. I'd make a spastic pumping motion like a lonely donor heart. I'd do the Cold Fish and make my hand a soggy dead thing. I'd run my middle finger seductively along his palm and wink like a prostitute and nod at the confessional. Dad ate it up; he was a sucker for irreverence. Morning mass acted on him just like laughing gas. If we were stationed for precaution at the rear of the church, I'd perform all the hymns like Marilyn Monroe, churning my hips and puffing out phantom tits. I'd always suspected Dad knew I was gay; he was easier about it, less uptight than Mom. I'd close the Ave Maria with *boop-boop-bee-doop!*, and Dad would choke my hand and say, "Jesus, would you *stop* it?" It wouldn't be long before I had him in hysterics, cheeks flushing purple, chest hyperventilating. "Last time I take you with me!" he'd mutter through his molars as we knelt down together at the slick communion rail. Once I plucked the Eucharist off my sticky tongue and pressed the pasty wafer to Dad's fat butt as he waddled down the aisle past appalled communicants. The altar boys died. The pastor called us over after.

"Mr. Sligh, if y'insist on bringing this boy with yar tuh mass, yar mustn't parmit 'im t'engage in such sarkrilege!"

"Hear that, Tobe? Say you're sorry, asswipe."

"I'm sorry, Fr. Tierney."

I really was, too.

I liked mass: I liked the clothes, I liked Jesus, I liked the songs, I liked the incense. I liked the dowdy widows with their impossible blue hair, like they soaked their ancient heads in Ty-D-Bol overnight. I liked the quiet of the church, and the cold smell of marble. I liked the icy water waiting in the baptismal font. What I liked especially was a priest named Fr. Diaz, a yummy young Spaniard straight out of *Latin GQ*. He played tennis with the best-looking guys in the parish, and I always saw him at the rectory court patting their asses with the head of his racket. I used to get a hard-on talking to him in confession. Fr. Diaz's words, warm and minty, blew at you through the grate, like a television lover's flawless morning breath. He wore his Izod shirtsleeves bunched tight against his biceps and always smelled of cigarettes and soap and Aramis. And he'd look at you like he was looking at himself, with the sort of silky bedroom smile that said, "We are a*dor*able." Too bad morning mass featured awful Fr. Tierney, a flatulent myopic wannabe Celt-poser who spoke with a sham brogue and nose-picked through the homily. Every time Tierney went digging for gold, I used to throw Dad a playful elbow in the ribs: "There he goes, Pop! Pick me out a Cadillac!" And I'd think of Fr. Diaz, in his Calvins, at the rectory, dark arms around a pillow, soaking up his beauty sleep.

"Peace be with you, Toby," my father said to me.

"Peace be with ya, Pops."

Our clammy hands unjoined.

 "IS LONELINESS GOD'S WAY *of punishing us for doubting His existence?*"

This was the question a visiting Jesuit had put before the student body that morning at Convocation. Except for me—who had been flogging spiritually dead horses since the tightened sphincter muscles of the early, early morning—we all sat slumped in the chapel half asleep, suffering in our Action Slacks, struggling with our starched collars, silent-but-deadlies wafting with redolent abandon up from squeaky pews to a sun-

bedizened altar. The priest was a tall, alarmingly gaunt fellow
with a Louisiana accent and a wasted constitution. I had never
seen him before, and I didn't catch his name when our principal—the Rev. Anthony McDuffy, S.J.—introduced him. But
from the way several teachers sat up at attention when, with as-
sistance, he ascended the pulpit, I knew he must have been a
familiar face to some. Even Ian, my boyfriend, the swimmer I
planned to accompany to the senior prom, straightened himself
and cocked his ear like a puppy, as if beyond the grave Barbara
Woodhouse tooted whistles. I felt a flush of envy: Ian had never
cocked his pretty ear before like that for me or, for that matter,
anybody. And he looked really gorgeous sitting there at attention: his carotids pulsing against his laundered Oxford, his just-
moussed crew-cut Olympic-trial hair aimed in aimless arrows at
a frieze of St. Sebastian, his rheumy glass eye angled thankfully
away. Ian was bright, the brightest boy in our class, one of these
freaks with genius coded in their genes. And he came across as
husky and indelibly straight; he excelled in nearly everything
but sexual expression. I, shameless *trop moderne* hussy that I
was, had been attempting, with some success, to coax him out of
his shell and, not without his shellshocked consent, into mine.
We'd been friends ever since his arrival from New Orleans and
had fooled around, well, you know, more than just a little. And
we really loved each other, though nobody would have guessed
it. We played it cool at school: all high-fives and hardy jock talk.
The only thing we didn't blow for each other was our cover.

    *"Does God confront us with human isolation as a terrorist tac-
tic to spur our flagging faith?"*

    It was a nifty theory, this loneliness one. I'd never thought
of God in such pathetic terms before. In fact, I'd never
thought of God that much at all. I was Jesus-fixated; I as-
sumed God *was.* And the way this Jesuit put his argument
across—his starved face pleading in a pained, sustained way,
not gloating in the usual pseudo-intellectual splendor of the
polished and pedantic Jesuitical wanker—made you want to

listen, made you want to take it in. He was one of those scary, charismatic fathers—seductive, hypnotic, alluring, all-consuming. A cross between the Reverend Billy Graham and Billy Idol. And apart from the fact that his body was collapsing, that he looked like a scarecrow whose pegs were coming loose and who would tumble any moment from his ramshackle cross, he had the careworn beauty of anything dying.

"Boys your age are too young to know the meaning of the word 'loneliness,' " he continued, looking more emaciated with each relinquished breath. "But a time will arrive in your complicated lives in which loneliness, with its endless corridor of empty rooms, will inhabit your hearts, will become reality. Will you wander the desolated mansion of your days as errantly, as despondently as God wanders His when He beholds a people that has turned its back on Him? Will you realize, as Jesus came to realize in the desert, that isolation teaches us to measure our true selves? To know loneliness, boys, is to know one's soul; and to know one's soul is to know one's God. Isolation may appear to be a trial at first, but through it we endure His most blessed, abiding test. Through it we commune with the Spirit who created us, who longs for our reunion, who suffers in our absence."

A far cry, indeed, from Tierney's crack-o'-dawn special about "Sinatra's famous ant" and the rubber tree plant: "Just what gives that parky little varmint such spirit?" I wished Dad were there so I could dig him in the ribcage and dolly-talk like Marilyn, all google-eyes and giggles: "Golly, Fr. Tierney! *Wubber twee plants?* I never knew prophylactics *gwew* on *twees!*" But I sat there, alone, God resounding in my head like a smooth pebble dropped from an impossible height into a pool of water too dark and too shallow.

✸ LECTURES THAT MORNING went by in slow motion; it was the last week of classes, and we were slouching toward the finish line. On this side of the tape were our teachers and ourselves, as familiar to one another as old shoes or married couples; on the other side lay college, independence, liberation—all of the illusions that the future always holds. And in between our routine and the prospect of our freedom was the celebrated prom, an intoxicated island where we would drink and dance and fuck and swear eternal friendships that wouldn't last the summer. By tradition our school held the prom on a Monday—this was sort of meant to have a sobering effect. But the figure of the Jesuit who spoke at convocation had already cast a pall across the prospect of our freedom, and I couldn't shake his image, or the words that he had said. So after morning classes, before I went to see my counselor, I tried to find Ian to talk about God. But he wasn't anywhere.

I mean Ian, that is.

✸ *WHEN I OPENED MY HAND and found my boyfriend's dick in it* was the answer I had given to Mr. Kickliter, the high school counselor's opening question: "When did you first realize you were gay?"

"That's not what I *meant*, Dr. Sligh," K. resumed, stabbing out his cigarette and firing up a new one.

Kickliter, smarmy slice of butt cheese that he was, always called me Dr. Sligh and grimaced at my humor in that endlessly patient, patently dismissive, underpaid and oversensitive high school counselor's way of his. You might confess to steamrolling a parade route of Shriners and he'd greet it with a shrug and a fresh cigarette.

"It's a stupid question, K.," I said, kicking back. "It's like asking me when I realized I had thumbs."

"Mine are double-jointed," Kickliter offered. He showed me. He wanted to Lighten Things Up.

"The point is," I resumed. "I fully intend to accompany my boyfriend—"

"And who might that be?"

"To next week's senior prom. And I want your estimation of the academic reper*cuss*ions of any such so-called ill-advised action."

"First off," K. evaded, "the whole issue's moot. You haven't even completed your community service hours."

Every senior, as part of his commitment to the lofty if laborious Jesuit ideal, had to perform fifty hours of community service before being permitted to attend the senior prom. This was our reward for serving the community. Failure to serve the community, however, came with its penalty: no graduation. Neither Ian nor I had undertaken our hours, and as we would be valedictorian and salutatorian, respectively, at the graduation ceremony the Friday after prom, we were facing a far less pleasantly sticky situation than coitus interruptus in the backseat of a limo.

"I'll complete my hours," I addressed the air.

"And neither has Ian Lamb," K. added, significantly, "if the little blue graph on my wall is correct."

"This has absolutely nothing to do with Ian Lamb," I protested, too vocally. "This concerns *me*."

" 'Me, me, me' . . . Ahhh, the middle word in life!"

K. was going under in a swamp of cigarette smoke; he coughed, then he surfaced, grin first, like a gator.

"Have you thought about a nunnery?" Kickliter suggested, twiddling his double-jointed digits with abandon and nigger-lipping the butt of his Kool something awful.

"K., my man, you haven't answered my *question*."

"Uh, Dr. Sligh?" Kickliter pursued, making a cigar of his cigarette, à la Groucho. "Is the door locked?"

"Yes."

He got up and double-checked it.

"Classified material. These walls have ears."

K. sat back and crossed his legs like a producer, flicked ashes on the floor: Who cared about the carpet? This was bottom-line stuff. This was seriously heavy. The baring of one human soul to another. Kickliter, to his credit, always kept things confidential. You had to give him that much. He was as Catholic as the pope.

"Your ass," K. said, exquisitely inhaling, "will be grass," K. concluded, exhaling brilliantly.

"Any reasons?"

"Just the usual medieval nonsense: intolerance, hypocrisy, fear of the unknown. Of course, it's your decision. Do your parents know you're gay?"

"I guess. I don't know. I think so."

"Pretty dodgy. Will they freak?"

"Will they what?"

"Will they *freak*, Dr. Sligh? Are you prepared to deal with, like, Major League Rejection? Rejection from your school, rejection from your family, rejection from your peers?"

"I think I'm in love."

"Love, well, *yeah*." The word made people nervous. "Love, well, *love*, yeah, love, um . . . *love*."

K. stood up and came around the chair behind me. He massaged my knotty shoulders. "Tension buster," he proclaimed. It was nice. It was kind. I was Jell-O underneath him. And he had fantastic hands. And I wondered, "Is *he* gay?"

"Dr. Sligh, I like you. You think for yourself. You're one of the last of the truthful, so to say. But think a bit about it. 'Bout the things you've got to lose. Unconditional acceptance at a reputable college. Scholarship money." He paused. "Your parents rich?"

"Nope," I conceded. We were colorfully poor.

"You do this thing, escort your boyfriend to the prom, you'll be a sort of hero. . . . But you'll give your life away."

"Like Jesus?"

I was always dragging Christ into things.

"Guy's a lie," K. responded.

"Just like me," I said, and left.

AFTER MY INFORMATIVE tête-à-tête with K. I came across Ian sitting by the swimming pool. His pants were rolled up and his feet were in the water. He dangled them gently up and down, like a kid. I didn't go to him; I just watched him for a while. He was staring at the pool as if it were full of jewels, as if the glittering map of its surface separated him from sunken treasure only he could see. For a while Ian sat there with his head between his knees, the sunlight in the water splashing him with coins of light, and every now and then he'd dip his fingers in the deep end and baptize himself and shiver in the awful heat. When I called over to him Ian came without running. His body, lithe and graceful, looked pavement-bound and clumsy as he shuffled dully over and said, not looking up, "Hey, Toby."

"Hey, Ian . . . I talked to Kickliter."

" 'Bout what?"

" 'Bout the prom."

"Oh, yeah . . . the senior prom."

"And I brought you a flower."

I handed it to Ian. It was pink. It was hiding in a brown paper bag.

I'd swiped it off a rosebush out back behind the Residence where the Society of Jesus lived and breathed and didn't breed. When I plucked it, I turned and thought I saw a pallid face disappear behind a curtain torn and blooming in a window. I found a paper bag and, like a robber, dropped it in it. And as I gave the bag to Ian I felt like Eve awry in Eden—righteous and romantic and profoundly paranoid: if Ian was my Adam, this was someone else's garden.

"What kind of flower is it?"

"Guess," I said and smiled.

Ian brought the bag up to his artificial eye.

"It's a rose," Ian said. "And it's *pink*," Ian added.

"And you're right," Toby said. "And it's *yours*," Toby added.

IAN HAD ARRIVED from New Orleans that year like God's gift to Sacred Heart and Jesus' gift to me. He was a mon-eyed All-American with a 4.0 average and National Merit standing and spiked hair and perfect teeth. I'd have been valedictorian if not for his arrival, but I couldn't have cared less. I was happy to be ruined. Something had happened to Ian in New Orleans and he'd lost his left eye, but he wouldn't talk about it. Like so many other things it only added to his charm: it cloaked him in the mantle of a living mystery. Ian wore his handicap like a badge of heroism and mopped the mucus from it with self-depre-cating flair. And he had a constant playful-dolphin energy about him, a grace in thought and movement other students emulated. But when Ian's mind was heavy, he seemed bedded to the ocean. You had to sound as deeply just to make him rise again.

"Everything OK?" I asked him in a whisper.

"Uh-huh." He just nodded; Ian's head was somewhere else. And his words were all imploding, like explosives in a Coke can. "That Jesuit this morning—"

"He was something," I began. "What he said about—"

"God. Uh-huh. What he *said*."

I was on Ian's left, peering into his glass eye, so I couldn't re-ally read him: I could only read his voice.

"You believe in God, Toby?"

"Never really thought about it."

"That's a lie, Toby Sligh," Ian said, and frowned a little. "God love you for a liar," Ian said, and dashed ahead.

When I caught up to him he was studying my flower. Ian held it, and he smelled it, and he dropped it in the bag.

"You gave me a bag. You said it was a flower. You told me to guess what kind of flower it *was*. I pictured a rose. A *pink* rose, Toby. I opened the bag. I was right. I was *lucky*. That's God, Toby. *That's* what your God is."

"And you're welcome for the flower."

We were headed for the library.

ON OUR WAY we came across a chlorinated pod of swimmers pitching quarters in a corner cordoned off against the heat. They hailed their sullen idol, and Ian gave them audience, and we squatted there awhile, losing money, talking crap. When we left, we high-fived, and we belched, and all that bullshit, and the music of their laughter hustled our footsteps away.

"K. SAID," I said to Ian, who was sitting in a cubicle in a wing of the library nobody used, except for maybe naps or doing drugs or jacking off, "if I try to take a guy to the prom, I'll be expelled."

"Expelled?" Ian wiped his weeping eye against his sleeve. "On what grounds?"

"You know K. He didn't get specific. Of course, there's the Church's stand on sexuality."

"Which is what?"

"Thumbs down. We were meant to sleep with chicks. And to multiply, you know. It's all there in Genesis."

"But half these priests are homos!" Ian whispered/shouted. "Fr. Clyde"—the swimming coach—"he sports a chronic flagpole!"

"That's a glandular problem."

"I've seen his fucking gland! Flashes it in the locker room often enough. *'Hey, fellas, any takers?'* "

I laughed.

"C'm'ere, Ian."

"Now, Toby—"

"Come *here*. . . ."

Ian smiled.

"Ohh, *okay*. . . ."

Ian rose, and felt his fly, and looked around, and sidled over. Genuflecting, he pressed his open mouth against mine. Our tongues found each other. When we finished, he was crying.

"Toby, *I love you*."

"Don't say that, Ian. It's stupid. You know we're both heading off for school."

"I love you. I *do*."

"I love you too, Ian."

"Kiss me please, Toby."

"Listen, kiddo . . ."

"Toby, *please?*"

I leaned in. So did Ian. When we kissed, I split my lip.

"Holy Christ! Someone's coming!"

We sat back and heard our hearts.

Two gawky feet were plodding comically toward us, as if the Jolly Green Giant had come to check out books. They belonged to Bubba Fishback, a meathead on steroids who confided all of his sexual secrets to Ian, most of which consisted of videotaping jack-off sessions in a sort of sick and shaky Sony handheld Technicolor. I pressed my broken lip between the pages of a book.

"Mouth's bleedin', Toby. Whatcha guys doin'? Sniffin' the lint in your assholes, har har har!"

A librarian, somewhere, shushed our commotion. Bubba pulled a chair up and camped beside Ian.

"Really, guys, hope I'm not interruptin' nothin'. You two, ya know, look mighty in*tense*."

Ian was smoother at this shit than I was. He draped an arm around me and shifted into Jock Gear.

"Just talkin' poontang. That's all, Bubba. Who we're takin' to the prom . . ."

"Toby *knows* who he's takin'!"

Bubba's plump fist shot out like a rocket and clocked me in the shoulder, which my dad had primed before.

"Easy there, Bubba. Wanna keep my motor skills."

"*Angelina!*" Bubba said, and preened for all to see. "My sister, Angelina! *That's* who he's takin'!"

It was true. Categorically. And it was news to Ian. At a weak moment, at a shopping mall, in an underwhelming outburst of phallo-Christian charity, I'd agreed to take Angelina to the senior prom. I liked her. She was smart. She was smarter than Bubba. She was bigger than him, too—and all that without steroids.

"And of course we all know who you're takin', Studly Morecrotch." Bubba winked at Ian, dipping Red Man in his cheek. "Primest piece of pussy at the Holy Dames Academy! Courtney A. Ciccone! Sex on the Beach herself!"

Courtney A. Ciccone was an edible cheerleader with tits like tidal waves and a blinding fake smile. She'd earned the sobriquet "Sex on the Beach" because of an escapade during spring break when a private detective freelancing for her parents photographed her groping half naked with a lifeguard in an observation tower on the Fort DeSoto shore.

"Awesome, dude!" I congratulated Ian, laying it on and slugging him hard. "How'd ya land *that* one?"

"My natural charm."

"And the size of his schlong!" Bubba chimed in, measuring a prize trout between his outspread hands.

For one thing, Ian's dick wasn't that big. It was big, all right. But it wasn't *that* big. A peculiar trait of heterosexual homo-eroticism I'd bothered to notice was that guys put guy friends' success with other women down to the exaggerated girth of their members. Ian did nothing to rebut his beefy legend, except to keep his legendary trouser snake trousered. Except for special viewings. Like mine . . . and *Courtney C.'s?*

" *'Miles Long? Miles Long? Paging Miles Long for Ms. Court- ney Ciccone?'* " Bubba improvised across a phantom loud-speaker.

We all giggle-grunted in that dumb gorilla guys' way. That's when my prodigious pal Juice sauntered over.

"Bubba! Ian Lamb! Toby *Sligh!* Whass*up!*"

Juice was jet black and just *smotheringly* cool. He wore Ital-ian clothes and sported thighs the size of juggernauts. Juice also dealt to all the other football players and made better money than my mom and dad combined. His real name was Leonard Compton, he glided like Blake's *Tyger*, and he hung out with me for reasons I could never figure: maybe because I didn't do drugs, maybe because I wouldn't give him my money, maybe be-cause I reminded him of someone. And Juice liked me a lot more than he liked Ian: he was straighter than a laser, but his eyes gleamed for me.

"What shit you all layin' down in the 'brary?"

Juice took some Skoal laced with cocaine and lipped it.

"Gimme some, Juice," Bubba begged.

"Gimme money."

They dealt. Juice offered us some. We declined.

Juice teeter-tottered on the chair that barely held him.

"Joo see that priest, Fr. Scarecrow, this mornin'? *Damn* that man skinny! I think he got AIDS!"

Bubba laughed at Juice and pinched another taste of Skoal. I stole a glance at Ian. He was staring at the floor.

"You okay, Lamb?" Juice said to Ian. "You look like somebody run over yo' penis."

"Just tired, Juice."

"I got somethin' for that. . . . His name is Benny." Juice produced amphetamines. "An' how much you want?"

Bubba said, "He ain't buying."

"I forgot—Lamb's clean," Juice said. "And Tobias?"

I looked at Juice's hand, then I swiped the bottle from it. I shook out a couple pills and just considered them awhile. This disturbed Juice: it was really rotten karma. My role was to refuse; I wasn't supposed to think about it. Juice's breathing grew audibly fitful and labored. I imagined I could hear the sad percussion of his heart.

"Whatchoo gonna do, Tobe, study it or taste it?"

I put the pills back.

Bubba said, "Sligh's a pussy."

"Sligh ain't no *pus*sy," Juice sighed, and smacked Bubba. "He just don't wanna go fuck hisself *up*. He ain't got no money to waste like you *rich* boys. He's a proletariat homie, like me. Ain't I right?"

"You're not a prole, Juice. You're petit bourgeois."

We shared the same desk in Political Science.

"Petit bourgeois? Fuck *that* shit, Tobias! I'm *major* bourgeois! I'm Captain A*meri*ca!"

We did a high-five; with Juice, it was different. It was like punctuating a really clever sentence, not the awkward body language of two guys afraid to touch.

"I don't understand what you're talking about," Bubba complained, and Juice smacked him again.

"You wouldn't understand, you stupid-ass fucker! You about as dumb as that man this mornin' skinny!"

"You think he's got AIDS?" Bubba said, and nursed his jaw.

"See that priest's *body?*" Juice said. "He's a *goner!* Seen guys like that, crosstown in the projects, when I visit my daddy—me and Mama got *out.* They starvin' like Marvin? I mean i'ss like '*Seee* ya!' That boy be so skinny you could *fax* him to his grave."

"I liked what he said about God," I interjected.

"Yeah, you into that *deep* shit, Sligh. You always got yo' mind on some *deep* shit or other. You gotta start thinkin' mo' *deep* with yo' *dick*." Juice grabbed my crotch and bolted, wailing like a banshee. I chased him and he wasted me. A librarian hollered and Juice let me up. "Still, I *smoked* you last Poli Sci test! I *smoked* you, Sligh, 'mit it! What'd I get?"

"96," I said. I decided to tease him. Juice was like my father: he needed to be teased. "But that's only because you were sitting next to *me*."

"You faggot," Juice said.

We were all very quiet.

"Tobe's a faggot," Juice said. "Uh-huh, I *know* he is . . ."

Outside, in the quad, somebody was whistling. It was just about lunchtime. We were all just sitting there.

"What was it Fr. Scarecrow said about God?" Bubba asked, with a cough now, and coming to our rescue.

"He said," Juice said, "God's a *lonely* motherfucker, like you gonna be, *G.*, 'less you *find* some for the prom."

"Who're you taking, Juice?" Ian said, coming around.

"My cousin Anquanna. And mmm-mmm-mmm. Girl's got more back than Canadian bacon! Who you takin', Ian?"

"Courtney Ciccone."

"Mercy!" Juice said. "Wear ten bags with that honey! She got every virus known to womankind!"

Bubba started laughing: "Fr. Scarecrow prob'ly fucked her!"

"Shut up," Ian said.

Bubba double-taked Ian.

"*Wha'd* you say, Ian?"

"I said shut the fuck up."

"*You* shut the fuck up!" Bubba bristled, devastated.

"No. *No*, Bubba. *You* shut the fuck up."

We all looked at Ian. He was looking at Bubba. Bubba's

mouth was dangling open. *Bubba shut the fuck up.*

Juice, who had surveyed the damage, popped his knuckles.

"Damn, Lamb. Ain't you'n a sweet mood today? Someone not suckin' your *dick* right or somethin'?'"

Ian looked at Bubba, and then he looked at Juice.

"I just get sick of hearin' Fishback talkin' bullshit."

"Like you don't!" Bubba blustered, really bleeding now.

"C'mon, now, Ian," I said to him finally.

"No," Ian said, looking straight into me. "I'm not gonna c'mon. Not *this* time, Toby!"

And then he charged out, smashing into a librarian who spilled a stack of books and banned us all from the library. Juice fetched the books and handed them to me and Bubba. We shelved them and left.

"Atom bomb," Juice said to me.

JUICE DROVE ME home in his convertible Porsche. It was as purple and as lethal as a kiss. We hadn't talked to Ian the rest of that day, and Juice was concerned: or at least he was intrigued. He kept inventing theories to explain Ian's outburst. It became his new obsession, like John F. Kennedy's murder, which, Juice would argue, had been plotted by Cubans.

"You don't shout 'Cuba libre!' to a buncha fuckin' *Cu*bans unless you intend to make *good* on yo' *prom*ise!"

Juice was a wiz at political theory. He really knew his shit. He'd be President someday.

"You think they're the ones who killed Marilyn, too?"

"*Boyeee*, J. was fuckin' a mafioso's bitch! Norma Jean Baker got caught in the *cross*fire! You listen to Juice, Tobe—he's *down* on the Ken'dys. You never seen a bunch uh G.'s so *hard* on their *wom*en!" We stopped at a crosswalk and dealt with a policeman. Juice pocketed a fifty and threw on some L.L. Cool J. "Marilyn

*Mon*roe, Chappa*quid*dick, that William Kennedy *rape* bullshit? Tyson been a pretty white Kennedy, *word,* he'd a got off, e'en though that boy be *guilty!*" Juice took his shirt off and fiddled with his nipples. He had the sort of pecs, like, *cardiac arrest.* "I mean, Jesus! What you Cath'lics got against *sisters?* Ken'dy boys, they got dicks like *hur*ricanes, leave a path of bitches in their motherfuckin' *wake!* It's like, *damn*—you beadbusters worship the Ma*don*na, kick the shit outta any honey *falls short!*"

"I like women," I said, not entirely convincingly.

"Uh-huh." Juice pumped up the bass real loud. "Yeah, Tobe. Yeah. I know you do, G."

We drove along awhile, not saying nothing.

At a traffic light a schoolgirl left her Audi running and bobbled over to us, and Juice sold her some X. *"Everything begins with an 'E,' "* she whispered to me as she leaned across the carseat, smelling of Chanel. When she kissed Juice's forehead he gave her some Acid, L.L. Cool J boom-boom-booming on the system:

> *Standing at the bus stop,*
> *Suckin' on a lollipop—*
> *When she gets pumpin'*
> *It's hard to make the hotty stop . . .*

At the green, Juice scoped me out of the corner of his eye and turned down the volume and cleared his throat a little.

"You like women, Tobe?"

I sat up.

"Uh-huh."

"Whatchoo like about 'em?"

I unbuttoned my collar.

"What do I *like?*"

"Yeah. Uh-huh. 'At's what I *axed,* didn't I?"

I stalled a little.

"You mean, like, *phy*sically?"

Juice started laughing.

"Yeah, uh-huh, *phys*ically!"

I sat there awhile. I was trying to think. I liked women, but not like I liked, you know, *guys*. I didn't like their bodies. I liked their *at*titudes. I liked the way you could say things to women and they wouldn't back off. I liked the way they took the truth.

"I like their . . . *asses*."

"Uh-huh. What about 'em?"

"How . . . uh." I scratched my head. "How, you know . . . how *round* they are."

Juice was chewing on a cinnamon stick. We drove for a while, Juice singing along:

> *If the Mona Lisa's name was Theresa,*
> *I'd get a piece a*
> *The Mona Lisa . . .*

"An' their tits?"

"Oh, yeah! I *really* like their tits!"

"How *roun'* they is, right?"

Juice was laughing *all over*.

"You a *trip*, Toby Sligh! You a absolute *trip!*"

We pulled onto the interstate, a siren screaming past us.

HALFWAY HOME, JUICE took an exit. We were in the projects. Folks were waving at us. We drove up to a yellow flat of crumbling apartments. A baby was chewing on a football in a gutter. Juice leaned over and wrapped an arm around me.

"That's where my daddy lives," Juice said, pointing. "He a crackhead now. He on his way *out*."

We pulled away then, and somebody hollered, "Leon!"

"All right," Juice spoke to them, softly, through the window.

✸ JUICE DROPPED ME off at my mother's place and asked, "Tobe, what the fuck you doin' *this* neighborhood?"
"Somebody I know."
"You fulla secrets, Sligh."
"And you know half of 'em."
Juice laughed. "*Seee* ya!"

✸ WALKING UP THE drive to Mom's drug dealer pad, I remembered something Juice and I'd seen while cruising past the Jesuit Residence that day.

In the little sandy garden at the rear of the building an ambulance had parked between two rows of peeling punk trees. Its taillights were on, so it must have been idling, and the driver just sat there, staring at his knuckles. This was usually a sign that somebody had died, that one of the older and more desiccated Jesuits had progressed to less strenuous *Spiritual Exercises* in the sky. I looked at Juice, who was looking at me, and then we passed Ian, who was walking to the Residence.

He didn't even see us; his chin was set and rigid. He walked with the steady, unencumbered stride of a George Romero zombie on the scent of fresh flesh. And I noticed Ian carrying my flower in his hand, which he turned in nervous circles, so the petals made a pinwheel.

Juice tapped his horn, but Ian didn't hear it. We turned around and saw him disappear inside the Residence. And though I know now, I could not have known then exactly why I half expected to see Ian's face plastered up against the glass of a crying ambulance when it passed us on the interstate just fifteen minutes later.

MOM WAS LYING naked on a paralytic lawnchair in the claustrophobic backyard of her new drug dealer pad. She shared the tiny weed-eaten lot with a bright blue dilapidated Chevy Corvair, its shattered eyes shining, its body up on blocks. Something in a junked car is like a crucifixion: abandoned, proud of it, and gloriously hopeless, its pose is no different than Christ crucified.

In her careless fashion Mom had left the frontdoor open, so anyone—a thief or a son—might walk in. The place had been stripped bare of furniture and carpet, and the walls were ripe with paint that smelled wet and fresh and woozy. A bottle of wine lay empty in a corner, with a pair of man's pants, stiff with paint, wrapped around it. Something was sighing, like a snake or a pipe, so I gave the apartment a precautionary tour. I sort of expected to discover some guy things, like the trousers of the lover she had chosen over Dad. Then I checked out the pants and realized they *were* Dad's—Mom had only worn them to protect her while she painted.

Somewhere underneath the delicious smell of Lucite hovered something more delicious—the smell of homemade pasta. In the kitchen I knelt and glanced inside a glowing oven. A pan of manicotti was bubbling cheesy lava. Because Mom was drunk, and delirious in sunshine, and drifting somewhere on that calm selfish island to which Dad and I were uninvited castaways, she didn't even see me staring at her through the window, her nipples flecked with paint, her tummy glinting in the sunlight. At last Mom had gotten outside herself completely; though anchored to the earth, her body all but levitated. And although I had never seen my mom so nude before—except for those pictures of her and Dad together Dad kept locked up in a strongbox in his cabinet at work—I found her body beautiful and new and fascinating: the dimple of her navel, her lush pubic mound, the way her pretty breasts sloped down to brush her midriff. I felt something rouse itself alive inside my trousers—but to my great relief, it surrendered just as quickly. I didn't want to claim the somewhat dubious distinction of being one of a select corps of young gay males whose only remotely heterosexual urgings were stirred by the prostrate, naked bodies of their mothers: it was all a little bit too textbook Oedipal for me. So when my mother's hands began to quietly meander from the region of her hips to more erogenous regions, and when her mute lips unfolded with the same mute abandon of even muter lips in more erogenous zones, you can understand why I left as quickly as I came, and why I even bothered to lock the door behind me, so Mom might be entitled (so to speak) to her peace.

IT TOOK ME forever to walk from Mom's place back to our house on the other side of town. I flirted once or twice with the idea of hitching, but every time I offered my thumb to the world, its owner felt exposed and absurd and obscene, as if other, more compromising bits of my anatomy were being displayed for passing motorists to see.

I'd forgotten that day to get a book from the school library, and after the incident between Ian and the librarian I didn't know when I would go in there again. And because I read religiously every night before bed, and because I had finished *The Idiot* in Theology and wanted to keep my Dostoevsky streak going, I headed in the direction of the decrepit branch library just a couple blocks from our neighborhood.

It was partially closed and being tented for termites. A polyurethane tarpaulin freckled with bugs' eyes blanketed the building and kept the pesticides in. I didn't like the idea of my favorite books and authors being blitz-bombed with toxins and noxious chemicals, but if anyone could withstand such a godawful onslaught, I figured my main man Dostoevsky could.

I say the library was partially closed because a city bookmobile was idling in the parking lot. It had a drive-thru window, just like a McDonald's, and a speaker through which you could order your McBooks. While inhaling lethal doses of carbon monoxide—not to mention whatever potpourri of poisons was leaking from flaps in the fluttering tarp—I stood between two eructing gas guzzlers awaiting my turn to put my modest order through.

"Welcome to the public library," an elegant, purling voice crackled through static. "Would you care to try a collection of Raymond Carver today?"

"No, thank you," I replied. Raymond Carver sucked. "I'll have the unabridged copy of *The Brothers Karamazov* by Fyodor Dostoevsky. And hold the cheese, please."

The speaker clicked dead: it was permanent-sounding. Then the voice came crackling through the static again.

"We're sorry, sir. We're out of Theodore Dreiser. Would you care to try something by Mr. John Updi—"

"I didn't say Theodore Dreiser," I said. "I said *F*yodor Dosto-*ev*sky."

"Could you *spell* that, please?"

Behind me, a car honked; I drew a fumy breath. I felt like a finalist at a Cyrillic spelling bee.

"Dostoevksy. D-o-s-t-o-e-v-s-k-*y*. Dostoevsky."

Now a car behind the *other* car was honking: it reminded me, in its own peculiar way, of applause.

"We have nothing listed under that spelling, sir. Would you care to try something by that 'modern master of horror,' Stephen Ki—"

"Sometimes it's spelled differently," I explained. "Try D-o-s-t-o-e-v-s-k-*i*."

A car burned rubber, its driver flipping me the finger—no doubt a Jackie Collins fan denied the nightly fix. Through the static came some hyperactive tapping at a keyboard, then the voice erupted crackling on the intercom again.

"Dostoevsk*i! He exists now!* Please proceed to the pickup station."

At the pickup station—which was really nothing more than a
tinted power window separating groundlings from the lofty driver's seat—a pale hand emerged and disgorged a slender volume, then vanished, displaying a sign that read: CLOSED. As the
bookmobile's engine spontaneously combusted, a prerecorded
message blared out across the lot, backed by a warped recording of the National Anthem: "Your mobile library is closed for
the evening. Please return tomorrow between the hours of eight
and eight. And remember: Truth is Fiction. And Reading is
Fundamental. Good night. *Y buenas noches.*" After which I became another gringo in Pamplona caught unawares at the running of the bulls, most of which were mad and manufactured in
Detroit. And it wasn't until I tiptoed into our kitchen and saw
Detective Thomas untangling Dad's spaghetti that I realized the
librarian had given me the wrong volume—not *The Brothers
Karamazov,* for which I had asked, but *The Double,* a novella I'd
never heard of.

DETECTIVE THOMAS RESEMBLED my father: same height,
same build, same hair, same features. They could have
been brothers. It was unbelievable. No wonder the guy jumped
back like a shot when I crept up behind him and locked him in
a bear hug: "All righty now, Pops, drop that fucking pasta!" Det.
Thomas did, all over the floor; and I stood there apologizing
flush-faced and flustered, to the visitor who, from the back especially, was my own dear father's motherfucking spittin' image.
But even from the front the resemblance was impressive. My
real dad, the one Det. Thomas looked just like, entered the
kitchen after having completed what he described as a "titanic
shit" and, seeing Det. Thomas beside me on the floor scooping
up pickup-stick piles of spaghetti, made me get up and made
Thomas get up, too. Then they stood cheek to cheek, beaming

like Siamese lighthouses as I walked circles round them and commended their resemblance.

"It's un*can*ny," I observed, like a Sherlock Holmes lackey.

"We never met until today," Det. Thomas swore.

"I feel like contacting Ripley or something!" Dad cried. "Isn't this the most incredible thing?"

"Incredible," I echoed.

The detective was blushing.

"I'm sorry, Mr. Sligh, about what happened to your pasta." Thomas turned to me then, like detectives do on television. "Your father was just telling me about your missing mother and—"

"You know how it *gets*, Tobe, I had to take a *crap*, and after all that *beer* I had—"

"My father," I explained, "moves his bowels, like, once a *year*."

"You can just imagine the *size* of it, Toby! Broke my heart to flush it! Swear to God it did! Today is a day of remarkable achievements and—"

"Yes, well," the detective interrupted, sticking his hand out and swinging back to me, "I'm Detective Thomas."

"My name is Toby."

We shook, like at mass.

"Now about the boy's mother . . ."

DET. THOMAS HAD the most transparent eyes I've ever seen—the kind that betray and wreak havoc on themselves, like the eyes of a tyke accused of swiping a cookie, who wishes he *had*, and finds himself declared guilty. And even though Thomas was asking me the questions, it felt like *I* was giving *him* the third degree. And what did *he* have to feel guilty about? I was the accessory to momnapping, not him. For all I knew he had pulled the same stunt when he was my age, he looked so sympathetic. His questions, in the end, were as limp as his spaghetti, so loath was he to pry, so disinclined to probe. And as we sat in a triangle at the Momless dinner table—my father like a floating partner in a parlor game—I kept tripping Thomas up on *his* inconsistencies, till Dad, embarrassed for him, fled our company for the kitchen.

"Let's begin again." Det. Thomas stumbled, and drew a leaky ballpoint from behind his squeaky ear. "You say you saw your mother last on Sunday evening, before you went to bed?"

"No. I said I saw my mother last on Monday morning, before I went to *school*."

"What time did she drop you off?"

"My *father* dropped me off. I told you that *too*."

"But your father says he saw her last before you went to school on Monday *morn*ing."

"I know. I *told* you. That's when we *both* saw her last."

"So where were you after midnight Sunday?"

"A*sleep*."

"Aha!"

I loved the way Det. Thomas said *"Aha!"* He bit the word off like the end of a good cigar.

"But I thought you said you saw her *Monday morning?*"

"I *did*, Det. Thomas. I saw her *when I woke up*. At *break*fast. With my *dad. We saw her both together.*"

"Oh," Det. Thomas said, looking crestfallen. "Right. Uh-huh. That would make sense. . . ."

In an effort to assist Det. Thomas in his troubles, my father, from the kitchen, offered him a glass of juice.

"We're not allowed to drink on duty." Det. Thomas rudely and sanctimoniously declined.

"But it's only orange juice!" my father bellowed.

"Well, in that case, if it's only *juice* . . ."

Dad brought out a weeping glass of Tropicana, and the detective drank it greedily, and set the glass down.

"Good juice," he declared, looking at me oddly. "You like juice?"

"Yes," I told him.

We stared at each other.

Well, that was that: we liked juice.

What the fuck?

"Those are all the questions I have for you, Tobe." I didn't like the way Det. Thomas called me Tobe; it made me feel vaguely like a big lumpy earlobe dangling there, cute and useless, being diddled to distraction. "And I'm sorry I seemed to get things in such a muddle." And here was something new, a detective who *apologized*—it was like Mahatma Gandhi doing Jack Webb on *Dragnet:* "You have the right to remain silent, very silent, and to fast."

"You see, well, um, I'm pretty new on the force and—"

"But I thought, looking at you, you're a *private* detective."

My father sat between us like a nerd interpreter: "Do you think we have the money for a *private* investigator?"

"But he hasn't got a uniform!"

"I'm a plainclothesman." Det. Thomas moped, as if spreading for a strip search.

"Yes, well, ahem, and what fine clothes they are," my father reassured him. "Like that Arrow jobbie, Toby?"

"Yeah, Pops, spiffy. Never seen a pattern like it. Maybe you two could swap outfits or something."

The two of them suddenly launched into laughter. When they settled back to earth, Det. Thomas smacked his lips.

"Excuse me, Mr. Sligh, but could I have some more orange juice? I'm kind of diabetic and I'd love another glass."

"Comin' right up. You wait here with Toby," my dad said, and left, and returned with more juice.

"By the way, Tobias," Det. Thomas said to me. "Who'd you ride home with from school this afternoon?"

I nearly said "Juice."

"Nobody," I lied. "I jogged the whole way."

"Over ten, eleven miles?"

"Toby's a track star," my father declared, and smote my leg biblically, as if my thighs were his thighs.

"Well . . ." Thomas rose. "We'll be saying bye now. With a little bit of luck, we should locate Mrs. Sligh. Good night, Mr. Sligh. And good night, Tobias."

"Good night, Detective Thomas," we called out from the door, and bolted it behind us, and surveyed each other.

"Nice fella," Dad said, turning suddenly away. "A good guy, don't you think?"

"Well, he certainly likes *juice.*"

THAT NIGHT, FOR dinner, we had Popeyes chicken—wings and breasts, biscuits, red beans and rice, and big cherry sodas that stained our lips red.

"What did you do after school today, Toby?"

"Popeyes is owned by the Vatican," I countered.

Dad's greasy mitts were tug-o'-warring with a wishbone. When he made no response, I advanced my private theory.

"Popeyes. *Pope-yes.* Check it out, Dad. At the way the letters slant. It's a covert operation."

"I never thought about it."

But he *would* think about it, from that day forward: Dad believed anything. A good lie, to him, was a balm and a blessing. It accounted for things. It helped him make it through his day.

"I suppose," Dad belched, "the Church has got to make money. Maybe we could get a discount. I'll ask Fr. Tierney."

We sat there, gauging the grease in our stomachs, running gauntlets through a slew of cable television channels.

"Oh, yeah," Dad addended. "Plus you got a phone call."

"From whom?"

"From the hospital. Some pal a yours."

"Ian Lamb?"

"Ian Something. Down at St. Osyth's. He says he'll call you. Look, Tobe! *The Liar's Club!*"

✺ BUT IAN NEVER called; I didn't think he would. He was scared fucking stiff of prolonged contact with my parents, as if they'd sniff out his sexual identity when, for all I knew, they hadn't even sniffed out mine. He also wanted me to keep away from his folks, which was okay by me—they didn't sound all that appealing. Lyle Lamb was a borderline alcoholic, Ian claimed, who'd finally crossed the border with the help of Edith Lamb, a displaced New Orleans high society diva who'd wilted in Florida like a hothouse orchid transplanted from her splendid, torpid Garden District soil. Ian's parents were a mess, my parents were a mess, their lives were a mess: *we wouldn't let them mess with ours.* It spoiled us, at worst; at best it insulated us, as if we existed in a world without family, as if we were foundlings in everything but love. I was amazed Ian Lamb had telephoned at all. And to give his real name? It was positively reckless. I put it all down as a personal triumph, Ian's first baby step toward our slow dance at the prom. And just that night I had made an appointment at the formal wear store where we would get our tuxes fitted. There was something romantic and casually erotic about the prospect of standing side by side in our underwear having our inseams measured by a stranger. It was vaguely ceremonial, like we were, um, en*gaged.* And it was nearly enough to drive out of my mind all my worries about why Ian'd phoned me from St. Osyth's. Was he sick? Was he injured? Was he visiting? *What?* And what would make him break with his anonymous routine?

IT WAS *a little before eight o'clock in the morning when Titular Councillor Yakov Petrovich Golyadkin woke from a long sleep, yawned, stretched, and finally opened his eyes completely. He lay motionless in bed, however, for a couple of minutes more, like a man who is not yet sure whether he is awake or still asleep, and whether what is happening around him is real and actual or only the continuation of his disordered dreams. . . .*

TRY AS I MIGHT, that night I couldn't sleep: couldn't sleep, couldn't read, couldn't do a blessed thing except lie awake and fret and wrestle naked with the sheets. I kept reading and rereading the opening paragraph of *The Double,* but none of it seemed to make any sense to me. Not even Dostoevsky and his rollercoaster prose could lift me high above the littered midway of my love; and for a while that night, acting on the theory that if reading cannot transport, it at least can tranquilize, I forswore Fyodor for the Sleepy Shelf Selection, hauling down some Hermann Hesse and roach-egg-dappled old *New Yorker*s. Off I nearly glided to the Land of Dreamy Dreams, magic carpet–riding on a mat of catatonic fiction until, semi-tranced at four o'-clock in the morning—Dad Bud-snoring on the living room sofa—I heard someone tapping tentatively at our frontdoor.

I was sure it was Ian. It was a tender kind of tapping.

"TAXI FOR TOBY Sligh," a lady in a Malcolm X cap said to me. She was black, and in the doorway her cap seemed to hover, a big white X-marks-the-spot on the night.

"Didn't hire any cab," I said, spitting whispers, and watching my back in case Dad had gotten up.

"Hired it for you, boy name of Ian."

She took off her cap and disappeared into the night.

"Excuse me," I said, and bolted to my room. I hopped into my clothes and scratched a message for my father: *Track before school. Got a ride with a pal. Didn't want to wake you. See ya, Pops. Love, Toby.*

And I got into the cab that was rumbling and glowing on our runway-looking driveway like a UFO in heat.

THE CITY THAT morning looked dead and deserted, as if a neutron bomb had leveled every living thing. It was pretty, and quiet, and peaceful, and poetic—I expected to see ghosts crossing streets and taking buses. Beside me, the lady cabbie lit a stinky joint, and sucked it till it sparkled, and offered me a toke. "Shit," she said, and stubbed the roach out as a cop car approached, "they been following me." The officers pulled up beside us and smiled, saluting us with two cups of Circle K coffee. "Been following me ever since I went to *get*choo," the lady cabbie grumbled, and smiled back at them.

ON THE WAY to St. Osyth's, suddenly and stubbornly, the sleep I'd been craving all night fell upon me. Like a slapstick piano it came crashing down, and I lay tangled up in a piano-wire cradle until I felt the lady cabbie's warm hand tousle mine.

"We here," she announced.

We were idling at a stoplight. The hospital was looming up a couple blocks ahead.

"Must've fallen asleep."

"Uh-huh, boy, you musta . . . *lamb* this, *lamb* that. Countin' sheeps in yo' *sleep.*"

As we pulled into the lot the lady cabbie flashed a fifty and said, "Ian paid," and put on some Bob Marley. But I didn't move a muscle. I just lay there, listening:

> *Old pirates*
> *Yes, they rob I—*
> *Sold I*
> *To the merchant ship—*
> *Minutes after they took I*
> *From the bottomless pit. . . .*

"You like this song?"

I was thinking of Ian; I was thinking of my parents; I was thinking of myself.

"Uh-huh, it's a nice one," I said, getting out.

"Room eleven-eleven."

The cab lurched away.

  > *But my hand*
> *Was made steady*
> *By the hand of the Almighty—*
> *We forward*
> *In this generation—*
> *Triumphantly. . . .*

The eleventh floor of St. Osyth's Hospital reeked of Lysol and Pine Wax and nuns, like a soul scrubbed clean of its malodorous body, like the timeshare temple of a fussy Holy Ghost. On the cold parquetry outside the elevator a guy about my age lay snoring on his stomach, a purple velvet sofa cushion covering his head. I expected to come across his loved ones in the lobby occupying davenports like storm evacuees.

I passed a sister holding an I.V. in one hand and perusing in the other the number one best-seller, *Whoever Dies with the Most Toys Wins*. It was the autobiography of a retired CEO who began his career shining bootleggers' shoes. The nun had an irresponsible, daffy look about her, and when I asked her what she thought of the CEO's book, she yawned and called it caca: "But it's fun between colostomies." And she didn't try to stop me when I hurried down the hallway—which was curious, I thought. But I just kept walking.

Room 1111 was at the end of the corridor, hidden in a luscious recession of shadow. The oaken door open-sesamed at my touch, revealing a room with a four-way partition. Behind the first partition stood a Plexiglas shelter housing an infant who looked pink and premature. Its brittle little arms were crucified with tubes and needles, but its mouth was gulping air, as if it wanted just to breathe. A sign on the Plexiglas cage said Temporary, and a Temporary sign announced the neighboring partition. Behind the second curtain lay a black kid on his belly, arms and legs spraddled in that absolute abandon only tiny children know when they give themselves to sleep. The child's body twitched beneath a skimpy yellow blanket, his legs kicking out in a learners'-pool paddle. The third partition opened on a Cuban in her twenties, body gaunt and sucked in like a wasted paper straw; her eyes, bulbed and heavy, protruded from their sockets and strained at the jaundiced lids that covered them like tape. I was terrified, suddenly. *Why was I here?* Something swept upward from my chest to my throat and moistened all my mouth with a taste of copper pennies. I felt as if I were being forced to witness something, as if I alone could prevent a tragedy if I could simply keep my hand from drawing back the curtain. Pain is only there if we see it, after all. I could still turn around. I could turn and walk away. But I didn't. I stood and I spoke the name, "Ian." And as my fingers palsied out to draw back the last partition, a hand like a claw landed firmly on my shoulder and I turned to face the sister I'd eluded in the hall.

"Young man," she demanded, "what's your name?"

"Toby Sligh."

"And I'm Cynthia Rose. But you can call me Sr. Cindy. We're so crowded we've had to put some of them together. *Even the baby's got the virus, you know.* Now, you don't want to be bothering poor Fr. Scarcross. He just got to sleep after *such* a long night. And Night Owls, you know, they should keep to the lobby. Though, really, I think you'd be more helpful in the day. *Why, To*by*, you're* crying! You're as bad as that other! It's only sick people! . . . *And your boy is here for you!*"

SR. CYNTHIA ROSE—with that casual brutality nuns alone occasion, assured of their impunity—steered me past two hostile nurses back toward the elevator, removed the purple cushion from the sleeping boy's head, and with three quick kicks, booted Ian awake.

"Christ!" Ian cried. "Fucking hell, Sr. Cindy!"

"I kicked you 'cause I knew that when you woke up, you would say that," Sr. Cindy declared, and glared at Ian, and left.

"*Toby!*" Ian sang, sitting up. "Hey! You made it!"

"Yeah." I nodded. I wanted to hold him; I wanted to hit him. "What the fuck is going on?"

"Siddown," Ian whispered. I sat. The floor was freezing. "You met Cindy Rose. She's a regular cunt."

Somewhere down the hall a nun cleared her throat.

Ian laughed and shivered: "Be careful . . . *voices carry.*"

For a while we sat there staring at each other, our legs crossed like Indians, Ian half asleep.

"Are you going to tell me what this shit is all about?"

"I will. In a minute. Be patient with me, Toby."

Outside, in the street, another siren was singing. I remembered my vision of Ian before, in the back of the ambulance, face pressed and screaming. I thought about Juice, and the pink rose I'd stolen, and my mother, and my father, and the priest at convocation. I thought about Det. Thomas and the lady cabbie. I looked at Ian's arms. They were creased and cold and blue.

"Why in the hell are we sitting on the floor?"

"Those sofas in the lounge—I kept rolling off 'em. I had this falling dream, and I fell, and hit the *floor.* I mean, *I really hit it! I dreamed* it, then it *hap*pened! When you're a kid," Ian said, and yawned big, and mopped his eyeball, "you're told, if that happens, you die in your sleep. But I didn't die, did I? *I'm right here, Toby!* But it shook me up, ya know? S'from now on, I'll take the floor."

Ian looked me over with his good eye, searching: "You've been crying, Toby Sligh."

"You know that I have."

"So you do love me, then! That's great . . . no more lies."

I was disappointed in him.

"That's right . . . no more lies."

ONE DAY AFTER Christmas in Chemistry class a new guy arrived with a patch across his eye. Without introduction he sat next to me, opened up his spiral notebook, and began to scribble notes. He had the finest handwriting I had ever seen; I got a little dizzy just following his pen. Halfway through the lecture Brother Loyal, our teacher, introduced Ian, and Ian said hello. He learned all our names and sat back in his seat and looked at me and smiled, and leaned his knee against mine. We sat there for half an hour, our quiet knees touching, Ian's pen decorating his paper with ink. I was already, then, a little bit in love with him. His hair smelled of chlorine. His skin was bleached and clean. And his knee leaned against mine with a soft, milky pressure; I felt drunk and stupid, and when the bell rang, I jumped. After class we ate lunch in the shadow of the chapel, me and Ian and Bubba and several other idiots. But I didn't say a word. I just sat and watched and listened. Ian told stories, and Ian told jokes, and he bragged about the girls he had screwed back in New Orleans. Ian lied to everyone, and everyone believed him, and when we asked him what had happened to his eye, he wouldn't say.

By the end of lunch he had already become the most interesting and popular boy in our class; and by the end of the day, when I asked him for a lift, and I told Juice not to worry, I had found a ride home, Ian took his patch off and showed me his stitches and the blue mucky bulb that looked like a dirty marble. "Can I touch it?" I asked. He pressed my hand against his wound. "What's it like?" I whispered. "I only see half the world. And I lied," Ian sighed. "I didn't screw all those girls. I'm a *virgin*, Toby Sligh. Are you?" I said I was. We played Ping-Pong that day at his parents' country club and went swimming in the pool, and I touched him underwater. "You don't mind my eye?" Ian asked later on, when we were in the shower at the country club, together. "No, I don't mind. What really happened to it?" "Just an accident, Tobias," Ian Lamb confessed to me.

✸ IAN STOOD AND stretched and shook the sleep off of his body. He offered me his hand; I looked, but wouldn't take it.

"I'm glad you came, Toby. I need you tonight. I need you more than ever. . . . Get off of that floor."

"I'm not budging, Ian, till you tell me what's up."

"I'll show you what's up. Ever worked in a clinic?"

"A what?"

"We're on duty. Community service. Kickliter okayed it. Me and you, kid. You'll have to get permission from your mom and dad, Toby."

"I can't."

"Why not?"

" *'Cause my mother moved out.*"

I was crying then, *again.* Ian Lamb looked embarrassed. He might have touched my shoulder. If he did, I didn't feel it.

"When was that?"

"Yesterday."

"And you didn't tell me?"

"How could I tell you?" I erupted; I was pissed. "You've been acting so strange! How the hell could I tell you? I give you a flower, you don't even *thank* me! You blow up in the library! You freeze Juice and me! You phone from St. Osyth's! I thought you were dying! How could I tell you? *How the fuck could I tell you?*"

"Quiet, now, Toby." Ian's arms closed around me. "Let's go get some coffee." We kissed cautiously. "It's all right. Shhh. I'll get you some coffee. We're all right, Tobe. *It'll all be all right.*"

IN THE ST. OSYTH'S snack bar I told Ian everything. I told him how my mother had yanked me out of school and about how I'd helped her set up her apartment and about how my dad was half crazy with worry and about how, well, I wasn't all that well myself. Ian asked me what I thought had really happened to my mother and I said I didn't know, I didn't have a fucking clue. I described Det. Thomas and his lame interrogation, and I told him how my dad had sworn he hadn't ever cheated, and how he swore on Mom's behalf that Mom hadn't cheated either, and how I believed him, how I had to believe him, how I didn't have a choice, *how the truth is never chosen.* And I told him how my mother had had me lie to Dad, and how I felt like shit for playing his trust off of hers. Then Ian swore he'd help me any way that he could figure, and as we sat huddled over a rickety table in the cozy buzzing shadows of the Koffee Mate machines, our fingers almost touching, our eyes in each other's, we'd never felt closer or deeper in love.

It was an oasis, the St. Osyth's snack bar, at five in the morning—an oasis of us. The room was packed to insomniac capacity, each sleepless soul in his or her own weary world—worried spouses or lovers who wouldn't or couldn't sleep and overworked doctors who couldn't and shouldn't sleep and hunchbacked chainsmoking gossiping nurses who rubbed each other's wrists and wore their nights beneath their eyes. The air was infested with secondhand smoke and everything seemed filtered through carcinogenic dreams as Ian, who'd dismantled his empty coffee cup, blew a flurry of Styrofoam chips in my face.

"I'm blind!" I cried.

He brushed the snowflakes off my lashes.

"Well, open your eyes, because I've got a secret, too."

I'll always remember the way Ian looked, that dreamy, smoky morning, when he told me what he told me. His face was pinched and flushed and excited, caffeine rushing in percolated surges to his cheeks. But his eye was downcast and water-blue and shattered-looking, like the headlights of Christ's Chevy in my mother's backyard. And his voice was filled with something I had never heard before, a language he had shared with no one else until now.

"He's here."

"Who is?"

"That man at convocation."

"What man at convocation?"

"That Jesuit *priest.* . . . 'Fr. Scarecrow,' Juice called him. He talked about God."

Ian stood up and dug some quarters from his pockets. He got fresh cups of coffee and handed one to me.

"Drink up," he told me. I did and scorched my tongue. "I'm gonna tell you something."

"Okay."

"He's got AIDS."

We were silent for a while; we were looking at each other; we were looking for an exit; we were looking at our hands.

"How do you know?"

"It's an AIDS ward, Toby. The clinic where we're working. You saw the patients there."

I remembered the baby crucified with I.V. needles, the skinny black kid swimming laps in his sleep, the gaunt Cuban woman with the paper straw body, the limp partition separating someone's pain from mine.

"His name is Fr. Scarcross—Sr. Cindy let it slip—and he used to be principal of Sacred Heart High."

"So much for patient confidentiality," I mumbled.

"She's dumb and indiscreet," Ian said, and spilled some coffee. "She knows we shouldn't be here. She's an idiot, Tobe."

"She didn't try to stop you?"

"She did, but I sweet-talked her. Said we were Volunteens for a program called the Night Owls. Nuns can be so trusting."

"She'll be sore tomorrow."

"I'll just say we thought we had the graveyard shift or something. Don't worry, Toby. I've got it figured out."

"And McDuffy and Kickliter?"

"They won't mess with me. I'm valedictorian. I'm going to Yale. I'm the motherfucking Jesuit ideal made flesh. They'll slap my wrist, kiddo. I'll play the innocent."

"Do they know about Scarcross?"

"If they do, it's hush-hush. A Jesuit with AIDS? That's lousy PR, Toby. And Sr. Cindy said AIDS wards are so overcrowded Fr. Scarcross is lucky to get a bed at all. But he's Catholic, you know. This is a Catholic hospital."

Outside, a paramedic unit splashed our faces pink. Ian stuck his finger in his coffee cup to test it.

"Aren't McDuffy and Kickliter and the others afraid that if we volunteer here we'll talk to somebody?"

"To somebody 'bout what?"

"About Scarcross being here."

"But we won't talk about it. It's *our* secret now, Toby. We'll have to take a vow of confidentiality."

"Just like Sr. Cindy."

"Just like Sr. Cindy." Ian's eyes were in mine. "But we'll keep our vow, now won't we?"

Outside the windows of the snack bar the night was caving in. It lay like scattered ashes on the quiltwork of the dawn.

"Have you talked to Fr. Scarcross?"

"I haven't. But I'd like to. That rose that you gave me, I left it for him. What he said about God—ya know, it really moved me. He's dying, though, Toby. And it kind of frightens me."

"That rose was for you."

"I know it. I'm sorry."

I looked at him and nodded; I wondered if he was.

"Yesterday, Ian, when me and Juice passed you, I saw you with my flower, but you didn't even see me."

Ian looked around and let his hand dandle mine. Already there was something unfamiliar in his touch.

"Yesterday, Tobe"—Ian's tone was low and plaintive; his glass eye jiggled up in jerks and zigzagged down again—"when Scarcross was speaking, when he was speaking to us, I swear to you, Tobe, he was looking right *at* me, and I wanted to help him, he wanted me to help him, can't you understand, Toby? *I wanted just to—*"

"Shhhh!"

An eleventh-floor nurse, harried on her coffee break, hurried over to Ian and plucked at his shirtsleeve.

"Whoever you are . . . Sr. Cindy wants you *now.*"

SR. CINDY WAS standing by a doctor in a scrubsuit with his village smithy forearms folded fiercely on his chest. The doctor was blushing all the way up to his forehead, and Sr. Cindy wore the chastened aspect of a truant.

"Why are you here at this hour of the morning? Who gave you permission? Answer me! *Now!*"

The doctor shoved his face in mine as if I were the problem.

"I—" I began, and cast a help-me glance at Ian. Ian was admiring the polished parquet floor.

"The other boy, the *quiet* one," Sr. Cindy intervened. "He claimed that they were Night Owls. Volunteens from Sacred Heart. This boy, doctor, he only just arrived. I really don't think he quite knows what's going on."

The doctor lunged forward and grappled Ian's shoulders.

"Who are you?"

"Ian Lamb."

"Why did you lie?"

"I wanted to see Scarcross."

"Goddamn it!" roared the doctor. "I'll call your principal!"

"Toby had nothing to do with this, sir," Ian said. "I told him to come here."

"And I let him in," Sr. Cindy admitted.

"Yes, well, all right," the frustrated doctor blustered, descending on Ian like a localized squall. "As for you, Mr. Lamb, you won't set foot in here again! This is a hospital!"

"Yes, doctor," Ian said.

"There are sick people here!"

"Yes, doctor," Ian said.

"You could put them at risk!"

"Yes, doctor," Ian said.

"I'll escort you out my*self.*"

"See you," Sr. Cindy said.

✹ FROM THE ELEVATOR we spied Sr. Cindy at her station leafing through *Whoever Dies with the Most Toys Wins*. She was humming a tune, a forgotten playground chant, and it spidered like the hand of a child up my spine as I stood behind Ian, who was singing sotto voce:

> *Liar, liar,*
> *Pants on fire,*
> *Hang your britches*
> *On a telephone wire . . .*

We could also make out, as the elevator closed, the still-open door of room 1111, behind which lay a stranger I would meet the next day, not out of any real curiosity of my own, but out of a curiosity Ian Lamb had thrust upon me.

✹ THAT DAWN WE made love in an industrial park, me and Ian, in the dark, behind a wall of damp cement. I remember Ian's tongue, and the pressure of his body, and the chlorine in his hair, and his cock against mine. I remember the words that we said to each other, and the words we didn't say, and the ones we didn't dare. I remember the way we slid apart from each other, after we had both come, and how I wanted just to hold him. As we straightened our clothes, and let our hands lose each other, and walked the crooked quarter mile back to Sacred Heart, I would agree to apologize to St. Osyth's Hospital and offer my services as a clinic volunteer. Ian, who would receive exactly as predicted a slapped wrist from McDuffy in response to St. Osyth's call, would be forced to content himself with the Gospel of Scarcross secondhand and second fiddle through his second ear: me. And Ian would select for his new community service project, at my and Kickliter's enthusiastic behest, outreach interaction with a crosstown shut-in: a shut-in who had no idea, in fact, she *was* a shut-in; a shut-in who had no idea, indeed, who Ian Lamb was; a woman who, against her better judgment, would snap up Ian's offer of yard work and home repairs and befriend the secret boy who loved her son in secret; the boy who, in her son's name, and in the name of Fr. Scarcross, would go about getting at the truth behind the lie that like the dark and lightsome seeds of a common garden weed would scatter upon touching and breed so many others.

WITHOUT EVEN HAVING done anything wrong, I felt an overwhelming urge to go to confession.

"Father, forgive me, for I have sinned. It has been two weeks since my last confession, and these are my sins."

Unfortunately, the voice that responded to my plea reeked unenticingly of corned beef and cabbage—and when you're anticipating the hot, lusty sizzle of paella, or the sweet musky tang of nutmeg-dusted white sangria, nothing's more unappetizing than an Irish potluck dinner.

"I'm sorry, Fr. Tierney, I need more time to contemplate. Would you excuse me?"

"Again? As yar wish."

In my bimonthly version of "The Lady or the Tiger"—or "The Laddy and El Tigre," as Ian jokingly called it—I made the Sign of the Cross and beat a hasty retreat from the rank little booth that stank of moral suffocation. Passing the scandalized Ty-D-Bol widows, I waited patiently in line for the confessional across from Tierney's, the booth containing Fr. Diaz—in his underwear, I hoped.

"In the name of the Father, and of the Son, and of the Holy Spirit. Amen."

I hadn't even finished crossing myself and already carnal thoughts were mounting upward to the ceiling. I breathed Den-

tyne, nicotine, Aramis, sweat: all my favorite smells except the
smell of Ian Lamb. In the checkerboard of shadows beyond the
iron grating a beautiful open-throated Ralph Lauren shirt revealed a crucifix nestled in a dark nest of chest hair, a slender
thumb and finger fondling Christ's pinioned body.

*"Father, forgive me, for I am sinning. It's been five minutes
since my last confession, now drop your Calvins and show me
your birthmarks. . . ."*

On hearing my voice as I proceeded with the more familiar
but less appropriate opening appeal, Fr. Diaz scratched his chin
and cupped his hands and softly lit a cigarette. He always had a
postcoital air around me. Once he even offered me a Lucky
through the grating. He said that it kept him from smoking too
much, but really it was like breathing his breath into mine.

"Dispense with the preliminaries," Fr. Diaz ordered. "*Cómo
estás*, Toby? When will we play tennis? I have this new racket
with an oversized head. Do you like bigger rackets?"

I told him I did.

"Good. We will play. Now, what is your trouble?"

"My mother moved out of the house, Fr. Diaz."

I sounded so pathetic. It really was erotic.

"Your father has not told me."

"He wouldn't. He's ashamed. And three days have gone by,
and I know where she is, but still I haven't told him. I swore I
wouldn't tell."

"Has your father hurt your mother?"

"Not that I know of."

"Have you hurt your mother?"

"I—I don't think so."

"And she wants to be alone?"

"For a while, I think."

"So what is the problem?"

"I feel like a liar. Dad asked me where she was and—"

"You said you did not know." Fr. Diaz sighed a swoony blast
of Scopy lover's breath. "Press your hand against mine on the

grating, Toby Sligh. Press your hand against mine and listen carefully to me."

A fine, slender hand came to rest against the webbing. Behind it, two eyes smoldered wetly in the darkness.

"Do you love your mother?"

"Yes."

"And your father, no?"

"I love him too."

"And you love yourself?"

I stuttered that I did.

"And do you love Jesus?"

"Yes, Fr. Diaz."

"Then pray every night, and have faith in God, and faith in yourself, and everything will be fine. I have spoken to your mother. She still loves your father. I swore I wouldn't tell you, but I've broken my vow. There, now! I'm a liar like you, Toby Sligh!"

I got, at that moment, the most incredible erection.

"But my heart is full of love. Do you understand, Toby?"

"Yes," I responded, full of something else entirely.

"So keep your heart happy, hopeful, and patient. And don't do anything hurtful or stupid. And lie if you have to, but only if you have to. Then it isn't lying. It's a subtle kind of truth. Will you promise me?"

"Yes."

"We will play tennis?"

"*Sí.*"

"Have some cigarettes. Go."

I plucked two Luckies through the grating.

"DIDN'T KNOW YOU smoked." Juice spoke from behind his Ray-Bans, sprawling in star-spangled Speedos in his Porsche convertible. It was a gorgeous day, Juice had put the

Porsche's top down, and he lay there like a bronze god on hiatus from Olympus, his running back's body lathered up with Coppertone.

"Juice! I can't believe you! You want some nun to see you?"

" 'Bout time they seed a real man," he said, and squeezed his balls. "Gimme one uh d'em Luckies."

"No way. They were a present."

"Gifts make *slaaaves*," Juice drawled, and rolled over. "What took you so long? I know you can't be *that* bad."

"Scoot over," I said. I got in the front and shoved him. His body, as always, gave way beneath my touch. "The line to confession, you know, was a long one."

"Uh-huh, I bet it was. You be jackin' off in there." Juice yawned, and pinched my titty, and nodded at a wad of clothing. "Gimme d'em, my Versaces. . . . I finna, Tobe, get dressed."

EARLIER THAT MORNING, before convocation, me and Ian had been summoned to the principal's office and given a mildly flattering tongue lashing for the previous night's escapade at St. Osyth's Hospital. McDuffy couldn't have been too upset about the matter: through the passive-aggressive length of his tepid reprimand he kept putting golf balls into an automatic gadget that spat them back at him with a gleeful clucking sound.

"Hoodwinking nuns," McDuffy said, "is verboten. And the ward you were at is chock-full of sick people."

Ian again took the blame upon his shoulders. McDuffy, a stork with a tubercular complexion, heard Ian out and even chucked his dimpled chin.

"Because you two are among my best students, I'll let you off this time with only a warning."

"Thank you, Fr. Tony," we said and stood to go. McDuffy waved papally. We halted at the door.

"Father," Ian said, drawing in a measured breath, and seizing McDuffy's clement mood by the *cojones,* "we need passes to complete our community service hours."

"Passes?"

"Yes, passes. Excuses from our classes. We've been accepted to good colleges and—"

"Shhh. Say no more!"

With a bureaucratic flourish of his faux Cross pen, McDuffy wrote out two elaborate passes—Ian's for morning classes, mine for afternoon, so that we couldn't work together, crime partners that we were; but so that, if we were crafty, at our break for senior lunch, we might see each other briefly, if only for an hour.

"But Lamb, stay away from St. Osyth's. Do you hear me? And, Tobias, get some sleep. You look horrible."

IT WAS TRUE. I'd hardly slept in over forty-eight hours, what with Dad and Ian's sticky nocturnal missions. Before chapel I'd pulled an alarmed Juice aside and begged him for a benny, but he said he'd sold them all. Then I asked him if he'd drive me to confession at lunch, and then to what I said was my first community service session, and though he agreed with affectionate suspicion, when Juice got word of our passes from McDuffy he kept muttering "Shit" all the way through convocation and casting sour glances first at Ian, then at me, as if we were privy to insider's information, as if we knew some angle even he had never figured. "Wha'd you two do, lick McDuffy's rectum? I hope it taste good. You wanna lick mine?" Like all the other seniors, Juice got an hour for lunch, and it really pissed him off: here we'd snagged a half a day.

"You know how much money I'd make with that schedule?"

We were driving to his cousin's public school to score some drugs. After that, Juice would drop me off at my mother's, where

Ian was waiting; he'd been waiting all morning; he had parked out of sight, so Juice wouldn't spot his car.

"McDuffy go an' han' me a schedule like that, I could buy and sell Ian's daddy's stanky rich white bootie twice," Juice declared, and hocked a loogie out the window, and mangled the stickshift, and threaded cufflinks through his shirtsleeves. "An' what am I doin'? Chaufferrin' you! *Drivin' Miss Toby!* An' can't even bum a smoke!"

"A priest gave 'em to me."

"Like I'm believin' *that.*"

"You can ask him yourself."

"I had enough a priess."

Juice, it was true, had had enough of priests, had had enough of churches, had had enough of God. He wouldn't even step inside St. Pat's while I confessed. Religion was a joke, and I was just a sucker: "I'm a chill out in the Porsche. I be sick a sin and shit." Juice's mother had enrolled him at Sacred Heart High when he was small enough for her to let him take her in a fight, but Mrs. Compton was hardly what you'd call a Catholic. Valilian Compton was a misanthropic realist who managed a motel and believed in little else besides her monthly paycheck and herself and her boy Leon. The Jesuits, she claimed, had saved her son from public school, which had taken most of the men she had known, including her ex-husband, and Juice's half brother, and prepared them well for prison—or for smaller, darker cells. Little did she know that her baby was a dealer.

Juice was clever at it; he made sure she didn't know. He parked his Porsche convertible every night in a garage he rented from Koreans and drove a shit-car home. He tucked his fatter earnings in mutual funds and spent his funny money on fly clothes and French cologne. And he told Mrs. Compton, who had reason to believe him, that he'd won a scholarship to a Pac-10 college where he'd pursue a B.A. in Political Science with an undeclared Minor in Psychopharmacology. In fact, it was true: Juice *had* won a scholarship, but it wasn't a full ride, it wasn't even close. So Juice whipped out his American Express and with only a minimal amount of ceremony awarded himself a Leonard Compton Fellowship. Juice's entire labyrinthine existence revolved around conducting his clandestine operations in a manner sly enough to support a clever mother without her ever guessing, without her ever cluing in, Mrs. Compton was his God; she was *all* of his devotion. His drug deals were the mysteries he offered up to her. "As for God," Juice would argue, delivering the coup de grâce, "in *Capital,* Karl Marx stuck his jimmy in religion."

"Hold on, you lost me there."

Juice's beeper started beeping.

"He just opium, Tobe. . . . We got our *own* product t' sell."

A PUERTO RICAN honey in a pink body glove was waiting for Juice by a huge water tower with "TROOTH" in fat graffiti letters smeared in gold across it. She was staring at her nails, which were wet with black enamel, and puffing them dry with pouty collagen lips. Behind her, her friends were conspiring in the shadows. A coach with a whistle was approaching in the distance. A car was circling. It was a white Plymouth. The girl was very nervous. She was holding someone's bag.

"That ain't Anquanna," Juice said, pulling over.

The girl was looking at us.

"You Leon?" she said.

"Uh-huh. Where's Anquanna?"

"She at the bloodmobile. I got what she give me."

She handed Juice the bag.

"Who's he?" She nodded at me. "He selling shoes or something?"

"My name is Cracker Jack."

Juice stuck his finger in and . . .

"*Shit!*"

A prankster in the shadows set off a ladyfinger. The girl whirled around and hurled curses at the joker: "Reggie, you dumb motherfucking cocksucker! I kick yo' butt, Reggie, you. try that shit again!"

Everyone was laughing. I'd almost crapped my pants. Juice was glancing in the rearview at the Plymouth circling.

"This is half," Juice declared, and tossed the girl the plastic bag.

"It's like a hot potato!" she laughed, and tossed it back.

Juice pulled out an envelope and took some money from it and gave it to the girl and handed me the bag.

"Give it to Anquanna, but say it's only half. She better find the other half," Juice added, like a gangster.

"Yeah, yeah," the girl said, puffing on her fingernails.

"You hear me?"

"I hear you . . ."

"You don't hear—"

"Shit!"

Something suddenly exploded. Somebody blew a whistle. There was fighting. There was shouting. The Porsche was pulling *g*'s. I thought I heard a siren, but it was only fear as I watched the water tower in the rearview mirror, shrinking.

"HOW YOU LIKE Sacred Heart now?" I asked Juice.

He was parked behind a billboard staring at the steering wheel.

He said, "Fuck you, Toby."

He was shaking like a baby. He was struggling with something. He was trying not to cry.

JUICE DROVE TO my mother's like a driving school instructor, all textbook stops and D.O.T. turns, swearing up and down someone was following us: the white Plymouth we'd seen outside the school, to be specific. He wanted to tear off, but he kept the Porsche purring until we were only half a mile from my mother's, when he hollered, "There they is!" and put the pedal to the metal. The squealing purple Porsche plowed through a row of tinpan trashcans that clanged across the pavement like a symphony for pots, and we glimpsed through hooded eyes the white shadow of the Plymouth as Juice spun into an alleyway a few blocks from my mom's.

"Ain't diggin' this, Juice—"

"It's like a episode a *Chips!* How far I gotta *take* you?"

"I can walk to there from here."

"Take my stash."

We got out.

"Take your what?"

"Take my stash! If they undercover, Sligh—"

"This is bullshit!"

"Toby, *please!*"

I was holding the bag. It felt awkward in my hands. Juice looked at me and coughed and stuffed a gun and money in it.

"Here they come," Juice said. "You git on up my shoulders, Toby."

"You're kidding me, right?"

"This ain't time to fuckin' kid!"

"But the gun'll go off!"

"No, it won't!"

"Yes, it will!"

"No, it won't! It's a old one. . . . *Up ya go, Toby Sligh!*"

And I couldn't help thinking, "Gifts make slaves," as I mounted Juice's shoulders and let him flip me up and over the steep wooden fence that bordered the alley where Juice lay waiting like a fugitive, trapped.

✳ AT FIRST I couldn't budge. I was p-paralyzed with fear. I felt the damp nose of a dog on my arm as I lay in the weeds with Juice's stash underneath me. Through the gaps in the fence I spied Juice's purple Porsche sticking out like a thumb someone had caught inside a cardoor. Juice was in the front seat chilling out to En Vogue:

> *I wear tight clothing*
> *And high heel shoes,*
> *It doesn't make me a prostitute, no . . .*

When the Plymouth pulled up, two guys in Wayfarers stepped out.
"Get outta the Porsche."
"Wha'd I do?" Juice said.
"Get out, you fuckin' monkey!"
Juice stepped slowly out.

> *I might date another race or color,*
> *Doesn't mean I don't like*
> *My strong black brother . . .*

I could see Juice spraddled at the side of the alley as the taller guy frisked him and the shorter one searched the Porsche.

> *Free your mind,*
> *And the rest will follow.*
> *Why, oh, why must it be this way? . . .*

"He's clean," they both said.
"He's lucky," they both said.

> *Can't change your mind,*
> *Can't change my co-lor . . .*

"You treat me like a King."
There was a sharp punching sound.

> *Before you can read me*
> *You got to learn how to see me, I said.*

"We don't wanna see your nigger ass again."

Juice was clutching his stomach. Beside me, the dog barked. I grabbed its mouth and held it. The men spun around.

"What was that?" one said.

Juice coughed. "Was a dog."

The taller guy approached him

"You're so fuckin' lucky."

"I'm charmed," Juice said.

"You're what?"

Juice spat.

"I said," Juice said, *"I said I'm fuckin' lucky ch—!"*

Then the taller guy did something and laughed when Juice shouted. It went through me like a blade—their laughter, not the shout. They left Juice lying in the dirt, like a rag. And I would have gone to him if he hadn't started talking.

"Oh, E-Eye! *I'm* sorry!" Juice's face was in his hands. He was rocking back and forth. He'd forgotten I was there. "Oh, E-Eye, I'm so*rry!* I fucked dat shit *up!*" He was crying. "Oh E-Eye! Oh, *Jesus!* *Oh, God!*"

ONE DAY, FOR a lark, I watched Juice at football practice. Inspired by something on *The NFL Today,* the coaches had strapped parachutes to all the players' backs and made them, upwind, run a hundred-yard dash. The sharp resistance offered by the mini-parachutes was supposed to give the players—running backs especially—superhuman speed when the chutes were removed. And though I had to admit that the concept looked ingenious, the players regarded the devices with distress, as if the coaches were purchasing sports equipment from de Sade. One by one the skittish players plowed the field, like scandalized skydivers, looking landlocked and ridiculous. The coaches timed them and called them wussies. They collapsed in the end zone clutching their chests. When it came Juice's turn, he tightened his chute with casual disdain and glanced archly at me. Juice was fast; he had always been fast; and he'd been snorting tons of coke, so his heart was souped and pounding. I remember abandoning my seat in the bleachers and going to the fence just to watch him make his run. All the other players were sitting up, too. The coaches were tense, in that lazy-tense coach way. Juice stood poised with his arms at his sides, cocked a little at the elbows, like wannabe wings, and the chute drooped behind him in a flaccid flaxen pouch, waiting for the wind to give it force and breath and vigor. When the whistle erupted, I remember getting goosebumps as the chute leapt to life behind Juice's chugging shoulders; I remember the way Juice's clumsy cleated feet dug and dug into the gridiron's hard uncompromising earth; and I remember how, right before the fifty-yard line, only a couple of feet from where I stood stone-still, Juice—whose face had been contorted in pain—broke suddenly into the most shit-eating grin I'd ever seen anyone grin in all my life. He didn't slow down; if anything, he sprinted faster. But as he overtook the forty, and the thirty, and the twenty—at a speed that seemed impossible and made the chute complain—a laugh, a colorful, rich, delicious laugh escaped Juice's lips and furled a rainbow in his wake. I was running by then, if a tiny bit behind him, Juice's music like live firecrackers underneath my feet, and my heart was filling up, like that stupid parachute, with the strength and joy and power of Juice's crazy jubilee. When at last Juice collapsed in a heap in the end zone, the coaches' eyebrows hooking at his otherworldly time, it was several minutes before Juice's laughing fit subsided. The players massed around him, and somebody fed him oxygen, and Juice lay there sucking it and sputtering hysterically, giggles spraying from his nose and lips like guzzled seltzer water. When the players hit the showers, and the coaches followed suit, Juice was left alone in the sunlight in the end zone, winding down like a laughing box whose batteries were dying. He sat there examining the limp chute in his hands, dandling it gently up and down in his lap, tossing it and smiling as it wafted back to earth. He knew I was watching (Juice had always been a poser), and he rose and wiped his face off with the chute and slouched away. At the doorway to the locker room he pitched it in a trashcan. "See ya," he told it. "Wouldn't wanna *be* ya." But I rescued Juice's parachute and have it to this day.

ALREADY I COULD recognize my mother's neighborhood. Her place crouched in a cul-de-sac behind a clot of sawpalms, and I spied her in the gutter prodding something with a shotgun. Her hair was bound up in fat rabbit-ear ribbons, the kind Carol Brady wore for epic bouts of spring cleaning. And across the street from me, behind a charred apartment complex, Ian's car was parked and sparkling, far from my mother's view, a Mercedes rising up from a tenement of ashes like a diamond from a valley of incinerated coal.

I took a back way and snuck into Mom's yard with the idea of stashing Juice's drugs in the Corvair. By then Mom was washing her hair in the kitchenette. I saw her through the window, her shoulderblades working, her long arms searching for her head down in the sink. It was after lunch, too, Ian nowhere to be seen, as I crept to Christ's Chevy through the Calvary weeds. I opened the car door to a spray of cockroaches and muscular black lizards running relays on upholstery and Ian, paint-stippled and snoring up a storm, mouth open to flies and other curious vermin. Without waking him, I shoved the drugs beneath the carseat, brushed an earwig off his lip, and went to see my AWOL mom.

✺ WHEN I WAS a kid and had done something wrong and Mom asked me if I had, knowing fucking well I had, and I lied and said, "No, Mom, I have not done this thing," she would seat me on a barstool, place her right hand on my forehead, and slowly lift my bangs and read across my traitor's skin: *"L-I-E,"* as if I'd blushed my own betrayal. *"L-I-E!* Toby Sligh is telling *stories!"*

✺ "RANDALL!" MY MOTHER shouted. "Hand me that towel!" Her head was underneath the faucet and her soapy arms were flailing. "It's baby shampoo, but it stings!" she complained. "Hurry, please, Randall!"

"Okey-dokey," I replied.

I went to the counter and scooped up the towel that lay beside a basket of my father's folded laundry. I handed it to Mom, and she said, "Thank you, Randall."

"Who's Randall?" I asked.

Mom turned around and screamed.

"To*bi*as!"

"*Mother!*"

"What are you doing here?"

"I asked you the same question three days ago. Who's Randall?"

"Who's Randall?"

"That's right. Who is Randall? He the guy that you left me and Pop for?"

"Tobias!"

"Well, is he? I think I'm entitled to an answer. If I'm lying for someone, I'm entitled to the—"

"*Shhhh!*"

Ian came sleepwalking into the kitchen.

"Some'in' wrong, Mrs. S.?"

"Nothing's wrong, Randall."

My mother plucked a tear from her eye and went to Ian. She took him by the shoulders and steered him toward me.

"Toby, this is Randall. He's sort of my helper. Randall Webster, this is Toby."

"Hullo, Toby."

"Uh, hullo."

Well, there was certainly egg on my face. I'd picked the wrong time to call someone on a lover. But my mother, though rattled, was as oblivious as ever. Her son was just a bastard; he hadn't been found out. And I felt really guilty: Mom had lost her giddy glory; her face had that look of a drained toddler pool. I had taken Mom's peace with herself and destroyed it, and her nervous hands were working: I had done that to her, too. In the midst of a catastrophe my mother had a habit of going ballistic, as if cossacks were approaching. At home she would rearrange the spices on her spice rack, or index all her paperbacks, or baseball-bat the rugs. Now, because her Spartan pad was absolutely spotless, she had nothing to do but glance helplessly about her. And I didn't like that idle-looking shotgun in the corner. It said, "Pick me up!" It said, "Fiddle with me!"

"Toby just scared me. He didn't mean to, Randy. I was washing my hair, and I thought he was—"

"You."

"But I'm not," Ian told me, with a smile. "I'm me."

"That's right," my mom answered. "You're you."

I was dizzy.

"God, Ma, I'm sorry, I really didn't mean to—"

My mother rushed forward, and her hair dripped about me. "It's hard for you, Toby! I know! All this lying!"

Ian shuffled his feet, like a houseboy.

"Mrs. S.?"

"What is it now, Randall?"

"Can I go for the day?"

"Stay and talk to Toby! Randall's new here, just like I am!"

"I'm painting the house for your mother," Ian muttered.

"Just the outside," Mom added. "I've already done the inside."

"Where are you from?" I asked Ian, feeling seasick.

"New Orl'uns," he drawled.

I had the most terrific headache.

"Randall graduated from Sacred Heart of New Orleans," Mom offered, nodding. "His girlfriend lives round here."

"I can't find work, so I'm doing odd jobs."

"His rates are very reasonable."

"I'm poor."

"He needs money."

"I want a new truck."

I thought of his Mercedes.

"Mom, have you got any Advil or something? I'm feeling kind of funny."

A chair screeched beneath me.

"He looks faint," said Randall. Ian said, "I think he's fainting."

My mother's face was spinning.

"Toby Sligh, *are you all ri . . . ?*"

TEN MINUTES LATER I was at the kitchen table with my mother and my boyfriend sitting straight across from me. Mom and Ian looked like lovers, but really they were strangers. Me and Ian looked like strangers, but really we were lovers. And this was what we'd wanted. This was what we had arranged. Ian'd help me with my mom; I'd help him out with Scarcross. Already all I wanted was to call the whole thing off. But we were in this thing too deep, like doomed lovers say in movies. We were lying on margin and were waiting for the crash.

An Alka-Seltzer sizzled in a jelly jar before me, and I guzzled it, and belched, and felt like a million bucks. Ian Lamb was looking at me with a "Hold on, Toby" look. Things were back in focus, but they weren't any less distorted.

"I've got to get to Sacred Heart," I said, and stood to go.

"You're pale! You should rest!"

"I can take him in my truck."

"We need to talk, Toby!"

"I'll get in trouble, Mom! I'm late from senior lunch and Mc-Duffy'll suspend me!"

"You're sick! You just fainted!"

"I'm not! I'm exhausted!"

"Why are you exhausted?"

"Dad keeps me up all night! He drinks! He's pathetic! He contacted a detective! He's scared to death, Ma!"

"He is?"

"Yes, he is!"

"How sweet," Mom said.

"This is bullshit! I'm leaving!"

I took a step, swayed, and sat quickly down again.

She said, "You're still poorly!"

"Of course I'm still poorly! This whole thing's a nightmare! Why the hell are you *here!*"

"Should I leave, Mrs. S.?"

"Yes, Randall." Mom nodded. "And take that dead snake from the gutter."

"Dead snake! *What snake?*"

Ian/Randall left us, and my mother squeezed my hand. I was looking hard at her. I was looking hard for answers.

"Randy's doing odd jobs. He's not doing me."

"I know."

"Oh, you do!"

She looked a tiny bit offended.

"Do you want him to?"

"Now you're insulting me, Toby!"

"Mom, this is crazy! This whole thing's to the *curb!*"

"I did your father's laundry."

"Hooray! You did Dad's laundry! What's that shotgun doing in the corner there, Ma?"

"I shot a snake with it. A rattlesnake, Toby."

"Ask a silly question . . ."

"Don't take that tone with me! Yesterday I was sunbathing, and I left the door open, but when I came in, it was locked. Someone came inside and locked it. I was worried. So I asked the landlord for a gun."

"Did he show you how to shoot it?"

"She did: the landlady. So just now I found a snake. It was coiled up in the closet, and I chased it to the gutter, and I shot its stupid head off! When I came back inside I found Randall in the garden, asleep in that infested matchbox cluttering my yard. He watched me shoot the snake, then he left, *and fell asleep!* Must be something in the water, all you young strong kids exhausted. And I think you've got a fever—Toby Sligh, you're just a mess."

"Of course I'm a mess! I'm everybody's punchline! You're torturing the only two men that you love!"

"You didn't see me sunbathing yesterday, did you?"

I looked at her. "What?"

"Did you see me sunbathing?"

"No, Ma."

"No?" She shoved my bangs up off my forehead. "All right. I believe you."

I was learning how to lie.

"In a way I wish you had," Mom went on, and smoothed my forehead. "Then I'd really know for sure some pervert hadn't been in here."

"If the perverts don't get you, the rattlesnakes will. And who's this Randall fella? He could be anybody!"

"Are you jealous, Toby?"

"What?"

She was smiling. "Are you jealous?"

"Am I jealous of what?"

"Oh, you know . . ."

"No, I don't!"

Across the table Mom was staring mischievously at me. Her eyebrows were arching. She pressed her nose against mine.

"Are you jeal-ous, Toby Sligh?" she was singing. "Are you *jeal*ous?"

"Am I jealous of what? Stop talking in riddles."

"That I have my own place?"

"That you 'have your own place'! Is that what this is all about? You having an apartment?"

"Are you and Dad jealous that I'm living on my own?"

"Is that why you're here?"

"I don't know why I'm here!"

She was crying.

I shouted, "I'm sick of people crying!"

Mom wiped her eyes. "Sorry . . ." She sat up. "No, I'm not! This is my place! I'll cry!" So Mom wailed even louder.

Ian stuck his nose in.

"You okay, Mrs. S.?"

He was holding a snake with no head.

"Mind your business!" My mother stopped crying. "Toby's color's better, Randall. You can take him back to school now."

"Oh, Christ, Ma, I'm sorry!"

"Go, Toby!"

"Look at me!"

"Next time you'll be invited!"

"Mother, please!"

"See you, Randall."

"C'mon, Toby," Ian said.

 THINGS HAD GONE from weird to weirder, and they'd only just begun, and I didn't foresee any letup in the future.

All the way to St. Osyth's, in Ian/Randall's Mercedes/truck, I was lectured/harangued about keeping my cool—a headless rattlesnake in a garbage bag between us. "You have to learn to be a better liar, Toby Sligh. I've only known your mother for one afternoon, and already I know more about her than you do."

"What's that s'posed to mean?"

"I'll tell you what it means . . . after you and Fr. Scarcross have had your first talk."

"This is like a hostage deal!"

"What's wrong with you, Toby?"

"This whole thing upsets me!"

"You think I enjoy it?"

"Yes." I looked at him. "Yes, I think you *do!*"

Ian's right eye—the good one, the real one, the *living* one—was brilliantly, ebulliently, bloomingly blue, like a violet in a time-lapse Botany movie. And Ian seemed happier than I had ever seen him: he was fresh and rested-looking and slap-happy with good health, he gleamed like a porpoise in a pool fat with mackerel, his once sloppy posture was Mary Poppins perfect, and there were dimples in his cheeks I had never seen till then.

"Dimples don't lie."

Ian said, "What does that mean?"

"It means that I hope that you know what you're doing."

"I do."

"Because I don't."

"I love you," Ian told me.

"Do you really?"

Ian nodded.

"Then prove it."

"Oh, okay."

The Mercedes swerved off into a Spanish-mossy alley, and Ian switched the engine off, and kissed me on the mouth. It was the slowest, sweetest, deliciousest kiss I had ever tasted in all my kissing life. I felt like a body wafting backwards into water, soft water, with a softer body buoying me up. Then Ian unzipped me and slurped me like a sno-cone, and he tucked me back in, and his lips nibbled mine.

"I love you," Ian whispered. "Now do you believe me?"

"How can I believe you?"

"Because it's just the truth. Do you love me?"

"I do."

We kissed.

"I believe you."

"How?" he said, and shuddered.

"Because dimples do not lie."

I'D NEVER KNOWN what sex was until I met Ian.

Let me rephrase that: I'd never known what making love was until I met Ian.

No. Hold on a second. That's not right either. Let me take a deep breath and try one last time. . . .

Before I met Ian, I had known what sex was, I had known what making love was, I had known what these things were, but I hadn't really known what they *were,* if you get me. When Ian Lamb kissed me, I knew what mouths were for. I knew what *lips* were for. I knew what *tongues* were for. It was nice to know that mouths, lips, tongues—when put together—could do things other than gossip, curse, and lie. They could say, "You're my angel." They could say, "My darling boy." They could say, "Never leave me." They could say, "I love you so." They could say these things, and more than that, they could *mean* them. They could mean them just like mysteries denied you all your life. Ian's kisses were better than a sea of Alka-Seltzer. They cleared my head, and my heart, and my soul, and my stomach. They became like Juice's mother: they were *all* of my devotion.

And so many of those things I had thought were just corny before I knew what love was became wonderful to me—pop songs,
roses, couples kissing in a corner, going places together, just
missing someone. Even the thought of my parents making love
made a smile of complicity curl across my lips. Ian was my
boyfriend. Ian Lamb was my lover. He loved me. *Ian loved me!*
Ian's love was all my truth.

THE MERCEDES WAS idling outside of St. Osyth's. We sat in
air-conditioned splendor staring at each other.

"You gonna be all right?" Ian asked me, very softly. "You
wanna see Scarcross?"

I nodded.

"You sure?"

Upstairs, on floor eleven, Fr. Scarcross was waiting—the
man I thought might have been Ian the night before. This time I
would meet him: I would draw back the curtain. It scared me. I
could taste the copper pennies on my tongue.

"When will I see you?"

"Tomorrow at lunch."

"Take care of my mother."

"Your mom is all right. Take some money for a cab."

Ian gave me fifty dollars.

"Call Peaches."

"Who's Peaches?"

"The cabbie. *I love you.*"

"I love you too, asshole."

"And don't you forget it!"

"Five days to the prom."

"Five days to the prom!"

SOMEONE WAS HAVING a birthday, I could tell, because while Lucinda Delaney, the social worker at St. Osyth's, briefed me on my duties as an AIDS ward volunteer—transporting patients to and from their rooms, reading to them, just helping pass the time—Sr. Cynthia Rose, with the crack deliberation of a bomb squad expert jerked away from Happy Hour, poked a handful of candles in a lopsided cake that was less cake than candles, and about as appetizing.

"Keep an eye out for this one," Sr. Cindy warned Lucinda, a modish young woman with a gold spike in her tongue. "He's full of shit and mischief. At least last night he was."

"Toby Sligh's a baby," the social worker lisped, and tightened the spike in her tongue once, and coughed. "That's what disturbs me. Can you handle this, Toby? These people aren't projects. They're *people*."

I said I could.

"It's better that you focus on just one patient," Lucinda continued, taking out some Murine. "Though it tends to be harder on you when they go—Jesus, these contacts! You guys wear contacts?"

We told her we didn't.

"Fucking things," Lucinda said.

"I've got some idea who Tobias wants to talk to," Sr. Cindy interjected, pointing at me with a candle. "Fr. Scarcross."

"Fr. Scarcross? Why Fr. Scarcross?"

I didn't have a reason.

"He spoke to us at school."

Lucinda looked at Cindy, who was humming at the cake. Scowling, she whipped a scythe of black hair from her eyes.

"Fr. Scarcross is brilliant, but his mind is going, Toby. He's liable to say anything."

Sr. Cindy said, "Who isn't?"

"Two days ago in chapel he made perfect sense to me."

"Two days is a lifetime for someone with AIDS," the social worker said. "You like William Shakespeare?"

"Who?"

"William Shakespeare. He's kind of this writer. Like Aretha Franklin sings."

"I might have heard of him."

"And that other one," she added.

"Mrs. Dickinson."

"*Ms.* Her name's Emily, Sister."

"Yes, Mrs. Dickinson. And Blake. And the Bible! He likes to be read to. And sometimes to perform. He's a marvelous—"

"Actor!"

They chortled at each other. Their in-jokes were unsettling. I let their laughter curdle.

"What kind of an actor?"

"A performer, you know," Sr. Cindy said demurely. "Eli is a performer."

"Eli?"

"Elijah. Father's Christian name's Elijah." Lucinda sucked a Tic-Tac. "But we call him Ja for short."

So they called him Elijah. And Eli. And Ja. And I hadn't even been introduced to him yet.

"You know," Lucinda told me, tossing Sister her Zippo. "We try to keep things at St. Osyth's confidential. The fact you go to school where Scarcross has spoken, where he might even have friends—"

"I won't tell a soul," I swore.

"It isn't that, Tobias," Lucinda said measuredly. "It isn't not telling. It's much, much more than that. It's listening so . . . Well, so they know they're being heard."

"Like confession?"

"Like confession." Sr. Cindy backed me up.

"You can't bare your heart to someone who doesn't listen. Confidentiality is just the better half of compassion. It isn't not telling. It isn't just that. It's caring so much that all you *want* to do is listen."

"Like God," Sr. Cindy said, getting metaphysical, and continuing in a vein that made the social worker squirm. "God is the Listener. The priest is just the ear. What if you told God your sins and He squealed?"

"Maybe He does," I argued. "Maybe that's history."

"Gawd! Another deep one!" the social worker hooted. "Don't get deep, Toby Sligh! Get stupid!"

"Okay."

They lit the candles. I swiped some waxy icing.

"How'd he get the virus?"

Their looks were licensed weapons. I was trying to be clever, but I was weakening inside.

"That isn't a question we ask here, Tobias."

"I'm sorry," I apologized. "I'm curious. I'm stupid."

"There's stupid and there's stupid," Lucinda said, and stood.

"Talk with your ears, not your mouth," said Sr. Cindy.

"You're weird, all you Catholics," Lucinda said, and left.

 Hap-py birthday to you!
Hap-py birthday to you!
Hap-py birthday, Fr. Scarcross!
Hap-py birthday to . . .

 "I'M TWENTY-FIVE years old," Elijah Scarcross lied, in response to the chorus: "How old are you now?" He lay still in bed with his cake in his lap. He wasn't twenty-five. He was double that, at least. And in his drawn condition he looked older than the earth. His shoulders tapered down beneath a translucent nightgown, giving his head a totem's disembodied bigness, and what remained of his frame lay immobile on the bed that buoyed up his body like a dead man on a liferaft. He lifted some cake to his lips and chewed slowly, the outline of his jaw exaggerated through the skin as if illuminated by subcutaneous lanterns. And his neck and chest were speckled purple with lesions. They looked fresh and glossy, like flowers after rain.

"Twenty-five?"

"I'm incapable of telling a lie. Tell this young person I'm incapable of lying."

Lucinda, who was distributing cake to two men who might have been twenty-five but who looked similarly ancient, called out in Spanish to the starved Cuban woman, who barked and made a fist. Lucinda hurried over.

"It's true, Toby Sligh. Elijah doesn't lie. He's the only honest Catholic I've ever met."

"This cake, for instance. This is horrible cake. Who made this cake?"

"I did," said Sr. Cindy.

Fr. Scarcross clicked his tongue and took another wary bite.

"This cake is what you give to someone you want to kill. Do you want to kill me, Sister?"

"Sometimes, Elijah, yes."

Scarcross's laughter extinguished several candles on a slab of cake Lucinda had left burning at his bedside.

"Another honest Catholic!" Fr. Scarcross declared, his laughter erupting into hyperventilation. Lucinda rubbed his shoulders while the spasm subsided. Scarcross settled back into himself like potter's clay.

"How are your eyes?" Sr. Cynthia asked him.

Fr. Scarcross touched his face and smiled wistfully at no one. "I'll just have to see with other things," he said and shuddered. His hands fluttered down to his sides like lighting birds. "Is this young man honest?"

He was talking around me.

"Why don't you ask him?" Sr. Cynthia said.

"Are you honest?" Fr. Scarcross repeated, very slowly. Though thick with medication, his voice was musical.

"That's a question you should never ask a liar," I answered.

He was quiet for a while.

"He's honest," Scarcross said.

"I want to introduce him to your roommates, Elijah," Lucinda interrupted, and took me by the hand. "This is Peter," she said, and introduced me to a frail man fiddling with an I.V. needle dripping from his chest. "Peter, this is Toby."

"Hi, Moby," Peter mumbled. "My needle is infected."

Lucinda made a note.

"Be careful around Eli," Peter said. "He thinks he's God."

"I am!" Scarcross shouted.

Peter huffed, "Stupid queen! You really have to whisper! 'Sgot ears like fucking Dumbo! You fart and it's a headline! Fr. Ja hears everything!"

"I'll get another needle," Lucinda promised Peter, and left him fumbling idly with the leaky yellow tube.

"We call him 'Fr. Ja' because Ja is love, Moby," Peter informed me as we headed away.

"It's Toby, not Moby."

"It's what?"

I turned to him.

"It's Toby, not Moby. My name is Toby Sligh."

"Too bad," Peter sighed, and smiled semi-rudely. "In that case, me and André won't get to see your d—"

Lucinda cleared her throat. "Be nice now, Peter."

"I'm always nice, girlfriend! See ya later, Missy Thang!"

I shook my head vaguely and followed Lucinda to the bed beside Peter's, where another man lay.

"This is André," she began. "André Lopez, this is Toby."

André Lopez didn't answer.

"Toby Sligh," Lucinda said.

André Lopez tried to smile, but his lips were caked with ul-

cers, and his tongue, faint with thrush, strained in vain to pry
them open. He was handsome for a man who was dying, I
thought, his face drawn back by an invisible hand. Underneath
the muslin blanket you could make out where his body, once
muscular and hardened, had given rein to AIDS. André closed
his eyes and sighed an infantile sigh, and I was reminded of the
baby in the cage the night before.

"Yesterday you were a child," I told him inexplicably.

He cast a glance at Lucinda that said, "Translate, please."

"André was a dancer in Miami," said Lucinda.

André smiled at me.

"Wanna . . . dance?" André said.

After a while Lucinda leaned over, pried our fingers apart,
and escorted me away. She mumbled something to me I couldn't
understand and led me to the bed where the Cuban woman lay.
Underneath her arm was a box of Havatampas—empty, I would
learn, except for orange peels—and she lay there tense and
coiled as a jack-in-the-box, her unblinking eyes glowering up at
the ceiling as if through sheer volition she held the clinic up. I
wanted to speak, but I could only stare.

Lucinda said, "Magda doesn't talk much, Toby."

I said, "*Hola,* Magda."

"*Maricón,*" Magda said.

"Do you understand Spanish?" Sr. Cindy called over.

"No," I informed her.

"*Es mejor,*" Lucinda said.

THE NEXT THING I knew, I was sitting beside Scarcross,
who was staring at his hands, and the partition had been
drawn. I could make out Lucinda's and Sr. Cindy's footsteps disappearing in a military tattoo down the hall, and the curtained-
off space containing me and Fr. Scarcross was filling up with

silence and pneumoniac breathing. Outside I heard a kettledrum of early summer thunder, and through a V in the curtains I saw thunderheads form. Scarcross's dead eyes were pivoting toward me. They were terrible with mucus. He began to speak to me.

"Books . . . I want books. . . . I made a list for you . . . Can you read, child?"

"What?"

"Can you read?"

"My name's Toby."

He coughed into his fist and cast a doubtful glance at me.

"Can you read, Toby Angel?"

"Toby Sligh . . . I can read."

"How old am I really?"

"Twenty-five, like you said."

A spasm rocked his body and his hands gripped the bedrail. He was groaning. I rose from my chair.

"It will pass!"

Outside, it was raining. I stared out the window. I watched two water droplets running races down the glass.

"There now, it's gone. The pain is gone, Toby. It's raining. I can hear it. . . . Will you give me your hand?"

The hand in his lap reached for mine, and I took it. He held on to me lightly. It felt like we were floating.

"You aren't afraid, are you? I thought you might be frightened. I feel your heart beating through your wrist. Feel my heart."

His fingers pressed mine to his pulse, which was racing. Every other second it would drop an awkward beat.

"That's where my life will fall through," he confided. "I've always lacked grace. . . . I've always made a sloppy exit."

He coughed and his hands wafted up to his face. His fingers pressed his eyelids and collapsed into his lap.

"My eyes—it's a cytomegalovirus. It means I'm going blind. I can't read anymore. . . . Come closer. Lean in. I can barely see you. We only have words now. Describe yourself to me."

"I—"

"Let me guess. I'm good at guessing, Toby! I can make you out a little, if you lean closer in. . . ."

I drew a sharp breath as I leaned into Scarcross. He was wheezing. His breath fanned my eyes. It was sweet.

"You have soft eyes . . ."

"Yes."

"And dark hair . . ."

"Yes."

"But your soul is light, Toby. It's lighter than air! How old are you?"

"Seven—" I stumbled. "Seventeen."

"You sound older."

"What?"

"You sound older, Toby!"

"I feel older."

"No. You feel seventeen. And you wouldn't think, to look at me, that I was twenty-five. . . . Are you frightened yet?"

"What?"

"Are you frightened, Tobias? So many people are. Are you frightened of the truth?"

I said I wasn't.

"That's good. You shouldn't be. Because lies—" He was trembling. "*Because lies are God's weeds.* We'll tend to our garden. Be lieless, like children."

"About what?"

"About *what?* About *every*thing, Toby! . . . We'll talk about our life and our friends and our family and be absolutely honest. I would like that very much."

"More than books?"

"More than books. Because words, these words we say . . . These words are not books. . . . These words are not lies. . . . These words are our spirit. . . . These words are our truth. Will you do that for me, Toby? Tell the truth. Will you promise?"

"I . . . promise."

"When I ask about your day, will you tell me every detail? You won't say it was okay and just let it go at that? Will you tell me what happened, and how it made you feel? It would make me so happy if you did that, Tobias. To hear an honest person, to hear one authentic voice . . . All our lives, you know, we're searching just for that. All we ever want is to speak honestly to someone. You'd think it would be simple, to speak the way we feel, but—"

"It isn't."

"No, it isn't. That's the virus that we carry. We save honesty for God and lie to everybody else. . . . A waste of precious breath. A precious waste, Tobias. *Would you like a lie?*"

"What?"

"Would you like to have a lie? Just one, a free one, to carry round in your pocket?"

I looked at him.

"Now, now . . . You go ahead and take it."

He plucked something from the air and he handed it to me.

"I don't want it, really."

"You tuck it in your pocket. . . . One lie is not a lot, when we consider all we've got."

"Do you get a lie?"

"What?"

"Do you get a lie, Eli?"

Fr. Scarcross touched his throat and turned his face away from mine. It felt as if we were in the room with someone else. Far away, across town, I could hear a siren singing. In an intimate voice, Scarcross spoke to no one there:

> *Little Lamb, who made thee?*
> *Dost thou know who made thee?*
> *Gave thee life, & bid thee feed*
> *By the stream & o'er the mead;*
> *Gave thee clothing of delight,*
> *Softest clothing, wooly, bright;*

> *Gave thee such a tender voice,*
> *Making all the vales rejoice?*
> *Little Lamb, who made thee?*
> *Dost thou know who made thee?*

"Dost thou know?" Scarcross whispered. "Do you know, Toby Sligh?"

When I told him I didn't, his reply filled the room.

> *Little Lamb, I'll tell thee,*
> *Little Lamb, I'll tell thee:*
> *He is called by thy name,*
> *For he calls himself a Lamb.*
> *He is meek, & he is mild;*
> *He became a little child.*
> *I a child, & thou a lamb,*
> *We are called by his name.*
> *Little Lamb, God bless thee!*
> *Little Lamb, God bless thee!*

"*List, list, list* . . . My list is on the table. You tuck it in your pocket. You have a little lie."

Outside, it was pouring. Fr. Scarcross touched my eyes.

"God bless you, Tobias. God bless you, Toby Angel!" He was falling asleep now. "You guard me while I dream."

The Tempest, Shakespeare
Experience & Innocence, Blake
The Bible
The Complete Poems of Emily Dickinson

FR. SCARCROSS NEVER woke—at least not while I was there. A nurse padded in and gave him an injection, changed his I.V., and said I had to go. I'd been sleeping for hours, through the rain and clumsy thunder, in the chair beside Eli, clutching his list. I'd awakened from a dream to see a doctor staring at me with curious amusement as he checked Elijah's pulse. He said, "You're the other one," and made a wry face. I'm the other one? I wondered. I'm the other what? I drifted off again until a second nurse came in and shook me by the shoulders and said, "Up and Adam." I shuffled off my sleep and unpocketed the money Ian had given me to catch a cab home. I was glad that he had. Outside, it was a deluge. And the room was strung with lightning as I passed by Peter's bed.

"Moby! Psst!" a voice whispered to me.

The nurse was in with Scarcross, so I headed for the voice.

"How's it hangin', Moby?"

"It's Toby," I yawned.

"You yawned in my face!" Peter shouted, scandalized.

"Now listen," he continued, talking like a junkie. His face was streaked with lightning and his eyes were quick and red. "I have something for you." He produced an envelope.

"What is it?" I asked.

"You can open it downstairs. . . . You'd better go, girlfriend."

I took the envelope and left.

PEACHES PULLED AROUND so I wouldn't get soaked and seemed more than pleased when I slipped her Ian's fifty. "That boy be livin' *large*," she declared and lit a joint. I was sitting by a pretty little three-year-old kid.

"That's Donna," Peaches said. "My dead sister's baby. This be mobile day care."

"Hullo, Donna," I said.

"Say hello, girl!" Peaches ordered.

Donna coughed.

"It's the smoke," Peaches told me. "Little Donna, she doan mind."

Donna smiled shyly and, noticing the envelope, tried to snatch it from me with her quicksilver hands.

"Donna, stop dippin'!" the lady cabbie scolded. "She always got her little hands in everybody's business!"

Lightning struck a tree and Donna shouted, *"Jacaranda!"*

"She get some Hershey Kisses if she say that," Peaches said.

When the cab pulled away from St. Osyth's in the downpour, I sneezed and felt my forehead and found out that I was hot. In the mirror I discovered that my tongue was white and coated—like André's, the patient I had seen, who had AIDS.

"You sick?" Peaches asked.

"I might be," I told her.

I fingered my throat: my glands were taut and swollen. I looked down at Donna—she was fingering her throat.

"Monkey see, monkey do," Peaches commented.

I made a face at Donna; she laughed and grabbed for me.

"Doan you let Donna crawl over you, honey! She jess like her mama—she all over white boys!"

Having overcome any preliminary shyness, Donna settled like an oversized doll in my lap. Her small head was cushioned in the pit of my arm as I opened Peter's envelope and Peaches prated on.

"Sho' you ain't sick?"

"I'm not sure at all."

"Got AIDS in that place."

"Uh-huh, yeah, I know."

"Want a condom?"

"A what?"

"You never know, baby."

"You never know what?"

"When you got to scratch the itch. You got AIDS?"

I looked at her. "Excuse me?"

Peaches coughed. "I said, You got aches?"

"I thought you said—"

"*Donna!*"

Donna, who thought I was a playground contraption, had scaled my upper body and was hanging round my neck. Peaches was staring in the rearview skeptically. She gave a little grunt and pitched her dead blunt out the window.

"Mama say, 'Girl, you feel under the weather, you take a little child and you hold it to your chess. You feel better no time.' Donna-honey he'p you *out*."

It was true: there is something restorative in children. Holding Donna, I felt like I was holding my own heart.

"Of course, then ag'in, you might give her what*choo* got," Peaches concluded, cranking up Bob Marley. I looked once at Donna. She was looking at me. Her eyes had that bottomless look of acceptance only little children know, and only children outgrow.

> *How long shall they kill our prophets*
> *While we stand aside and look?*
> *Some say it's just a part of it—*
> *We've got to fulfill the book. . . .*

"That baby girl, shit, she as strong as two fellas. I be there when they had her," Peaches said. "Kid come out swangin'—"

Suddenly, Donna grabbed the envelope from me and tore it in pieces as I scanned Peter's note. She'd also found the twenty-dollar bill he had inserted and examined it with interest, then stuffed it in an ashtray. Donna settled back into the cushion of my lap and tried to pick my nose as I read Peter's letter:

> *Moby,*
>
> > *My brother says he will pay you*
> > *more money if you can find me the*

drugs we read about in journals.
Can you get them for me? if not I
understand. I think you are very
sweet like my brother. Kenny's gay
too are you? I thought so! I am
sorry Moby if I embarass you by
asking you are awfully sweet.
Destroy this letter because of
course St. Oz's will be SO PLEASED
to here that I am looking for other
treatment! It is all too slow and
then we will be dead. Can I call
you Moby girlfriend don't take
offence its only a joke!

—*Love & Tongue Kisses, Peter*

"Lemme ask you something," Peaches was saying. "Ian, he tell me your name is Tobias, my name be Peaches to my family an' friends—"

Behind us, a patrol car cruised around a corner, then another one like it started cruising at its side. I gave Donna Peter's letter and she put it through the "shredder," then she stuffed it in the ashtray with the twenty-dollar bill.

"Toby, you in any kinda trouble with the law?"

"No," I said. "Why?"

Peaches grimaced at the squad cars.

" 'Cause every time I getchoo the man be on my tail! I ain't never seen someone like you for fetching cops!"

"Jacaranda!" Donna squealed.

"There she go," Peaches muttered.

The police pulled away, and behind them, in the storm, a gorgeous tree exploded with color in the wind, its long arms heaving with violet flowers, the wet ground around it spilling purple in the rain.

"Jacaranda!" Peaches sang, and Donna shrieked sweetly. "Every time she see one, she say it, Lord have mercy! Her auntie give her Kisses when she do that, so she do it. She think it make her smart, but she ax juss like a ho'."

Donna curled up in a ball against my chest.

"She like you," Peaches said.

I stroked her hair.

"I like her too."

"She strong as two men," Peaches said. "Ain'tchoo, honey?"

Donna was sleeping.

"Rain'll do that," Peaches said.

PEACHES DROPPED ME off at the end of our block so my father wouldn't see that I'd been brought home by a cab. I sprinted through the squall and almost tripped across two cats who were hunchbacked and howling, hypnotized by coming violence. They looked like they'd been delivered by or from a hurricane, and I would've separated the two with my shoe if I hadn't been vaguely aware of a rebellion in the pit of my bowels as I hurried up the drive. Dad's car was missing, in itself an odd thing: he never went out weeknights; the TV tethered him. *Ahoy there, Pops!* My shout echoed down the hallway as I burst into the house: it ricocheted in emptiness. On the counter in the kitchen lay a photograph of Mom looking forlorn and forgotten. It was pasted on pink paper. Above Mom's photo Dad had written in Crayola "Have you seen me lately?" several times, and crossed it out. At the bottom of the paper, under pencil erasures, was a word Dad had scribbled and obliterated: "Tom's." I didn't know a Tom and neither did Dad, and neither did Mom, as far as I knew. And the windows and curtains in the house were open wide and little pools of rainwater had stained the windowsills. I called out for Dad, but he wasn't anywhere as I ran about the open house battening down the hatches; and outside my parents' window I could see the same cats turning threatening circles and shrieking at each other. They weren't any neighborhood toms I'd ever seen. They looked like they'd been born to fight and frighten each other. I slammed the window shut on their god-awful music and, impelled by a matter just a little bit more pressing, rushed into the bathroom and let my trousers drop. A great spray of diarrhea flooded the toilet and a wave of itchy sweat unfurled across my chest. I sat there, reeling, and hoisted up a paper basket. I dry-heaved a little, then when my bowels regained control, I wiped my throbbing asshole and hobbled off to bed. I was sick. The house was empty. I had a whopping fever—103°, Mom's thermometer read—and though I'd always been inclined to mild hypochondria, even I knew that a flu was just a flu, that you had to ride it out, that you had to get rest. The fact that I'd been sleeping with a guy I'd only known for five, six months, a guy from somewhere else, a guy who seemed less experienced than I was—except at matters like, um, head and French kissing—had not permitted darker thoughts to steal inside my mind. I hadn't been eating. I hadn't been sleeping. I was under stress. I had sprinted through a storm. My aches, my diarrhea, the glands expanding in my throat had nothing to do with the boy I had kissed, the lips I had tasted, the body I had shared. And I was sufficiently enlightened to know that the hands I had held that day at St. Osyth's were far more likely to feel the effects of any virus I might carry than any they might transmit, *than any they could transmit,* ravaged as they were. I had seen enough pandering public service announcements to know that you couldn't get AIDS just through touching, that only blood and semen were the bearers of bad tidings, messengers whom—in this case—you couldn't kill, but messengers who, in any case, could kill you. I'd never let Ian Lamb come inside my mouth. And we'd never had each other up the butt, or anything. Except for the occasional backseat blow job, our activities had been confined to deep kissing and rubbing. But how deep did we kiss? And how hard did we rub? Once, after serious foreplay with Ian, I'd noticed an abrasion on the shaft of my dick. I dabbed it with alcohol, lightly; it stung. That stinging told me it had opened on the bloodstream; and I thought about Ian, and a past I didn't share. Just because Ian seemed more innocent than I was didn't mean he *was*. So he *said* he was a virgin . . . I loved him so much I couldn't think about his past. The present is future enough for anybody. I knew I was clean; I'd had a couple quick encounters that were more guilt-inflicting than anything else. Then I'd met Ian and we'd fallen in love. We were young and attractive and healthy and safe. We wouldn't hurt each other. We couldn't hurt each other. AIDS was something other, older, gayer people got. But that night, in bed, quilts and blankets wrapped around me as another arctic cold front descended on my room, I thought about Ian, and the things we had done, and I sweated so much that I left a silhouette of my body on the bedsheet that lay suffering beneath me. We'd kissed in the library, that week, and I'd bled. I'd cut my lip open, Ian's spittle had entered, and if for any reason . . . I couldn't think about it. Ian loved me. I loved Ian. We were smart. We were careful. We didn't use condoms. We didn't need condoms. We didn't share needles; we shared, instead, ourselves. My temperature was 103° from the flu, my body was sweaty and aching from the flu, my mind was worried and reeling from the flu, people got the flu and it was really *just* the flu. Still, the empty house was as jolly as a morgue. No father, no mother, no Ian, nobody. Just me. In the storm, in the cat-howling storm, in the nobody storm, in the nobody darkness . . .

And two days later, after lots of crap TV, convinced that I was better—though I hadn't seen a doctor, and no one except McDuffy's receptionist had called, and the people from St. Osyth's, to say Scarcross was dying—I got dressed Friday morning, determined to be better, and stood beside the porchswing staring at a purple sky. As the sun rose before me like the Champion of Dark-

ness, I was even more frightened, because everything had
changed—the sunlight I had loved, the sky I had prized, everything now held a promise of disaster. And still I had a fever; I
could feel it, very slightly. It was burning in my head like a
thought I couldn't shake. I was really all alone. And my mother
was alone. And my father was alone. And my Ian was alone. Nobody had phoned me; and I had phoned no one. I had ridden out a
tempest and no one had seen me do it. So I got dressed and
prayed to a new sort of God—a God not of love, but of fear, deliv-
ery—and as I stood on the frontporch waiting for Juice beside several tidy piles of immaculate laundry someone had delivered to
our porchswing in the night, I thought, Take a breath. Take a deep
breath, Toby. This is just the beginning, *and you're in it to the end.*

I EXPECTED TO spy a FOR SALE sign sprouting up like a re-
altor's weed from our yard as I waited for Juice's dilatory
Porsche to show. I had called Juice at dawn and had spoken to
his mom, who had said, "Leonard's outside trying to start the
Buick." The only time Juice ever made it late to school was
when the shit-car he dròve to his Porsche wouldn't start. Mrs.
Compton said, "Who *is* this?" "Toby Sligh," I told her. "I go to
Sacred Heart, and I need a ride to school." It was the first time
I'd ever heard Mrs. Compton's voice, and it was a lot less black
than her son's, I noticed. Juice was like Ian: protective of his
parents, though his protectiveness was born more of love than of
dread. Juice tried to keep the world at arm's length from his
mother; his father was a world he kept an arm's length from himself. "You'll have to wait a minute," Mrs. Compton announced,
and set the receiver on the counter with a clang as she hollered
through the kitchen window: "Leonard! Telephone!" I heard an
engine hacking like a lion with a hairball, and a distant voice

shouting, and a train rattling by. When Juice got on the telephone he seemed surprised to hear me.

"Where you been, boyee?"

"Sick," I said to him. "Can you take me to school?"

Juice said he could, but he'd be a little late; he had to fetch his cousin.

"And Anquanna's on the rag," Juice added, sotto voce, as if his mother didn't know what periods were.

"You remember where I live?"

"I remember, G-money! Don't play me like d'at! I ain't some fuckin' *Alz*heimer's!"

Juice knew where I lived. He'd been there lots of times. He used to play Scrabble with me and my folks before Ian came. He was a super player. Juice had a gift for forming seven-letter words, and he and my mother would team up together against my dad and me and kick our asses off the board. Once my mother laid down the word "galatea," and I reached for the *Webster's* and Juice snatched my wrist. "You doubtin' your moms?" Juice asked me, aghast. I looked at him and smiled. "It's a *word*?" I said to him. "Of course it's a word! So is 'mom'!" Juice shouted. I looked it up later. It was a word, too.

"Is Leonard in trouble?" Mrs. Compton asked me, when Juice ducked off the telephone to go and take a leak.

"Not that I know of."

"If he were, would you tell me?"

I can't remember what I said.

"If you were his mom, you would."

Juice stopped coming to our house to play Scrabble because he tried to sell my folks a bag of pot. I'd found an old bong on a shelf in the garage where the four of us used to hold our epic Scrabble tourneys, and not knowing what it was, had asked if I could use it for a hydraulics project overdue in Physics class. Mom and Dad and Juice had all pissed themselves laughing. "Haven't you thrown that thing away, Timothy?" "No, Bea," my

father said, opting out on "Beatrice." My parents only used their
first names for company; otherwise, it was endearments: Snug-
gle Pie and Cuddle Buns. Beatrice and Timothy were someone
else's parents—people you played Scrabble with on Sunday af-
ternoons. "Well, put it in the trash, Toby Sligh," my mother ordered. "We should've thrown it out with those old Procol Harum
records." But when I came back, the garage was deserted and
Mom was in the kitchen brewing up a pot of coffee. Dad was on
the frontporch yelling at Juice, and Juice looked embarrassed;
then he slunked away. When Dad came inside he wouldn't say
what had happened; Mom was playing dumb, but was upset that
Juice had left. "Would've sold it to 'em wholesale," Juice explained to me later, "in exchange for the Scrabble and Doritos,
don'tcha know." Till Juice filled me in on exactly what had happened I thought Dad had run him off because Juice had kicked
his butt in Scrabble. And ever after that, Juice never came
around—even though there was a picture of the four of us together we had taken with an old-fashioned automatic camera
and tacked to the door of our Sears refrigerator underneath a
silly frame of smiling pomegranate magnets; even though my
mom often asked about Juice and longed for the marathon sessions of Scrabble; even though my father had confessed one afternoon after losing to my mother in a blitzkrieg round of Risk:
"Except for certain *hobbies,* that Compton kid's all right."

"YOUR FOLKS AIN'T around?" Juice asked, lying low. He
was hunched down in the frontseat, hands across his eye-
balls. "That thing is Anquanna," Juice said. "This is Toby."
   I nodded at the girl who was crashed out in the back.
   "Hey, Tubby," she mumbled. "You homies with Leon?"
   She had a sort of store-bought Salt-N-Pepa accent.
   "Uh-huh."

"Doan know why . . . he a sorry-ass fucker."

Juice put on some Anthrax and cranked it till our ears bled.

"You ress your pretty head, Robobitch," Juice said, and spat out the window, and put the Porsche in reverse.

 FIRST ANQUANNA LAY with her head in her arms, then she rolled over and lay on her back, then she sat up and shoved her head between her knees, and I thought I heard crying, but the music drowned her out. When at last she looked up from the cradle of her thighs I saw the most amazing face that I had ever seen. Her eyes were like prizes under carnival glass, her lashes were fat and swept back with black mascara, her lips were thick and slick and licked wet with fleshy lipstick, and her face was as ripe and as polished as a plum. Add to that a look of immeasurable contempt for any object caught in her immediate line of vision and you had, in a word, the most fascinating creature I had ever felt the urge to let my fag's eyes linger on. Her face was so arresting, I could almost overlook the vestige of the black eye disappearing on her skin. But I couldn't overlook, because of that same battered beauty, the fact that it was Juice who most likely gave it to her, whose "on the rag" alibi, so ugly in itself, became a euphemism for something uglier. When Juice dropped her off and kissed her wetly on the cheek she said, "Fuck you, Leon," and she murmured in my ear: "Leonard Compton's full of shit. Don't believe a word he says. I trusted his ass. *Look what happened to me.*"

ON THE WAY to Sacred Heart, Juice dropped me at St. Patrick's—I wanted to see if my father was at mass. Inside, there was the usual flock of old ladies, their blue hair like a bumper crop of van Gogh's irises. On the altar Fr. Diaz was blessing the host, and when he saw me, he lifted it high like a tennis ball, and made a serving motion. I smiled and waved. Then I surveyed the aisles. And I checked out the pews. I even peeked in the confessionals. But my father wasn't there.

BECAUSE OF ANQUANNA we were late for convocation. Or so Juice claimed. It was all because of me.

"Who cares?" Juice yawned. "Motherfuck if I do. I on in-school suspension already, Toby Sligh. McDuffy nail my ass fuh being late from senior lunch."

"You're lucky you're alive."

Juice didn't say a word: what happened in the alleyway on Wednesday was behind him.

"Maybe I let McDuffy fuck me up the ass the way you an' Lamb do, I get outta my suspension," Juice said. "*Shit,* I wanna play hooky *too.* You the only two out in the whole senior class. We thought you was doin' community service, or maybe each other—ahem-ahem-ahem."

Juice slapped the stickshift and hit the interstate. He was doing eighty, easy. I'd never seen him so uptight.

"I was sick as a dog," I told Juice. "I still am. My folks have flown the coop. It was like *Home Alone.*"

Juice's voice dropped an octave. "You playin' me, Toby?"

"It's the truth, Juice," I told him. "I never been so alone."

We drove along awhile, Juice staring at me. When he spoke, his words became sticky with something.

"Whatchoo been sick with?"

"The flu."

"And the symptoms?"

"Sweats, squirts, vomiting, fever, the works."

"You still got a fever?"

I nodded. "A little."

Juice was looking at me. He reached out and touched my forehead.

"Toby, you hot."

He slowed down a little. He was looking at me softly. He turned the Anthrax down.

"You seen a doctor, boyee?"

"I haven't got the money."

"I'll give you fuckin' money!"

"God, Juice, I'll be okay."

"Don'tchoo gimme that *Little Homeboy on the Motherfucking Prairie* 'Juice, I be okay' big-man bullshit! You gonna see a doctor. I take you during lunch."

"You can't take me, asshole—in-school suspension?"

"Fuck d'at shit! Like somebody finna catch me."

"They'll expel you if they do."

" *'They'll expel you if they do.'* . . . Lemme worry 'bout that, you faggot-ass fool! I getchoo to a doctor, you cracker-assed Q-Tip!"

He popped out the Anthrax and slid in some Kenny G. Juice was the kind of guy whose moods were in his music.

"Lemme see your tongue."

"Go fuck yourself, 'boyeee.' "

He grabbed my jaw and laughed.

"Dr. Feelgood say *'Ahhhhhh!'* "

I opened up and showed him. He whistled like a redneck. I opened up wider, and his hand shook a little.

"Your tongue's all coated. You on antibiotics?"

I told him I wasn't.

"How long i'ss like that?"

"Two days," I mumbled.

"Ain't gettin' any better?"

"A little," I lied. "Now you're scarin' me, Juice."

"We'll getchoo to a doctor," Juice said, and hit the gas. "Best damn doctor plastic money can buy. Where's your moms and pops, T.?"

"Fuck me if I know."

"Tha'ss to the *curb*. Ain't you called the police?"

"Is Leonard Compton telling me to call the police?"

Juice was looking at me; he couldn't *stop* looking at me.

"You was sick by yourself and you didn't even *beep* me?"

"Didn't want you to worry."

"You so full of shit. I betchoo called Ian."

"What's *that* supposed to mean?"

"I betchoo called Lamb."

"*Just fuck off!*" I shouted.

We drove for a while. My ears were burning up. Juice could be a bastard. He could really cut you deep.

"I'm sorry, Tobias," Juice said, finally. His hand fell on my shoulder. "Sorry, Tobe," he said to me.

AT SCHOOL I asked Juice what had happened to Anquanna. We were in the parking lot. "What happened to her face?"

Juice cut the engine, stepped out of the Porsche, and engaged the car's high-tech security system. A voice like Hal the Computer on steroids said: "System deployed! Step *away* from the vehicle!" Far away across campus we could hear students singing: mass for our last day of classes, thank God. In four brisk movements Juice tied his tie and brushed designer lint off his Polo and said, "Anquanna got jumped by a Puerto Rican posse didn't even go to the school that she be at, and they held her at knifepoint somewhere in a bathroom while that body-glove cunt took our money made the deal."

"That's how she got the bruises?" I said. "You didn't hit her?"

Juice jacked up an eyebrow and took a step toward me.

"Compton hits no one. I mean it, Tobias. Anquanna my cousin."

I looked him in the eye.

"All right," I said to him. "All right, I believe you."

"Don't give a fuck, Toby Sligh, *what*choo believe."

HEIDI, MCDUFFY'S RECEPTIONIST, seemed pleased to see me. "How are you, Toby?" she said and swept her hair back, then wrote out late passes for the two of us in pencil so we could manipulate the time of our arrival and go to Circle K and get bum bottles of beer. Juice was the only guy, apart from my dad, with whom I ever had the least desire to drink. Juice had seen me drunk, Juice had gotten me drunk one morning on a thermos of mint Jagermeister and steadied my shoulders while I vomited schnapps all over a rival class's Homecoming project. Our favorite place to get blasted was mass. We'd pass a flask between us underneath our missalettes and experience the spins staring up at stained glass. And since, after mass, we had classes together—Ethics and Latin and Political Science—we would sit in the back making sarcastic comments and burping with abandon while our buzzes tapered off.

"Did you have the same bug Ian has?" Heidi asked me.

I said that I had. "Is Ian still sick?"

Heidi shrugged: "Dunno! Yesterday his mom called, right about now, which was sweet, ya know, really, 'cause it saved me from calling, and I have so much t' *do!*"

Heidi said Mrs. Lamb reminded her of something (the Lambs were recluses and subject to speculation). Then she asked me if my mother was feeling any better.

"Yeah, uh-huh." I coughed and looked at Juice. He was whistling at the ceiling. "Mom is feeling much better."

While I was out Heidi had phoned our empty house and I'd
said that my mom was even sicker than I was. Because Heidi
liked me, and because she was busy, and because I had
sounded like I had the flu I had, she hadn't pressed the matter
or put up any fuss.

"Oh yeah, could I have Ian's telephone number," I asked her,
"to phone up, to find out how he's doing?"

Part of Ian's paranoia, ever since I'd known him, was never,
never, *ever* to give out his parents' number, as if I'd call his folks
and say, "This is Ian's boyfriend. Are you Lyle and Edith? Your
son is great in bed!"

With a wink, Juice said, "I'm going to mass," and headed for
his Porsche while Heidi seized her Rolodex.

TEN MINUTES LATER, outside the Circle K, guzzling Magnum malt liquor out of brown paper bags, I called Ian's
number. It rang ten times, and a tranquilized voice staggered on
the line and said, "Hello, you have reached the Lamb residence. Lyle and Edith are on business in Barbados. Ian is the
temporary master of the household. If this is an emergency,
phone our attorney. If this is for Ian, call his private number." I
didn't even know Ian had a private number. "At the sound of the
beep, please leave a message." The beep was interminable. I
hung up and left.

WE MADE IT to the year-end mass just in time for the reces-
sional, a rousing revisionist Muzak rendition of the paranoid classic "I Am Behind You." While the seniors and the
bishop massacred the lyrics:

> *I am your shepherd,*
> *I am your friend;*
> *I am be-hind you—*
> *Until the end. . . .*

Juice and I, reeling, improvised our own version:

> *I am your shepherd,*
> *I am your friend;*
> *I am be-hiiind you—*
> *Right up your end. . . .*

Afterward we swapped hissing shots of Binaca and dunked our bleary heads in the sacristy sink while the altar boy, a freshman, looked at us in wonder.

"Oh, Rrrochester," Juice addressed the boy, "our towels!"

In the next room, the bishop washed his face sloppily.

"My name isn't Rochester," the freshman protested.

"Rrrochester!" Juice groaned. "We're making *such* a mess!"

"Who's there!" yelled the bishop, splashing in the sink.

"Oh, Rrrochester, hurry!"

We received our towels and left.

ATTACHED TO A corner of my towel with a pin was a simple gold key in the shape of a cross. It was the key to the chapel tabernacle. I detached the key and let it drop into my pocket.

INCREDIBLY, THE LAST day of classes had arrived. The weekend was for study, and exams were on Monday, followed that evening by the celebrated prom. And even though all

I could think of was Ian—whom I wanted to see, whom I wanted
to talk to, whom I wanted to dance with, whom I wanted to hold,
who had become in the course of my lonely viral trial a memory
and, worse yet, a vague kind of threat—everything was so
chaotic, everything was so anarchic that I found my worries
swept up in the giddy rush of things. Seniors were arriving at
school in gaudy ties, violating every conceivable rule of the
dress code, and talking back to teachers in a way that was un-
heard of: in a way that suggested a subversive affection. In
Ethics we got into a one-sided slugfest about whether homosexuals should be permitted in the military—a topic not to touch
with a ten-foot pole, let alone a ten-inch one, on previous occa-
sions. Knowing that only a majority of hard-ons could set anybody from the opposition straight, I buttoned my lip and
swallowed a chill pill and imagined the entire class arguing
nude. It was Juice who interrupted my fantasy in flesh, just as
the school quarterback—a closet queen if e'er there was one—
retreated to his seat from my mental undressing none the worse
for wear and calling for the deaths of fags. "I got something to
say, Dr. Zipser!" Juice proclaimed, and rose with a Magnum-
sized belch from his chair.

Zipser was a Sartre-eyed former Scholastic addicted to coffee and the conservative press. On his desk he kept a picture of
William F. Buckley only slightly less offensive than the connect-
the-dots portrait of the Assumption of Mary he'd propped up beside it. In this particular connect-the-dots portrait, Dr. Zipser's
niece or nephew had mixed up a couple of dots, so the Blessed
Virgin looked like a trapeze artist plunging to her death with
Bill Buckley looking on. *"Egad!"* Buckley seemed to be saying
from his armchair. *"Let us hope she who's born without sin has a
net!"* On Zipser's file cabinet an imported coffeemaker brewed
an endless succession of double espressos, which Zipser
knocked back like Juan Valdéz on a bender. In his chronic hy-
pertension Dr. Zipser couldn't process any talking head any
less wired than he, so Juice's slurred musings, outrageous as

they were, became 33s set at 78 rpm, and didn't really play on Zipser's zippy turntable.

"I can't speak for the rest of the fellas," Juice was saying, fingering his nipples to erection through his shirt, "but, umm, I kinda dig it when somebody check me out. I mean girl, guy, Hindu lady in a shower cap— Word, I ain't playin' you, gives me a thrill. So this shit, you know, about showerin' together . . . You fellas be lyin', 'cuz you know you dig it, too."

If Juice hadn't been so massive, and so dangerously cool, and so sexy in a way even straight guys could admire, he would have paid for that comment in the parking lot at night. As it was, and as Juice was most these guys' dealer, the whole class hooted and pounded on their desks, versed as they were in that school of boosterism promulgated by Hitler and Arsenio Hall—and taking the sting out of what Juice had said with a chorus of the Juicy Fruit chewing gum theme:

> *Take a whiff!*
> *Pull it out!*
> *The taste is gonna move ya*
> *When you pop it in your mouth!*

The more time I spent at Sacred Heart High, the more I realized it really was *the* place to be gay. Except for the intolerance demonstrated by the students, and the indifference demonstrated by the majority of the faculty, and the hypocrisy of Jesuits who kept their legs crossed as if their penises were Christ's own portable cross, and apart from the horseplay that bordered on foreplay, and the obsession with athletics that was almost obscene, and the banishment of women from the Kingdom of the Cock—a kingdom Christ himself would have had no earthly part of—it was nice to be with guys, I had to admit it: students, teachers, young guys, old guys, middle-aged guys who wished they were young guys, elderly guys who longed for middle age. Everybody had a real male affection for one another that went way beyond all the gay-straight posing. We were "Men for Oth-

ers"—that was our motto. We were "Men for *Each Other*": we
were really all we had. Sacred Heart was set in a testosterone
ocean; the secretaries, the cafeteria workers, the former female
teachers who had shattered their fair share of hetero-hearts
were like creatures on loan from some exotic girl zoo, endan-
gered species on display in our masculine menagerie. Because
there were no mothers, no sisters, no girlfriends, no future wives
or daughters to coddle us along, you would have thought we
might've learned to take better care of ourselves. But we didn't;
we retreated behind our Y chromosomes and waged a private
war that was in fact a war of love. No wonder gay guys came out
of Sacred Heart flaming and straight guys came out of it defensive and confused. It was like the military: we *were* showering
together. But the lines had been drawn, the trenches had been
dug, the enemy was us: we didn't dare enjoy each other! In saying what he said, Juice had stumbled on a landmine, and glad it
wasn't them, the class awaited detonation.

"A healthy self-image is a wonderful thing," Zipser conde-
scended, shotgunning an espresso. "But should the army com-
promise preparedness for ego?"

"Ain't that what the Cold War was all about, Zipser?" Juice
persisted, sounding like Kissinger guest-hosting *Soul Train*.
"Show me yo' missile, I show you my mine? Maybe we both take
a peek at our pee-pees the worl' won't explode, an' all that
Strangelove bullshit?"

The class greeted this with a megablast of laughter. Zipser
licked his coffee cup and fixed his eyes on Juice.

"Mr. Compton, are you kidding me? A big strong—"

" *'Buck-naked nigger like you!'* I know!" Juice shouted, com-
pleting Zipser's sentence to a horrifying, bonafide, Ground Zero
hush. "It's the same kinda prejudice makes QB Butch say 'faggot,' the same kinda shit you teachers *never ever* jump on, leas'
not 'less you *have* to, leas' not till it's too *late!*" Juice drew a
breath, luxuriating in the fallout; then he glanced around
fiercely, catching everybody's eye. "You fellas, I mean it, you

better check yo' heads! And you too, Zipser, especially you! I'ss Millennium #3 comin', you ready? We gotta throw all that ol' shit out the window."

Juice took his seat and snuck some cocaine from his pocket. Faking the sniffles, he snorted half a line.

"What do you say, Toby Sligh?" Zipser segued, focusing on me for reasons I could live without.

Everybody in the class had turned silently to me. I felt like the Resident Expert on Fags.

I stood up and said, "I think Compton's full of bullshit," and sat back down, and wouldn't meet Juice's eye.

"Thank you, Mr. Sligh," Dr. Zipser responded.

Juice was staring at me.

Yeah, I know: he'd been betrayed.

THOUGH I NEVER understood what inspired his forgiveness, halfway through Latin Juice sent me a note via several random hands, written in a dead language: *"Conticere est concidere."* I sent it back to him with the message crossed out and another underneath it: *"Iam negate."* Juice smiled at me. Then he put the paper in his mouth and swallowed it.

AT LUNCH I didn't have much of an appetite—and I didn't have money, so my appetite was moot. I was wandering round the lunchroom fingering my glands and swiping orphan french fries when Kickliter idled over.

"Howdy there, Toby," K. said and lit a Kool. He exhaled a plume of smoke at the ketchup-stained ceiling. Occasionally a packet would dislodge and pelt his head. "How's that new community service project coming—the AIDS ward at St. Osyth's? You're quite the brave lad."

"I just want to go to the prom," I assured him. "Bravery has nothing to do with it, sir."

"Does a certain somebody have something to do with it?" K. asked insouciantly.

"Maybe you should ask him."

"I'd like to, I've *tried* to. That's the problem, Dr. Sligh. Seems his mom and dad have been out of town all week and somebody's been phoning in sick for him, Toby."

"Really? And are you as free with my secrets as you are with Somebody's?"

"You are Somebody's secret."

Juice walked over, and K. turned to greet him. He liked Juice a lot; Juice probably sold him pot.

"Do you like me, Dr. Compton?" K. said.

Juice shrugged.

"Am I one of the good guys?"

"I'd say you was, K."

"Then how come your buddy Tobias doesn't like me?"

"I don't know, sir. Maybe you should ax him."

Kickliter put a hand on Juice's shoulder and inhaled. I was feeling faint again; I decided I'd hold on.

"Have you ever, Dr. Compton, thought someone was your enemy, when all he really wanted was to help you out a lot?"

"Yeah, G., been there. The other way, too. Like when you in tight an' they stab you in the back."

Juice blew a smokering; Kickliter blew one through it. I could feel a wave of sweat breaking out across my forehead.

"Toby doesn't trust me."

"Why should he truss you?"

"He's taking somebody to the prom."

"I know he is."

"Who's he taking, Juice?"

"Who you taking, T-Sly?"

"Angelina Fishback," I said, and stared at K.

"That's not what *I* think," K. answered, singsongy. "I heard from someone *else* that he was taking someone *else*."

"Well then, I guess you heard wrong, Kicks my man. 'Cause Toby himself say he takin' Angelina. You can ask Bubba Fishback. He right over there. An' Bubba kill Toby if he doan', you know tha'ss right."

Across the cafeteria we could see Bubba Fishback, two cheese-toasties dripping grease from either fist.

"All I know, Juice, we counselors hear things, and we'd really like to help, before things get outta hand. You tell your friend Toby I'm one of the good guys. You tell him he can trust me if he wants to talk it out."

"You tell him yo'self. He right here," Juice told him.

K. walked away, whistling.

"Cocksucker," Juice said.

JUICE HAD TO catch me in a wrestler's headlock to get me to go with him to Dr. Wu's at lunch. And though I felt faint, and my temperature was zooming, and I didn't have the energy to put up any fuss, the funny thing was it made me feel sorta better to be nestled down deep in Juice's Brut-smelling armpit. But I told him he was crazy; he'd get caught and be expelled. *And then who would I have left to love me in this world?* Juice just ignored this and shoved me into his Porsche, and we drove past Kickliter, who was waving bon voyage.

"Now Kickliter saw you and he'll go tell McDuffy and your ass will be grass," I said, using K.'s pet phrase.

"No it won't, Toby," Juice said and cracked a smile. " 'Cause that pot I couldn't sell to your moms and pops, remember? I sold it to K. An' I got him tape-recorded."

Juice produced a shoebox from underneath the carseat. In it

were dozens of microcassettes—some with teachers' names, some with coaches' names, and one with "Kickliter" scrawled in marker across it.

"He ain't gonna squeal to nobody, Tobias."

I blinked and leaned over and spoke into Juice's cufflink.

"One, two, three. Testing one, two, three. My name is Toby Sligh, and for the record—I am innocent!"

AFTER DESCRIBING MY illness to Dr. Wu, a stylish young woman fresh out of Johns Hopkins, and after she had taken a look at my tongue, the first question she asked me was "Like, are you *gay?*" At the same time she jabbed a syringe into my forearm and drew a vial of bubbling purple blood from my vein.

"Have I got AIDS?" I asked her.

Wu giggled. "It takes more than two days of flu to get AIDS! Have you had anal sex?"

I answered in the negative.

"Oral sex?"

"Yeah, but I never, um, swallow."

"Have you ever shared needles?"

"Only with doctors."

"And are you a hemophiliac?"

"Emotionally, yes."

Wu left the needle in and drew a second tube. I was looking away: I always had to look away.

"I don't know how much you know about these things," Wu continued in an alarmingly lighthearted tone. "But you don't get AIDS until you get HIV. First you get the virus, then the other stuff! Someone who tests positive for antibodies, Toby, they may have eight, ten, twelve years to live! We can't even be sure that they'll get AIDS at all!"

"But they usually do."

"Yes, they usually do."

"And they usually die."

"Yes, they usually die."

Wu drew a third tube of blood from me now; I felt like a Last Chance Texaco in Transylvania.

"Why do they call it 'positive' if you've got antibodies?"

I already knew the answer; I was just messing around.

"Keep still!" Wu said. She slapped my head. "Excuse me?"

"Why do they call it 'positive'? Shouldn't it be 'negative'?"

"The results are positive. It makes you feel negative."

"So negative is positive?"

Wu coughed slightly. "Yes."

"And they're called antibodies 'cause they don't like your body?"

"Antibodies are good!" Wu cried. "They fight the virus!"

Having just drawn a fourth tube of blood from my arm, Wu pulled up a stool and sat squarely on it and sneezed into a handkerchief and wiped her nose and said, "Enough of your questions. Now let me ask you something."

I was saying a rosary over the vials of blood that lay benignly in Dr. Wu's lap.

"Shoot."

"Are you gay?"

I nodded.

"Are you happy?"

I thought a bit about. I finally said, "No."

"So if it's positive when you're negative, and if antibodies help your body, how can you expect to be gay and be happy?" Dr. Wu concluded, and stood up, and clicked her pen, and wrote me a prescription for antibiotics plus a note for McDuffy—both impossible to read.

"But we have so much help from *society*," I told her.

"Since when did society ever help anybody?"

I took the slips of paper and rolled down my sleeve.

"The least you can do is be happy," Wu said, and took Juice's credit card, and zapped it with a laser.

"So that blood there, um, it's going to be tested?"

"Not for AIDS, Toby. For the HIV virus."

"Can I go on kissing my boyfriend on the mouth?"

"With your tongue, do you mean?"

"Mm-hmm, with my tongue."

"And with his tongue on your tongue?"

I nodded. "Uh-huh."

"Well, as far as we know, you could spend a thousand hours liplocked and slobbering and you wouldn't have to worry."

"Unless our mouths were bleeding."

"Unless your mouths were bleeding."

"But that's just your opinion."

"Everything is my opinion. That's what doctors do; we give informed opinion. In many ways, we do not know shit about AIDS. The only thing we know is, if you don't want to get it, you have to—"

"Stop having sex."

"Yes, stop having sex. Which is okay, you know, if you don't like sex, or if you're a eunuch, or if you're not in love. Are you in love, Toby Sligh?"

I looked at her and nodded.

"Love makes you stupid. Are you stupid, Toby Sligh?"

I told her I was.

"Then buy lots of condoms. They're a bargain compared to, like, terminal illness."

Wu opened the door.

"You'll have the results in—?"

"Two weeks. Think positive!"

"I think you mean negative."

Wu smiled. "I think you know just what I mean."

As I went out, Wu bowed theatrically and said, "And tell Leonard Compton I would like to see him, please."

JUICE WAS IN with Dr. Wu for over half an hour, so when he got back to Sacred Heart, he would be late, and if he got caught, he would be expelled. Unless, of course, he had micro-cassettes of McDuffy and the Jesuits negotiating crack deals, which I would not have put past him, not at that point. There had always been something supernaturally lucky surrounding Juice Compton from the moment we met. Our first day of school—freshman orientation, or freshman disorientation, as some pre-ferred to call it—my father had dropped me off two hours early and I'd wandered around the campus like an adolescent alien, a little blue space saucer beanie on my head that said to all preda-tors: "I am your prey." Several hours later, when I lay in the quadrangle wriggling on my back like a piece of frying bacon to the cackling approval of a pack of upperclassmen, I would expe-rience the first in a series of doubts about the efficacy of a Jesuit education—as would Leonard Compton, who lay wrigging be-side me, his mouth hissing *"Sssssss!,"* impersonating Sizzle-Lean. That morning I had seen him in the same quadrangle knocking over a statue of Ignatius de Loyola while no one was looking—no one except me, no one except me and the unfurling dawn that pointed accusatory purple fingers at him. The vandal had vanished underneath the chapel's eaves, his immaculate blue beanie wadded up beneath his arm, and when he'd gotten out of sight, I approached the toppled statue and stood looking at it, my back turned to Juice. I didn't even know who St. Ignatius was; I thought he was Christ's stunt double or something. All I knew was, he looked like a decent guy, and his nose was in the dirt, which no decent guy deserved. Would the freshman class deserve it hours later after lunch when all of us lay writhing in the same dirt together pushing number-two pencils with the knobs of our noses? Would the freshman class deserve it at the end of the day when we squatted with our heels under one an-other's armpits running wheelbarrow races through chattering sprinklers? Would the freshman class deserve it at the raucous pep rally when a barnyard of jocks gave us 'Wedgies for Others'?

No, we wouldn't; and neither did he. So even though I didn't
know who this angry black kid was, or why he had toppled this
mild white god who looked like your average messiah-in-train-
ing, I cast a quick glance at him over my shoulder as I bent down
to lift the stricken St. Ignatius up. I was just a tiny fella, just
turned fourteen, and the statue was heavy, much heavier than
me. How Juice had knocked it over was a thing I'd never figure;
he must have had a big bowl of Wheaties for breakfast. I strained
and I strained, but the statue wouldn't budge—till I managed at
last to roll it over on its back and it lay staring up at the blind eye
of God crying out, *"Help! I've fallen and I can't get up!"* After a
while, when I too had surrendered and lay beside Ignatius staring at the callous sky, Juice came over and said, "My name's
Leonard. Who bus' d'uh statue?"

"I dunno," I replied.

Leonard bent down and helped me up off the ground, and together we knelt and put our arms around Loyola. "The sun's
throwin' down like a motherfucker now," Leonard proclaimed as
we wrestled with Ignatius. At last, with a Jesuit watching from
the chapel, we succeeded in standing the statue on its feet; and
as it posed with its arms in a V against the dawn, like the night
had scored a touchdown, like the horizon's referee, the figure in
the chapel doorway disappeared within, and we gave each other
high-fives and headed inside, too.

"You know what?" I told Juice, upon entering the chapel to
stained glass and silence and lingering light. "I thought when
we finally got that statue on its feet it would come straight to life
and give us anything we wanted. What would you want from it,
Leonard?" I asked him.

"I would want outta here, damn it," Juice said. "What would
you want from it, Toby?" he asked me.

"I guess I'd want someone to help me up if I fell down."

✳ "YOU TAKE THE Porsche." Juice handed me the keys. There was a pinpoint of blood on his sleeve. "I'm taking a taxi. I'll get Baby later."

"Who's Baby?"

"My Porsche."

Juice called his Porsche Baby.

✳ OUT OF CURIOSITY, I checked out the shoebox of microcassettes Juice had shown me before. I inserted Kickliter's in a miniature recorder Juice had stashed in a Kleenex caddy underneath the dash. I could hear Juice's voice distinctly in the foreground; Kickliter's was somewhere in the background mumbling. The recording was brief. It was gnarled with static. If there'd been a drug deal, I couldn't hear it. But at the end of the tape Kickliter spoke clearly. He sounded as if he was leaning into Juice. Juice started crying, like he'd done back in the alley, and though I didn't want to listen, I couldn't help myself.

"Picture him, Leonard!" Kickliter was urging. "Picture—!"

He mentioned a name I'd heard before.

"He's running to me!" Juice was shouting. *"E-Eye's running!"*

Then there was a clicking sound: the tape snapped off.

Almost instinctively, I popped the tape out and popped in a new one, featuring a coach.

"To be a winner, Compton," a football coach was saying, "you gotta blah blah, blah blah, blah blah blah . . ."

The sermon dragged on for interminable minutes, then it concluded. But again, no drug deal.

And so on, with a dozen cassettes that I surveyed. Most were just lectures, or casual advice, or candid observations Juice decided to record. One—a cassette labeled 2BSLY—contained comments on friendship I'd made in Ethics class, comments I'd

forgotten and Juice had preserved: "Because you don't have to."
I was free-associating. "Because it's not a duty, because it is
your privilege . . ." On recordings featuring just Juice's voice,
the urban jungle jive and street profanity were missing. Juice
didn't come off so much white as less black, as if the private
Juice hated housing project patois while the public Juice prac-
ticed only rap attack patter. Arranging the cassettes in the order
I had found them, I realized that this was what I'd done with
people's voices—disassembled sound bites and pieces of their
lives, disassembled jigsaws I didn't dare complete.

I locked Baby up and walked across the parking lot, my tape-
recorded comments on a loop inside my head: "Because you
don't have to, because it's not a duty, because it is your privilege
to be somebody's friend . . ." And it occurred to me then that I
had chosen my friends, or that they had chosen me, or that we'd
chosen one another; and that it was my duty, my privilege, our
privilege, to love as best we could for as long as we were able.
And as I entered the lobby of St. Osyth's Hospital and spotted
Ian standing abandoned and exhausted like a child who's never
known a single moment's rest since he left his mother's breast,
and will never return, I took some money from him, and I purchased my prescription, and he led me to the men's room, and
he said, *"Toby, hold me."* And I held him, and he kissed me, and
I kissed him, and he held me—and already it was like we'd
never even been away.

 "I'M SORRY," IAN said.
"For what?"
He was crying.
"I'm sorry, Toby Sligh," Ian said. "For everything."

AT THE SNACK bar we had our customary cups of coffee and I asked Ian if he had recovered from the flu.

"I never had the flu, Toby Sligh," he confided.

"I didn't think you had."

Ian smiled and wiped his eye.

"I've been with your mother," he began.

"But your parents—"

"They've gone to Barbados."

"I know. I called your house."

"How'd you get my number?"

"Heidi gave it to me. You have your own line."

"Uh-huh, yeah, I do."

He admitted this as if it had been public knowledge; suddenly I felt like Det. Thomas, Jr.

"Has my mother been calling in sick for you mornings?"

"She doesn't have a phone. I go to Circle K. And if she called in, she would know we were classmates."

"Who does it then?"

"The Circle K lady. I give her twenty dollars."

Ian was a genius.

"Have you talked to Kickliter?"

He said that he hadn't.

"He knows that we're planning to go to the prom."

"Who could've told him?"

"Just you or me, Ian."

"It wasn't me, Toby."

"Well, maybe it was Randall."

Ian took my hand, and he held it in his hand, and he flipped it back and forth like a pancake on a griddle.

"How is my mother?" I asked him.

"She's fine." Ian let his head drop. "No, she's not. She's paranoid. She has this idea that somebody tapped your phone line and if she calls home—from the Circle K, even—they'll monitor the call and figure out her neighborhood. You told her yourself

your dad hired a detective. Bea isn't taking chances. She wants
to be alone."

"Why?"

"I'll tell you later."

"When's later?"

"Tonight."

"Is she having an affair?"

Ian coughed. "No, Toby."

"Is she having one with you?"

Ian laughed, then he shivered. "Bea's not having an affair
with anybody. Your mother—" Ian said, and stopped himself
from saying something. I looked at him closely. He was staring
at his hands.

"I've had the flu since Wednesday," I informed him. "Since
Wednesday. Nobody called me. Not you, not my mother—"

"You had your dad, Toby."

"No, I didn't." I got quiet. "My father has absconded."

"He's what?"

"My dad has left."

Ian bit his coffee cup and looked at me, troubled. He nibbled
foam chips off the rim and dribbled them. "What's that supposed to mean?"

"It means exactly that: my dad has left home. The place is
deserted. It's me and the roaches. We're the end of the line."

"So Beatrice was right."

It sounded funny: Beatrice.

"About what?"

"About what? About . . . Oh, never mind."

"You know," I said to Ian, and I took his hand in my hand,
and flipped it like a pancake, and looked him in the eye. "If I
didn't really love you, ya know what I'd do?"

He shook his head.

"What?"

"Oh, Ian, *never mind.*"

"I wanted to see you, Toby Sligh!" he protested. "But your mother! She won't let me out of her sight!"

"So when did you pay the convenience store lady?"

"When your mom was asleep."

"And the laundry?"

"What laundry?"

I told him about the fresh pile of laundry someone had delivered to our porchswing in the night.

"It was you or my mother."

"It wasn't me, Toby."

"Then it must've been Mom."

"Well, maybe you should ask her."

"Is she receiving visitors?"

"Not at the moment . . . though sometimes, ya know, she *acts* like someone's coming. She gets really nervous if a car drives by. And she sleeps with a rifle tucked underneath her mattress."

"And where do you sleep?"

"On a futon in the closet. She needs me, Tobias. I protect her from—"

"What?"

"From something."

"What's 'something'?"

"From *something*, Tobias . . . And you can't help her, and your father can't help her, and I can't help her. She can only help herself! But she needs me there with her. She needs me to protect her! She's told me things, Toby, she's never told another soul."

I looked at him once. He turned his face away. His artificial eye was like a boarded-up house.

"Where is she now? Is she here?"

"Is she where?"

"Is she here? At St. Osyth's? Is she dying, like Scarcross?"

Ian stood up and fished more quarters from his pocket. He got fresh cups of coffee and he drank from his and mine.

"Scarcross is dying?" he asked, sitting down.

"Of course Eli's dying! That's why he's here!"

"You said you would tell me the things that he told you."

"I've wanted to, Ian, but I've sort of had this flu and—"

"Just how sick were you?" He was looking at me closely. "I mean, how sick, really?"

"Pretty sick," I said to him.

"And what were you sick with?"

Ian looked a little worried.

"I have no idea."

His eyes were in mine.

"Scarcross," I continued, "is a mystery, Ian. His words go right through you. We even struck a deal."

"What kinda deal?" Ian spilled a pool of coffee. He was suddenly defensive. "What kinda deal, Toby?"

"We swore we would only tell each other the truth. No matter what happened. *'Lies are God's weeds.'* "

"The truth," Ian said, "the truth is a bastard."

"But Scarcross is dying because he tried to live a lie."

"What lie?" Ian said, coughing nonchalantly. He was going to say something, then his voice split in two.

"What was that, Ian? You were gonna say something—"

"I was saying, I was gonna . . . but the words got in the way."

An old man in pajamas lumbered over to us. He sat down beside us. He heard every word we said.

"Tell me about my mother."

"I'll tell you tonight."

"You promise me, Ian?"

"I'll tell you everything. . . . Are we still getting fitted at Castiglione's?"

"*You* tell *me.*"

"What's that supposed to mean?"

"It's like we've forgotten."

"Like we've forgotten what?"

I was suddenly bleeding.

"Oh, Christ! Everything!"

One month before, in the back of Ian's Benz, at the Thunderbird Drive-In, we had made a lovers' promise: we lay naked underneath two Cub Scout blankets, and there was popcorn all around us, and the night was on our bodies. We swore we loved each other, and we wanted to prove it: we swore we'd do something to validate our love. That was when I asked him to take me to the prom: to take me there, and kiss me there, and dance with me before the whole student body. Ian said he would, but I knew he wouldn't; he said it the way that somebody says something when they want to make somebody they don't love less insecure. But ever since then I had clung to his promise as if it were something only time could nullify: I had clung to it the day Bubba's sister Angelina asked me to the prom and I said yes; I had clung to it when I learned that Courtney Ciccone would be Ian's escort after he had promised me; and I clung to it now after two days of fever when Ian's voice and face had become a memory. Who was Ian Lamb? And why did I believe him? And how far would I let myself fall before he caught me?

"I haven't forgotten," Ian whispered, with feeling. "I remember our promise—every word of it, Toby."

"Will you keep it?"

He blinked. "I don't want to be expelled."

"How can they expel us! We'll have finished our exams! We're graduating first and second in the senior class! All they'll do is laugh! Laugh at us and call us faggots! We'll make the evening news and get on with our lives!"

"I dunno, Toby." He shuddered. "I'm a coward."

"Then close your eyes, Ian, and pretend we're alone! In a room, just the two of us, you and me, dancing! I don't give a goddamn what people say! I love you! I know it! I didn't before! I've felt things for you I never felt for anybody. Isn't that why we're going through all this bullshit? Isn't that why we always lie to everybody?"

"Stop crying, Toby. People are watching."

People were watching; the snack bar was packed.

"You could kiss me right here, and then I'd believe you! In front of everybody!"

"Be quiet, Toby Sligh!"

"You could kiss me right now, in front of everygoddamnbody! If we were a guy and a girl, folks would smile! They would say, 'They're in love!' Everyone would be happy! If you only had the courage, if you only had the—"

But before I could finish my sentence, Ian kissed me. His tongue probed my mouth like a scavenger of love.

We sat there, blushing. People were leaving. Someone was shouting. My soul was in the air.

"How do you feel, Toby Sligh?" Ian asked me.

My arm was being punched.

"Um, I feel good. . . ."

"You better get out of here!" the old man was screeching, and pummeling my shoulder, and making lots of noise.

"C'mon, Toby Sligh," Ian said, and helped me up. "You feel okay to walk?"

I nodded and we left.

ON THE ELEVATOR up to the eleventh floor of St. Osyth's I showed Ian the list of books Scarcross had given me and which, I then realized, I'd forgotten to get.

"*The Tempest!*" Ian said. "I was in *The Tempest!* 'Full faggot five!' " Ian sang, and squeezed my hand.

The elevator opened and Sr. Cindy entered and looked at me and Ian, and coughed when I got off.

"Hi, Sister," I said.

"Hello, Toby," she answered.

She glanced once at Ian, then down at the floor.

"I'll see you tonight at Castiglione's!" Ian hollered at me as the elevator closed. "I'll bring my dancing shoes and we can practice our waltzing! And you can spend the night! Would you like to spend the night . . . ?"

And I floated, I glided past several LPNs to room 1111, where Fr. Scarcross lay—with a tube in his neck, and another in his chest, and another in his wrist, and a rosary in his fist; and he said, with difficulty, through a spiderweb of spittle, through a voice that broke in pieces every time he tried to speak, "After all this time, Toby Sligh, did you remember? Did you keep your promise to me? Have you brought my precious books?"

O Rose, thou art sick!
The invisible worm
That flies in the night,
In the howling storm,

Has found out thy bed
Of crimson joy,
And his dark secret love
Does thy life destroy.

HE LAY THERE like a mannequin contemplating air. Apart from the poem, Scarcross had said nothing. At one point I thought I heard him call me a liar. Lucinda came in wearing a surgical mask, so I couldn't see the nifty gold spike in her tongue. "May I see you outside for a moment?" she whispered, and handed me the mask that I should've been wearing. I looked at the Jesuit: his eyes were moving, speed-reading volumes in the study of his mind. And all at once his dead eyes pivoted toward me, pupils expressive and abject in their blindness. I couldn't meet his gaze; its flatness went right through me—as if he had finally recognized the world for what it was.

"HAD THE FLU," Lucinda said, pointing to her mask. "Me too. Majorly."

Our voices sounded blurry.

"It's a bitch, idn't it? Anyway, I'm good to *go*. Feelin' strong as Lynda Carter. What's going on with Ja?"

"Dunno." I shrugged. A shrug is shoulders lying. "I went in, said hi, he recited some poem, and now he's just lying there, absolutely silent."

"Eli's been wanting to see you so badly. He said you promised to bring him some books."

We both stepped aside as a gurney glided by. On it lay Peter, I.V.'s in his body. I smiled at him. He jerked his head away. I'd failed him. I watched as they wheeled the gurney off.

"Peter's been waiting to see you too, Toby. Did you promise him something?"

"I never promised him a thing!"

"Settle down! God!" She took some pills from her pocket. They were antibiotics. She offered me one.

"No. Got my own."

"Amoxil?"

"Augmentin."

"Oh, you're in the big leagues!" She popped one underneath her mask. "All I want to know is what's going on with Scarcross. Sr. Cynthia Rose is an emotional wreck. André died yesterday, and Scarcross is dying, and now even Peter is down for the count. The only stable one is Magda, who's crazy. We're out for two days and the world falls apart."

"They're sick because of me."

"That isn't true, Toby. They might've picked it up from you or me or anybody. Viruses are like love. You never know when you're contagious. That's why we wear masks. . . . Did you promise Ja books?"

"He wants to be read to."

"Why didn't you get them?"

"I was sick with the flu!"

"Then tell him that, Toby! Jesus Christ, kiddo, tell the poor guy fucking something! And get the books tonight and bring them in ASAP."

"Doesn't anybody visit?"

"Nobody, Toby."

"Why?"

"Who knows? He's a priest who has AIDS. Priests are like doctors. They're supposed to be healers. They aren't allowed to get sick, and to die—and all that."

I had taken off my mask and was looking at Lucinda. She had taken hers off and was looking at me.

"Why does Scarcross need me?"

The corridor was quiet.

"Why does anybody need us?" Lucinda said, and walked away.

I EXPLAINED TO Fr. Scarcross exactly what had happened, but still he wouldn't answer—not for several hours. He lay there, blind eyes staring deeply into nothing, dry mouth chewing, his tongue licking air. When the sun sank down and the night stained the curtains and they rolled Peter in and I awakened from a dream, I felt Scarcross's hand flutter down across my wrist, and his fraying voice unraveled like a promise in the night.

"Look beneath my bed. Beneath the mattress—lift a little . . . Do you have it? What is it?"

"It's a rose."

"Well . . . *yes.* I thought it when I *smelled* it. I thought it when I *felt* it. Someone left it for me, a friend, while I was sleeping. Did you leave it for me, Toby?"

"No."

"I didn't think so. What color is it?"

"Pink."

"Nice color for roses . . . Your voice, Toby Sligh—your voice is full of dreaming." He pressed the flower in my hand. *"Toby talks in his sleep. . . ."*

"I do?"

Scarcross smiled. "You do!"

"About what?"

"About waltzing! With someone! With someone you love! With someone you dreamed about the *first* day you were here . . ."

"I talked in my sleep the first day I was here?"

"You couldn't stop talking! I spoke to you through it."

"You did?"

Scarcross nodded.

"Did I mention any . . . *names?"*

"You were dancing with—"

"Who?"

"With a friend. With a loved one . . . You had another dream. Just now. Do you remember? You dreamt of a . . . friend. The friend was named—"

"Randall."

"Do your pockets feel lighter?"

"Excuse me?"

He was laughing.

"Your pockets, Toby Sligh—do your pockets feel . . . *light?"*

"THIS HAPPENS TO me sometimes," Scarcross said, and he shivered. His fingers were probing his throat in painful circles. "I used to talk quickly, and now it's all so slow. . . . Every word, like a needle and thread, in and out. Like a needle and thread through my throat, Toby Sligh."

His gorge rose a little, and I wiped his mouth of bile.

"It's the medicine I'm taking that's making me ill."

"Drink some water," I told him.

"I'd like some more water. You tell me your dream and I'll drink some water, Toby. You talk about Randall and I'll listen here and lie."

"You mean lie here and listen."

He took the water from me.

"We mean what we say . . . *and you're buzzing like a fly!*"

"That's my mask," I told him. "Lucinda made me wear one. I'm recovering from the flu."

"Take it off," Scarcross said.

I looked at him. "What?"

"Take it *off*, Toby Sligh. Don't imagine you have anything inside you that could hurt me."

I told him I didn't; he knew that I didn't; I should've worn one from the first day I arrived. But he started to cough and his hands began to twitch, and he said he wouldn't speak to anybody in a mask. So I looked around for nurses, and I thought a bit about it, and I looked at his body—which was dwindling away. Then I took off the mask and I handed it to him and I thought, Is this murder? Or is it making dying easier?

"Your dream—tell it truly. You've spent your lie, Toby. *Les enfants qui mentent ne vont pas au paradis.*"

"*A STORM . . . A tempest . . . a house with no roof . . . the rafters were bone . . . we lay huddled inside . . . on the floor,*

in a heap, with our heads between our knees . . . and the rain was
pouring down . . . and the rain was pouring down."

 "I REMEMBER, I think, you were talking to me, and then I must have . . . I—I must have drifted off to sleep. I'm sorry. . . . Is it night yet?"

"It's been night for quite a while."

"I'm sorry, Tobias. . . . I'm sorry I was cruel."

"Do you want me to go, sir?"

"Call me Elijah. Do you need to go, Toby?"

"I got a fitting for a tux."

"Will you come back tomorrow?"

"If you're well enough, Father."

"If I'm well enough, Toby? I'll be well enough for you! And your dream! I forgot it! I dream a lot, Toby! Even when I'm awake! And my books! Please don't forget!"

"I won't, sir, I promise."

"Elijah!"

"Elijah!"

"You know what you are?"

We could hear the sirens singing. His voice was paper tearing.

"You're my angel and my friend."

AT THE FORMAL wear store I was greeted by a tailor who wore a tape measure like a belt around his waist.

"Tim Sligh?"

"Toby. Tim Sligh is my father."

The tailor checked a list and looked a little bit confused.

"Timothy, Toby, I . . . Well, it does not matter."

Then he grabbed me by the elbow and steered me to a back room and ordered me in no uncertain terms to drop my pants.

"Has Ian Lamb been here?" I asked him, pathetically.

The back of his wrist was pressing up against my balls.

"No Lamb here," the tailor said, and made a note, and patted my ass, and said, "Turn around, please."

AFTER MY FITTING, back in our driveway, house lights on behind drawn curtains casting an eerie filtered light across our yard, I saw that Dad's laundry had been lifted from the porchswing and strewn like a massacre of Halloween ghosts across the front planter and a chinaberry tree my father had planted on the day I was born. Then a white Plymouth came roaring round a corner and burned a black patch of tire rubber on our lawn. I didn't see the driver. I didn't want to see him. I was crouched between two palm trees, their trunks protecting me.

That night I slept in my parents' big bed, the boxsprings underneath me protesting my invasion.

Where were my parents? And what were they doing?

Maybe they had found each other.

Maybe they were making love. . . .

BUBBA'S SISTER ANGELINA telephoned at midnight and apologized for having to call up so late, but the prom was on Monday, she'd been trying to reach me, and she hoped I didn't mind, but we had to get things *straight*.

Angelina Fishback was a wonderful girl. She had an extra-large body and an extra-large soul, and her mind was constantly

bopping with ideas like Ping-Pong balls in a bingo bin. Like
Ian, Angelina had been accepted to Yale, but she'd turned New
Haven down for a community college. She adored her family—
Bubba especially, whom she liked to slug full-force in the stomach in front of her friends, just out of affection—and she
couldn't bear leaving her home to go north, even though she had
an air of independence about her. "I bagged Yale for spite," she
said through her nose. The better part of Angelina's charm was
vanity. She had a tattoo displaying her SAT scores—which were
way off the charts, and eclipsed even Ian's. But her wit was so
sharp and her tongue so incisive you had to have a rhino's skin
to hang around with her. She intimidated Ian, who kept his distance from her, and she described herself aptly as a human tor-
nado—sucking friends and family alike into her wake and
spitting them back out again, loved but devastated. I'd always
had a spiritual crush on Angelina: if I had been a woman, I'd've
wanted to be her. She carried herself like a Mardi Gras float and
draped herself in pastels like one of Monet's haystacks and covered her girthy and ungirdled frame with dozens of politically
incorrect buttons—"Kill The Poor," "Right To Die," "PMS Is A
Lifestyle Option"—that were more humane than their self-
righteous targets. Angelina didn't like me—not in *that* way—
but we made a fetching couple, and we had a blast together.
What she wanted was a body to escort her to the prom: someone
to strut with, someone to gossip with, someone to get in everybody's fucking face with. And she was pissed off I hadn't telephoned her sooner, what with the prom only three nights away.
She woke me from a sleep I felt I'd never really earned, her
voice like a rape whistle shrieking through the phone.

   "Bubba's tux, Toby! It's *tangerine-colored!* He got it from,
like, a *televangelist garage sale!* He's going to be healing *fucking spastics* on the *dance floor! Satan, begone! SWEETJESUS-
YOUCANCONGA!*" There was something narcotizing in
Angelina's stridency as I lay beneath an open window drifting
off to sleep. " 'Big Brother!' I said. 'You look like a *circus*

peanut!' It sorta made him cry, but the moron needs to know." I
couldn't see then, or was only half aware of the shadow of a figure approaching the window. It looked like the trunk of a palm
tree swaying and taking two sinister steps in the moonlight.
"And then I got in trouble with my dyke Religion teacher—ever
notice, Tobe, how your class is called 'Theology' and ours is
called 'Religion'? It's so fucking sexist!—because I said that Jesus—have you ever thought about it?—was probably forced to
carry his cross upside down, with the arm bar dragging on the
ground. *It makes sense,* 'cause it would be more difficult to, like,
get a *grip* on, and Christ would get all these nasty splinters in
his fingers that would make the nails feel like—*GAWD!,
acutherapy!*" In the vanity mirror above my mother's dresser I
could make out the shadow in the window taking shape, arms
extended outward, no longer a shadow, but fleshy, and creeping,
and emerging in the moonlight. "Toby, you know, you are *shit* for
conversation! Whenever you guys get quiet on the phone I as-
sume you're masturbating. Put your cock away and *talk!*" But
the receiver was already tumbling from my hand as the face of a
stranger, damp with tears and crusted blood, blossomed darkly in
the mirror like a gory moonflower. *"Toby!"* I screamed and catapulted from bed. *"Toby! . . . It's me! . . . It's your friend! . . . Let
me in!"*

"I DIDN'T MEAN to scare you," Juice said, later on, after I
had put my mother's Ginsu away and let him, hyperventilating, in the frontdoor. He was bleeding. His hands fumbled for
a cigarette. He never carried cigarettes; Juice always mooched
off people. "I would've rung the bell, but in case your folks was
home . . . Can I smoke?" he asked shakily. "Can I have a glass
of water?" He landed on a barstool, head between his hands.
"I'm sorry, Toby Sligh. I'm sorry to disturb you. You the one,

Toby Sligh." I sat down next to him. "What's happening, Juice?"
"You my friend, ain'tchoo?" "I like to think I am." He looked at
me and blinked. "My moms, Toby Sligh—" He choked on cigarette smoke; his cough was deep and chesty, and it rumbled
through the house. "Somebody, Tobias, somebody talked to
Moms, some undercover agent, and he said I was a dealer."
"You *are* a dealer, Juice." He bowed his head and nodded. "I
know I is, Toby. I know I'm a dealer. *But not like you
think* . . . Could I have that glass a' water?" I went to the cup-
board and got him a glass, then I went to the refrigerator and
fetched the jug of water. On the door of the fridge, as I opened it,
I noticed the picture of my folks and Juice together, gathered
like a family around the Scrabble board. "Fuck the glass, Toby,
just gimme the jug," Juice said and grabbed it and put it to his
lips, and drank the gallon down in great greedy gulps. "You
might wanna wash that," he said when he had finished. There
was blood on the spout, so I pitched the jug in the sink. "It's not
like you think. Nothing ever is, Toby. I deal to people, I make
money off it, but I do other things—" "Like what?" "Never
mind. So anyway, Tobes, I'm home late from hoops, and Moms is
waitin' up, and I say, 'What's for dinner?', and she come over to
me, and ya know, she make this fist, and then she starts to *hit
me!* In the *face,* she starts to *hit me!* 'No son a' mine!' she
screamin'. 'No son a' mine!' And she say she seed the pictures
the officer showed her! An' I say, 'What pictures?,' an' I stan'
there gettin' hit! An' she juss keep screamin' and callin' me a
dealer!" Juice's body had collapsed now, and his shoulders were
heaving, and I got a paper towel, and I wiped his bloody face. "I
ain't a dealer, Toby! Not like they think! I mean I *am* a dealer,
but it's diff'rent, it is!" Juice, he was crying like a locomotive;
then his shoulders stopped churning, and he sat there cooling
down. "So I come to you, Toby, 'cause you the one, ain'tchoo?
Anquanna, she doan' want me. I ain't got nowhere to go. Can I
crash here awhile, till your parents come back? I shack up some

motel it juss remind me of my mama. I pay you for the room—"

"*Juice*—" "I pay you for the—"

Just then there was a pounding at the door. A car had pulled up, but we hadn't even heard it. The porchlight was out. Some-one stood beside the porchswing—a big, hulking person, loom-ing there, breathing deep.

"That your pops, Toby?"

"I don't know who it is!"

"He woan' wanna see me. . . . Maybe I should go!"

"You stay right there!"

"Toby Sligh!"

"It's a lady!"

"I recognize that voice!"

The voice spoke: "It's Ange*li*na!"

ANGELINA FISHBACK DIDN'T need to see Juice. She was the most extemporaneous gossip in the world, and if the story got out, the rumors would be rampant. So I led Juice around to my mom and dad's bedroom and told him to shower and sleep if he wanted, and then I threw some clothes on and staggered out-side. Angelina was sitting on the porchswing, swinging. It was creaking underneath her. She wore a pink plastic trenchcoat.

"Gawd, Toby Sligh, thank Christ you're alive! I heard you let out that bloodcurdling scream and I said, the poor boy has *cli-maxed* to death! I know the mere sound of Angelina Fishback is enough to send any mere lad into *rap*ture, but really, Tobias, this is phone sex in ex*trem*is! What is Mr. Leonard Compton's Porsche doing here?" she said as I sat down and stretched out beside her. "Is he inside, Toby? Are your parents awake? Mine are watching cyberfascist Schwarzenegger movies. I put on *La Strada*—are you *into* Fellini?—but my dad only watches, like,

colorized movies, and once he saw the subtitles and heard the
Italian it was time for, like, *Terminator 3: Paradiso.*" I leaned
my sleepy head against her plasticoated shoulder. It crackled
sympathetically. She fiddled with my hair. "Ya know, Sly Tobias,
I don't have to do the talking. I know I'm entertaining, but I
came to save your *life!* I think a thank-you is in order." I yawned
and told her thank you. "Just deliver your firstborn to the following address." She recited an address and shoved me rudely
off her shoulder. "We *are* still going to the prom, are we not?
There's this *fabtastic* rumor floating around school that two guys
in your class are attending the prom together! Is it you and
Leonard Compton? Is that why his car's here? Are you shacking
up together right now? May I watch? *Gawd!* I hope your parents
can't hear me, Toby Sligh! I know I'm overbearing—earth god-
desses are. Did I wake you up, kiddo? I really was worried. I
thought you had been murdered. . . . I'm even packing Daddy's
piece!"

WE GOT INTO Angelina's father's Continental and I told her
she'd phoned me in the middle of a dream, that I'd been
semiconscious, and that I'd sort of had a nightmare.

"It was thanatos, then! *What* a disappointment! I always
thought my dulcet tones might elicit eros! But I guess"—her bosom heaved, and she batted her eyelashes—"I inspire darker
things. *Je ne suis qu'une femme fatale!*"

We cruised around my neighborhood—her talking, me listening—till Angelina anchored her father's Continental at the
library that had recently been tented for termites. The tent had
been struck and lay like a busted condom, and the library rose
inside it, dusty and deserted, doors and windows bolted, and all
the novels sleeping. Angelina grilled me about Juice's Porsche,
and when pressed I said yes, that it was Juice's Baby, that Juice

had loaned it to me while my parents were away.

"Where are they, Toby?"

"Um, in Barbados."

"That's funny. Ian's parents are in Barbados, too. Maybe they're having a group thing, or something."

I thought a bit about it.

"Maybe they are."

We got out of the frontseat and squatted on the hood. It was very nice out. The moon was fat and pink.

"Bubba said you had the flu," Angelina stated. "And Ian has it, too. Sex on the Beach is worried."

"About what?"

"About what? *That Ian won't get it up!* Courtney heard he's huge! Well, is he, Tobias?"

"How would I know?"

"I thought you guys compared . . . in the shower and all."

It was true: we did.

"Bubba's is teensy. It's always peeking out. He's proud of it, though. He likes to show it off."

"Who is Bubba taking to the prom, Angelina?"

She took out a chic black cigarette and lit it.

"Clove?"

"No, thanks. They give you throat cancer."

"That's why I like them."

The air became delicious.

"Bubba is taking this shy little dormouse who was raised by Mormons and who looks like Cousin It. Her name is Grace Cage. She never talks at all, except to tell people that they're going to hell—like *moi,* in particular. That's why Bubba asked her."

We got up for a walk and strolled around the parking lot, and we made plans together while orbiting the building. At night Angelina's brassy voice became sultry, and she glided through the darkness on invisible coasters. It was a shame I didn't like her. In a funny way, I did. Unlike other guys, I wasn't put off by her size. She was just another sexless female specimen to me.

She could have been Madonna. She could have been Marilyn. She could have been a manatee. Her insides were important.

"Am I doing *all* the planning?" Angelina scolded. "You'll be alarmed by my consultancy fee!"

So we discussed what time I would be at her house—we were meeting at the Fishbacks' for a pre-prom get-together—and what she was wearing, and what I would wear, and the corsage she wanted, and the boutonniere I'd get, and where we thought the eight of us might want to go have dinner.

"There's this Japanese place that serves exquisite sushi. Have you ever had sushi?"

I told her I hadn't.

"*Ooo,* it's to *die* for! But expensive?" Angel whistled. "And, hey, I'm not cheap. Do you think I'm cheap, Toby?"

I told her I didn't.

"Darn tootin', I ain't! You'll be paying out the butt! *Out the butt,* Toby Sligh!"

At the side of the building we came to an alley blockaded by a dumpster overflowing with books. I reached in and grabbed one—*Arabian Nights.* It was covered with bugs. I wiped the cover clean.

"I've always wanted to read this!" Angelina shouted. "It's all about this girl named Scheherazade who tells stories to keep from being decapitated by this guy with a hard-on for chicks without heads!"

I gave her the book; she stuck it in her pocket.

"Thanks, Tobe," she said. "I'm sure it's a keeper."

Angelina and I bonded best through books; we both loved novels and had discriminating taste. Her favorites were French—Flaubert and Camus. All mine were Russian—Turgenev and Chekhov. We'd argue about Dostoevsky and Proust and the English novel, which I said was perverse, which she claimed was why she liked it: *Vanity Fair* especially and, in particular, Becky Sharp. The only novel we agreed on completely was Miguel de Cervantes' *Don Quixote de la Mancha,* which Angelina had read in the original Spanish. She claimed I couldn't appreciate Cervantes in translation, which I said was bullshit: all good novels translate. And we'd fight about when the Don was lowered in the well and whether the paradise he found was imagined; and we'd talk about whether he loved Sancho Panza and whether he had tried to fuck his best friend up the ass; but we never argued once about how hard it made us laugh, or how sad Quixote was when they put him in his cage. Angelina said, and I still agree with her, that the difference between a classic and a classic piece of trash is that trash always manages to lie in a true way and that a classic always manages to tell the truth through lies—which was why we left writers like Mailer in the dumpster and rescued a collection of Flannery O'Connor, which was why we bypassed Toni Morrison for Zora and rescued Sterne and Swift over Pynchon and Joyce. When we finished, our arms were overflowing with volumes. They reeked of pesticides. We breathed in their aroma.

"Let's put 'em back inside," Angelina suggested, and with the butt of Daddy's gun smashed a hole through a window, her big bulky body obliterating space.

INSIDE IT WAS pitch black, except for schools of moonbeams swimming through a skylight to a card catalog. Clutching her books, Angelina snatched her lighter and, before I could warn her, flicked on her trusty Bic. A leafstorm of roaches fluttered in our faces, hissing and beating their chocolate-colored wings, the sound like the sound of a million unturned pages flipping in the darkness, skimmed by phantom eyes. Angelina screamed and attached her body to me, and her lighter fell with an excruciating *click!* to the floor. Already we could hear the flying armies retreating and dropping to the tile in a pattering of rain. It was so dark in there that we couldn't get our bearings; we could only move together toward the distant, milky light. Our arms around each other, we advanced as a couple, roaches like potato chips crackling underfoot. At the card catalog, in a cataract of moonlight, we had a view at last of the library entire: it was like a battlefield, bug bodies rampant, on their backs and kicking their last and dying in droves atop Harlequin Romances. I left Angelina death-shuddering in silence and forayed out to find the books Scarcross had requested. Scanning the shelves with a blind man's intuition, I located Blake, and Dickinson, and Shakespeare, and even an edition of the King James Bible. When I came back, Angelina Fishback had fled, and I spied her cornfed figure in the underwater moonlight shelving O'Connor, and Hurston, and Sterne. Returning, Angelina wrapped her ample arms around me and said, "This is the weirdest thing I have ever *done*." I put my arms around her, and I looked her in the eye, and we both smiled shyly, and I asked her to dance. "You mean here?" she said. "Can't it wait until prom?" "No," I told her. "We have to dance now." . . . Because I knew at the prom I'd be dancing with Ian; because I knew, when I had to, I'd abandon Angelina. So to the fluttering of roaches, and the waltzing of our hearts, and under the restless eyes of a thousand unread novels, we joined our trembling bodies and began describing circles on the floor that crunched beneath us, in a cataract of moonlight, in the mutual assurance that the best lies are honest, the best dancers awkward, and the truest stories false.

"THAT WAS REALLY different," Angelina told me as she dropped me back off at my house later on.

I kissed her sweaty forehead. "See you at the prom!"

"And say hello to Juice!" she cried out, and tore away.

✺ WHEN I GOT in, Juice was spread-eagled on my folks' bed, in Bill Blass pajamas, and I crawled in bed beside him. His body was huge, and hot, and unruly. It sprawled across the mattress, his corded muscles twitching. When I woke up in the morning his arms were around me, and I lifted them off, and I climbed out of bed. I stood looking at him; he was snoring operatically. And his bloody mouth was open and drooling on a pillow. Juice was like a toddler who was sleeping off an illness, like a healthier version of the kid at St. Osyth's I'd seen the first night that I went to search for Ian. When I glanced out the window it was still dark out, so I crept back in bed and wrapped Juice's arms around me. It was nice, Juice holding me. We were funky brothers. But then he called me E-Eye and locked his arms around me and I could barely breathe until at last he loosened up. By then he was crying, and just as quickly he was snoring, and when I finally got up, he had fixed a modest breakfast. "Cornflakes or Cocoa Puffs?" Juice asked and shook the boxes. He wore my dad's robe and my mom's shower cap, and his cheekbones were creamy with Oil of Olay. "But you'll have to munch 'em dry, Tobe. The milk is all spoilt."

✺ SATURDAY MORNING AND most the afternoon we spent eating Cocoa Puffs and watching cartoons, for which Juice had an appreciation verging on the spiritual. "When I have rug apes"—Juice called children rug apes—"I ain't gonna give 'em no motherfuckin' Bible. Gonna sit their booties down and make 'em watch Looney Tunes." Juice could be Zen about the most unlikely subjects, and when I asked him why the Roadrunner never got caught, he shot me a look like I was some kind of pagan. "Just watch the *show*, Toby Sligh," Juice ordered. The Coyote was about to be crushed by a boulder. *"Bam!"* Juice reproduced the sound of the impact. Then he said, "Lookit! *He always gets up!*"

Later on I opened up to Juice about my parents, mostly my dad: I was worried about him. I knew where my mom was; I could find her if I wanted, though I didn't tell Juice that. I just said they both were missing. I sort of wanted Juice to talk to me about *his* parents, but his mother was a sore spot; she had kicked him out of the house. And his father, well, Juice wouldn't talk about his dad. And in the middle of our session Lucinda at St. Osyth's phoned up to tell me I couldn't visit Scarcross: "His throat is shot, Toby. He needs to rest today."

When I hung up, Juice said, "Who's 'at?"

"Angelina."

"*Bull*shit," Juice said. "Woulda *heard* Angelina." And when Juice was in his Porsche getting ready to go, he said, "I'll put an APB out on your daddy. Pops is always easier to locate than moms is. G.'s is always movin'; ladies keep still."

"Like the Roadrunner and Coyote?" I asked.

Juice revved the engine. "Them is both G.'s. . . . '*Bleep! Bleep!*' " he said and left.

IT WAS GETTING on suppertime, but the sun was still shining, and I had spent most of the day on the porchswing staring at a lawn I saw no reason to mow. Ian hadn't called; I was being forgotten. He had stood me up at the formalwear fitting, and for all I knew he'd do the same thing at the prom. And I could picture Fr. Scarcross alone across town, in bed, and sleeping, and dreaming of me. Then a carhorn goosed me and Fr. Diaz pulled up in a raffle Cadillac with blue-and-white pinstriping. He was brandishing two rackets and a fabulous smile, a cigarette pulsing on his heart-shaped lips.

"HOW ARE YOU, Toby?" Fr. Diaz began, and gave my forearm an affectionate pump.

"*Muy bien,* Father. And you?"

"I am *well!*"

Riding high around Diaz's tan, muscled thighs was a skimpy
pair of Izod-Lacoste playing shorts. A matching lavender shirt
with the alligator logo coming undone hung about his upper
body. Tennis balls dotted the floor of the Cadillac—tennis balls
and unopened packs of Lucky Strikes. There was also a *Sports
Illustrated* swimsuit issue open on a topless goddess pouting in
Barbados.

"Don't you have tennis shorts?"

He was looking at my crotch.

"I guess I don't, Father."

He handed me a Lucky.

"I am sure that we have a pair or two at the rectory. We always
have things in the Lost and Found closet."

"Will my parents be there?"

"At St. Patrick's, Toby?"

"In the Lost and Found closet."

Diaz smiled and squeezed my forearm.

THAT SHOULD HAVE been his cue to tell me what was going
on, but Diaz didn't say word one about my folks until we
were deep in the third set of the match, and then he only addressed the missing duo metaphorically. Diaz had taken the
first two sets 6–0, 6–0 with a capacity for cruelty I'd come to expect from close encounters with nuns but would never have
thought possible from any parish priest. I didn't hold serve. I
couldn't even score a point. And Diaz, his swirling hair plastered to his forehead, would curse stray services with sudden
shouts of "*Coño!*" and threaten phantom judges as ferociously

as McEnroe, then go all cute and cuddly like that cobra, Andre
Agassi. And then, right when I was catching my breath, he
would ace me with a service as fast as a *pelota*. At first I was dis-
tressed by Diaz's refusal to concede to me at least even one
mercy point; I thought he was taking his Wimbledon fantasy,
sexy as it was, a little too far. But every time we switched sides
he would pat me on the ass and flash that dazzling Latin smile
and say, "Do not give up! Never give up, Tobias!" And I'd come
back at him with miraculous rallies and volleys at the net I'd
never dreamed that I could make. But somehow, always, he
managed to return them—until we came to match point, and
Diaz was serving, and I found myself soaked head to toe in de-
feat, and Diaz lobbed the ball up with Pentecostal grace, and
brought his racket down, and smoked me with an ace.

"Six-love, six-love, six-love!" Diaz sang as he sprang across
the net like an antelope in heat and helped me up off of the
scorching concrete. "And the lesson, Toby Sligh, is that in tennis, as in life, it is okay not to win, if you do it for *love!*"

I was leaning on his shoulder.

Then he said: "Let's take a shower."

FR. DIAZ LATHERED up himself from top to bottom and,
bouncing on the balls of his feet like a boxer, began to
throw soapsudsy punches at me.

"Fight, Toby, fight! Don't you know how to fight?"

The only thing I was fighting at the moment was a—

"*No.*"

"Jesus said to turn the other cheek," Diaz counseled, turning
around and showing me *his:* they were buttered up with soap
and they made my stomach flutter. "But when Jesus was a boy, I
am sure that Joseph taught him." I could just picture Jesus going ten rounds with his stepdad: "*My father can beat up your fa-*

ther," he would brag. "But Mary probably taught him the best strategy of all—and that, Toby Sligh, is to sometimes keep quiet. Not to talk, but to listen, as Christ did with his accusers. If you can fight like you did on the courts today, Toby, can you keep still if you absolutely have to?" I was trying to keep still; I was, I swear to God. "Will you promise, Toby Sligh? I'll show you something if you promise." "I promise, Fr. Diaz," I said. I was waiting. *"Poom! Poom!"* Diaz hollered, whirling around. He caught me in a slippery clinch and pushed me away. This was too much: I had to play Hide-a-Woody. *"Muy bien!* You're a fighter! Now get dressed and follow me!"

I WATCHED DIAZ step into a pair of Calvin Kleins and drape a black linen alb across his tawny body. The blossomy garment billowed around him. He was going to hear confessions, and he wanted me to come.

"When I get into the confessional"—we were walking toward the church—"wait till no one's looking, then knock very gently, and I will let you in."

"But—"

"Silencio, Toby!"

He entered the church, and I followed in after. It was Saturday night—the usual old ladies. When the last had been heard I knocked at the confessional. The church bell struck eight. Fr. Diaz dragged me in.

"Crawl underneath my gown and say absolutely nothing!"

"Crawl underneath your—?"

"Gown, yes! Do it, Toby! *Shhhh!*"

I did as he asked and crept underneath his garment. His body was warm, like a puppy's, next to mine. I could feel the bristly hairs of his chest on my shoulders. I could feel his steel crucifix tickling my spine.

"Father—"

"*Toby! You promised silencio!*" He slapped my ass reprovingly. "*Now not another word!*"

Outside the booth we heard a single pair of footsteps. They were light, like a woman's. They were pacing back and forth. Then we heard the door to the booth before us open, and a dark figure cleared her throat and knelt and crossed herself. At the same time, in the booth that was opposite her, someone had entered and silently knelt. It was a man, I could tell; I could peek through Diaz's collar. He crossed himself quickly and spoke. It was Dad.

"Father, forgive me for I have sinned. It has been two days since my last confession, and, Father—*and, Father, I*—"

Dad started crying.

"*I love her!*" he blustered. "Oh, Father, *I love her!* I'm losing my mind! I don't know where she is! I've looked everywhere! You gotta help me find her! If I don't find her, Father, I don't know what I'll—"

"*Shhh!*"

Fr. Diaz rested his hand against the webbing. My father was sobbing. And I was crying, too.

"Have patience, Mr. Sligh."

"I've tried everything, Father! I've looked so hard I can't look anymore!"

"She loves you, Mr. Sligh."

"I know she does, Father! But if I could only find her, everything would be all right!"

In the dark booth behind us I could hear the woman moving. She smelled like suntan oil. She smelled like manicotti.

"You have to help me, Father. You have to help me find her! I know that she's seen you! I know that you've spoken! For the love a' God, Father, if you value the family—"

"I cannot tell you where she is without her permission," Fr. Diaz said.

"I know," my dad sniffled. "Does she *want* me to find her?"

"I think so, Mr. Sligh."

"I'm tired of searching. Every day we're searching."

"Who's we?" Diaz asked.

"Nobody," Dad said.

There was silence. In the next room, the woman straightened up.

"I better go, Father. I'm sorry to bother you. It's just that I love her. *Is that such a sin?*"

Lifting up my hand, Fr. Diaz blessed my father.

"We should have so many sinners. Now go and get some sleep."

Then my dad rose up, as if the world were on his shoulders, and right before he left he pressed his face against the grating.

"You gaining weight, Padre?" Dad said, leaning in.

"Good night, Mr. Sligh," Diaz said, and closed the grate.

When my father had gone, Diaz pivoted around and peered into the darkness of the booth that was before us. The breath of a woman wafted lightly on our faces. She sat there, huddled over. She didn't say a word.

"Did you hear him?" Diaz asked.

The woman only nodded.

"He loves you," Diaz said.

"I know he does."

It was my mom.

"He loves you a lot," Diaz said.

"I love him too."

"He wants me to tell him where you're living."

Mom exhaled.

"I'll have to think about it, Fr. Diaz," she whispered. She ran her fingers through her hair and rose up slowly from the kneeler. Then she knelt back down. "How is Toby?" she asked.

Fr. Diaz clamped my mouth shut.

"Just fine. We played tennis."

"I'll call you, Fr. Diaz," Mom said, and then she left.

We listened to her go, her footsteps disappearing.

✺ THAT NIGHT I slept in my parents' big bed. The mattress still carried the impressions of their bodies. There was room enough for two, but Juice didn't show, so the bed was all mine. I slept in it alone.

✺ NOW TWO BEDS were vacant in Room 1111. The third, containing Magda, had her sitting up in bed, eating an orange in methodical sections and concealing the peelings in her Havatampa box. Fr. Scarcross was lying in bed with his rosary, fingers ticking off the smooth porcelain beads, mouthing a meager Morse code of supplication. Sitting beside him, leafing through the Sunday paper, was the last man I expected to find there—Kickliter. He stood up when I entered and said, "Dr. *Sligh!*" and took the books from me and examined them with interest.

Scarcross dropped his rosary.

"Is Toby here already?"

His voice was much stronger than it had been before.

"He's brought you something, Father," Kickliter told him, and handed him the books, one after the other.

"I don't want the books! Not now, Jerry!" Scarcross scolded K., motioning for me.

I went over to him. His fingers were extended. He reached beneath my mask and began to trace my face—the lines of my mouth, and my nose, and my eyes, the lines of my neck, and my chin, and my forehead.

"You know Toby, Jerry?"

He called Kickliter Jerry.

"He's one of our best, Fr. Scarcross," K. said.

"I imagine he is. He's dreadfully honest! You can read it in the lines of his face. Go ahead!"

Scarcross's fingers reached out for Kickliter's and closed

down upon them, then pressed them onto me. K. traced the lines of my face with his fingers, and when he had finished, he said he had to go.

"Everyone at Sacred Heart is rooting for you, man."

"But don't let them come and see me!" Scarcross insisted. His voice was overpowering. "I'm in no condition to be seen!"

As K. turned to go Fr. Scarcross cried out and clutched the books close to his bosom and said, "Look at these books! All these lovely books, Jerry! We'll have so much to talk about, Toby and I!"

"THEY'RE OPERATING ON my throat this afternoon, Toby." It was hard to conceive of: his voice sounded strong.

"I don't understand it. Yesterday, it was in pieces! Now, I'm like a songbird!"

He trilled a nonsense song.

"Maybe you don't need surgery at all."

"But if I lose my voice"—he drew my mask away from me—"how will we talk and tell the truth to each other?"

"But talking," I said to him, "talking is lying."

"No, it isn't, Toby! Everything we say is true. But some things we say are just truer than others. For instance, if I told you that once I knew a man who lay down to die beneath a juniper tree, and an angel touched him, and brought him cake and water and said, *'The word of the Lord in thy mouth is truth'*; and if I told you, Toby Sligh, that I was that man, would you believe my story, or would you say I was a liar?"

"That's too imaginative to be a lie," I concluded. "Lies are ordinary. It must be the truth."

Fr. Scarcross smiled and caught my hands in his.

"Why couldn't I have met you when I was full of life?"

"You are full of life."

"God love you for a liar."

Outside, a bird flew against the windowpane. It struggled there awhile, and then it flew away. I watched it receding in the afternoon sky—just wings, then a smear, then a speck. And it was gone.

"Was Jesus a liar?" I asked for no reason when Eli's hands abandoned mine for his beads. "He said he was the Son of God. Do you believe him?"

Fr. Scarcross thought it over, breathing like a whistle.

"I don't believe Jesus believed *himself,* Toby. Christ didn't know whether he was a liar. He thought his dad was God. He thought he was the Savior. But how could he be sure? So he died to prove his love."

"Did Christ have to die to prove his love for his father? Couldn't he have, like, just *mowed the yard* or something?"

Scarcross let the rosary spill into his lap. Then he picked it up again and counted as he spoke.

"Would you die for your father if he asked you to, Toby?"

"I'd live for my mother."

Fr. Scarcross stopped counting.

"But would you die for anyone? Anyone you loved?"

I was thinking of Ian.

"Are you in love, Toby Sligh?"

I didn't answer right away: it wasn't any of his business. But I sighed, without knowing it. Eli opened up his arms.

"Love," he exhaled. He embraced himself sadly. "Here it is; there it goes." He released himself again.

I wondered if Scarcross had ever been in love. Jesuit priests took a vow of chastity. Had he broken his vow? Or had his vow broken him? Who was his undoing? And was it any of my business?

"Have you ever been in love?" I asked, with difficulty.

"Yes," he said and shuddered, and spat up a pat of blood. "I wasn't alive till I fell in love, Toby." He examined his body. "Now look at me."

"Who were you in love with?" I asked, very softly.

"God knows who it was. God knows who I loved."

I was looking at my shoes. I was thinking of my parents. The whole world was quiet. It was biting its tongue.

"Where is your family?" Fr. Scarcross asked suddenly.

He was sitting up in bed. He was staring at me, blindly.

"Away," I said, trembling. "My family's away."

"Here is your family," Scarcross said, and touched his heart. "Here is your family. Right here, Toby Sligh."

We sat there awhile. My heart felt abandoned. I was tired. I was empty. I was trying not to cry.

"If I lose my voice, will you be my voice; and if you become my voice, Toby Sligh, will you speak truly? When God lost his voice, Jesus Christ spoke for him. That's why they crucified him. Because he spoke for God."

"So God decides to pout and a man gets murdered. That isn't very fair."

"It's fair if it's love."

Outside, we heard a siren. It pined and died away. Scarcross lay back and clasped his books against his chest.

"Do you like the books I brought you?"

He gave each a kiss.

"They smell just like bug spray!"

I stifled a laugh.

"Read one to me."

"Which one?"

"Read *The Tempest*! We'll skip the first act, except for the shipwreck. . . . Would you like to hear the shipwreck?"

"Dunno. Is it exciting?"

"Is it *exciting?*" Scarcross said, and he bolted up in bed.

A maelstrom of noises—waves and shouts and rolling thunder—escaped Eli's lips and set the AIDS ward deep at sea. Magda chimed in and started groaning like weak lumber, and two nurses—boatswains—hustled in and out again. When Scarcross had finished, and the room hadn't capsized, Sr. Cindy and

Lucinda stood whistling at the doorway, two new arrivals clapping meekly at their sides.

"Pay no attention to Ja," advised Lucinda.

"Silence! We're conducting a performance of *The Tempest!*"

FROM WHAT I could gather—*The Tempest* was beyond me, though Scarcross provided a sort of running commentary—a magician named Prospero had been booted from his dukedom because he spent too much time nosing through his books. He landed on an island with his daughter, Miranda, and enslaved two inhabitants—a monster and a fairy—and began to make arrangements to win his dukedom back. Only thing was, it was nice on the island—good books, good food, good weather, good fun . . . like *Gilligan's Island* with a really good script. And Prospero hardly talked at all about his wife—if you asked me, he might have had a thing for the fairy, whom he was always calling "my dainty Ariel." My favorite character, Caliban, the foul-mouthed monster, got all the best speeches and took shit from no one. Scarcross would grumble all of Caliban's curses, his once-ravaged throat performing admirably. But Eli was really more suited to Prospero: both had an air of exiled royalty. Magda started crying when Scarcross mimicked barking in a scene in which two drunkards got chased by hunting dogs, but Eli repeated—virtually singing it—Caliban's speech about the noises of the isle, and Magda's weeping faded into sweet narcotic sleep:

> *Be not afeard; the isle is full of noises,*
> *Sounds and sweet airs, that give delight and hurt not.*
> *Sometimes a thousand twangling instruments*
> *Will hum about mine ears; and sometimes voices,*
> *That if I then had wak'd after long sleep,*

Will make me sleep again, and then in dreaming,
The clouds methought would open and show riches
Ready to drop upon me, that, when I wak'd
I cried to dream again. . . .

It made me sleepy too, in a delicious sort of way, like when you're young and drowsy in the backseat of a car and all you hear is traffic, and your parents, and Top 40. And I thought of all the voices on Juice's tape recorder, and the voice of my mother, and the voice of my father, and the voice of Ian Lamb—the voices of my world. Scarcross's words were like a jigsaw of them all, like waves of peaceful static, like a hurricane of calm. I reached for his hand, and I held it for a while. We were standing in a current, but his body was drifting. Something was tugging at it, something indistinct, and I could only stand there, anchoring him. I could have let go even then, if I wanted. But I held on to his hand until he drifted back to me. He opened his eyes: they were full of the world. They couldn't see a thing, but he was looking into me. And at last he sat up, and he clapped the volume shut, and he asked me for my honest opinion of *The Tempest*.

"I like Caliban," I said, "even though he gets screwed."

"Caliban's a monster," Fr. Scarcross informed me. "What does Prospero want?"

"Prospero wants power."

"No!" Scarcross answered. "Prospero wants love!"

"What about Ariel?" Scarcross continued. "Is he free in the end?"

I didn't know what he meant.

"Ariel," Scarcross said, "is he *free*, Toby Sligh?"

"You mean is he *released*?"

"*That's not what I mean at all!*"

Beside us, Magda started crying in her sleep. She was whispering a woman's name over and over. She awoke from her dream and looked over at us. Two orderlies entered with a chattering metal gurney.

"I give this to you!" Scarcross handed me *The Tempest*. "Hide it underneath your mattress! It's truer than roses!"

They hoisted Fr. Scarcross onto the gurney.

"True or false, Toby?"

He wouldn't let me go. They wanted to remove him, but his hand held fast to mine.

"Prospero is a good man! True or false, Toby?"

"False," I said to Scarcross: Prospero was a liar.

"True or false, Toby! Caliban's a monster!"

"False," I said to Scarcross: Caliban was true.

"True or false, Toby! Ariel is free now!"

I was looking at him closely; his hands abandoned mine.

"True or false, Toby!" They were wheeling him away. "True or false, Toby! *True or false, Toby Sligh!*"

WAS ARIEL FREE? Prospero had released him. He had done what he had to; now he was free to go. But would someone else enslave him? Did he even want his freedom? I thought I had my answer. What would Ariel's be?

WHILE SCARCROSS WAS in surgery I tried my best to study, but I felt the sudden urge to see the face of my mother. I didn't really need to see the face of my father; I only had to look into a mirror to do that. Fathers and sons are photographic negatives; a mother's face you sort of have to touch base with. So I said goodbye to Cindy and then to Lucinda, and they said to hurry back, because Scarcross needed me.

IN THE LOBBY of St. Osyth's I was stopped by a kid with a quarter in one hand and a lost look in his eye.

"Have you seen my uncle?" he asked.

I said I hadn't.

"Don't you have a nuncle?" the kid said, and cracked his knuckles.

I told him I didn't: in fact, it was true. For relatives, I only had my mother and father.

"I just have a mommy and daddy," I explained.

"That *sucks*," the kid said. "Here, you can have my quarter."

SINCE MY MOTHER and father'd moved out of the house, it had occurred to me that families, like figures in history, repeat the same mistakes with ridiculous precision. It was a peculiar trait of the Sligh household that we didn't have a family besides ourselves to speak of. And when I say "to speak of," I mean exactly that: my parents didn't speak of either one of their parents, nor would they speak *to* them. It was like they'd never been. And here I was, a third-generation talking cripple, miring in the quicksand of communication breakdown. My relatives were somewhere. I didn't know where. Something bad had happened a long time ago, scars had run deep, and now nobody spoke. So in a way I did and *didn't* have relations; and I couldn't bitch and moan about a clan I'd never known. Did I have aunts and uncles? If so, nobody'd told me. It was weird, the whole business; we were all the Slighs we had. And Mom and Dad wouldn't talk about the families they'd abandoned, or by whom they'd been abandoned, many bitter years ago. The topic of the breakup, in fact, was so taboo that something in it must have been awfully romantic; I imagined a spectacularly decadent elopement, shotguns and squadcars and squalid hints of incest, sins so enormous only love could hush them up. A world of shit had happened before my arrival and my folks were fools to think it wouldn't be my legacy. . . .

But I still believed in truth, in spite of everything. I knew it was somewhere, like the Loch Ness monster, waiting to rear its legendary ugly head. Mom had moved out of the house for a reason; my father had followed her lead for a reason; neither of them spoke to their families for a reason; and now, for a reason, neither of them spoke to me. Ian's glass eye, Juice's crying jags, Anquanna's battered cheek, Fr. Scarcross's illness—these things had reasons: I could learn them if I wanted; I could learn them if I waited: if I learned to be *sly*. The simplest revelations required simple patience: the blood that Wu drew from my arm taught me that. It was somewhere in a lab. Someone was looking at it. If they saw something bad they would make a note of it, stick the note in an envelope, and mail it to Wu. And if I tested positive for the HIV virus, somewhere in a baker's dozen years I would be dead—dead just like André, dead just like Peter, dead like Scarcross would be in a matter of days, dead like so many unfortunate others whose bodies told the truth because the blood never lies. And if I had the virus, Ian Lamb probably had it. And whomever he might sleep with, they would get it too. My parents had the Cold War, the Bomb outside the body. We had AIDS. The Bomb had moved inside. Nations once afraid to even look at one another were replaced by lovers frightened by the simplest touch or kiss. And the virus was alive in every truth we never told—alive in the laundry someone scattered in our yard, alive in the white Plymouth terrorizing me, in Juice's tape recordings, in Ian Lamb's equivocations, in the ravaged throat of Scarcross on the operating table. All these were lies or the products of lying. I only knew a few things that were absolutely true: that I loved my parents, that I loved Ian Lamb, that I even loved Juice and Fr. Scarcross in my way. These things were true things, plus one important other: *that I was a faggot, an incurable faggot, and that*

I had spent seventeen years on this planet denying the undeniable truth of my existence. Toby Sligh was a lie. Toby's world was a liar's. And now his biggest lie was multiplying in his blood. "The truth," Ian said, "the truth is a bastard." But Ian was wrong, and I was learning what was right. The truth—that men wanted, that men needed one another—was the truth of my existence, and to lie would be to die. I had lived long enough in my labyrinth of lying. I would tell my mom I loved her. And that Toby Sligh was gay.

THE FRONTDOOR TO my mother's efficiency was open, though it had been camouflaged over with fronds. I entered without knocking, without shouting out. I didn't want to shock her; after all, she had a shotgun. I was immediately struck by the way the place had changed: purple shag carpeting covered the floor, a half an inch thick, bouncy as a trampoline, and the peach-colored walls were covered with drawings of a nude guy who bore a resemblance to Ian. The kitchen was spotless and free of cockroaches. Something like gumbo was aboil on the stove. This was how my mother would have lived if she'd been single—surrounded by her drawings, and her cooking, and herself. The place was a mess, but it had a messy order. It was my mother's mess. It was *distinctively* fucked up.

In the kitchen I lifted the lid off the gumbo and was going to taste it when I heard my mother's voice. It wasn't so much my mother's voice as her laugh; it was shrill and schoolgirl silly, like a menopausal Mouseketeer's. Outside it was fantastically bright and hot, and the sun had emerged from a flock of fleecy clouds and was charging the backyard in great bursts of light. I looked out the window and could make out my mother standing in jeans by the dilapidated Chevy. Standing atop it, in my mother's wedding gown, was Ian, and my mother was making alterations. Neither of them saw me; they were horsing around. Ian said something and my mother slapped his ass. A bunch of pins were sticking from her mouth, and Mom would remove them and poke them into Ian. I thought I heard a siren, then the sun disappeared, and when it reemerged Ian hopped down off the Chevy and he and my mother started waltzing in the yard. They were turning in elegant, radiant circles, and my heart was in my mouth, and when the waltz stopped, they *kissed*. The kiss was delicate. My mother's lips were full of pins. . . . But already I was crying fucking buckets by then, my mind pregnant with a hundred dirty possibilities as I fled the apartment, Toby Sligh's truth in tow.

 ACROSS FROM SACRED Heart, there was a park. I went for a walk and a man followed me. He asked me for the time and I told him what it was. He went into the woods, and I followed him.

My mother groan'd! my father wept.
Into the dangerous world I leapt:
Helpless, naked, piping loud:
Like a fiend hid in a cloud.

Struggling in my father's hands,
Striving against my swadling bands,
Bound and weary I thought best
To sulk upon my mother's breast. . . .

THERE WERE TUBES and needles in Scarcross's body. The partition had been drawn, so his bed was in shadow. I removed the books covering the chair beside his bed and took a seat quietly. Eli was in a coma.

"It's something with his heart," Lucinda had informed me before she led me in. "It happened during surgery. They couldn't find out what was wrong with his throat. Then his heart sort of— quit. We're glad you're here, Toby."

Scarcross was dying. Pretty soon he would be dead. You could read it in his breathing. You could read it on his skin. And any fool could see the operation was disastrous. His neck was bruised and battered, like a lacerated flute. And his chest wore a massive black crucifix of stitches that would mark him forever when they thrust him in the ground. I picked up the volume of Blake at his bedside and read two poems aloud—"Infant Joy" and "Infant Sorrow." I didn't understand them; they got jumbled in my head. But somewhere in the limbo in between them Scarcross lay:

> *"I HAVE no name:*
> *"I am but two days old."*
>> (My mother groan'd! my father wept.
>> Into the dangerous world I leapt . . .)
> *What shall I call thee?*
> *"I happy am,*
>> (Helpless, naked, piping loud:
>> Like a fiend hid in a cloud . . .)
> *"Joy is my name."*
> *Sweet joy befall thee! . . .*

In the infancy of dying, Fr. Scarcross was reborn. The dangerous world was receding into death and his limbs were as disheveled as a baby's in oblivion. If he could see himself, would Eli be surprised? In the Gospel of Scarcross, sorrow equaled joy. And joy equaled sorrow. It was God's odd equation. Where we had come

from and where we were going to, God only knew: we lived, and
then we didn't. The least we could do, in the Gospel of Eli, was to
enjoy the lousy ride, however ugly it might get. And by the look
of Scarcross it could get pretty ugly: the lesions, the stitches, the
tentacles and needles, the skeleton like bikespokes poking up
beneath the skin—this was what happened when the hourglass
ran out, when you found yourself staring at the other side of being. "Our little life is rounded by a sleep," Prospero claimed
when we had read *The Tempest*. But Prospero was a liar. This
sleep didn't round you; it was all razor edges. What was meant to
refresh left you helpless and naked, like Blake's blasted baby.
Sleep was an ordeal. And what I saw before me was a man who'd
been stripped of all life like a twig being stripped for an inferno.
How did it happen exactly, dying? Conception is simple: sperm
meets egg. But when one begins to die, are there similar colli-
sions? What meets what? *And could you purchase contraception?*
I couldn't stop thinking of the things I had done in the park, with
the stranger, in the darkness of the trees. We'd looked over our
shoulders, the two of us, groping; there had been too much fear
to allow for any pleasure. When we'd finished, we left, and we
didn't say goodbye. We didn't say a word. We put our cocks away
and walked . . . while somewhere across town Mom was waltzing
with Ian, and Dad was waltzing with his shadow, and Fr. Scarcross lay alone. Was this Jesuit here because he'd done the same
things with a similar stranger in a deeper, darker wood? And how
long would it be before I lay here like Scarcross? Before Ian
Lamb lay here? And the strangers we had touched? You would
live just so long as you never touched anybody; to touch was to
die; and to love was to touch.

 I hadn't scrubbed up. I had taken off my mask. And I
shouldn't have done it, but I took Elijah's hand. It was as light
as a lady's empty glove as I lifted it up to my forehead, and my
chest, and my shoulders. I said, "Father, forgive me for I have
sinned," and I listed my sins to a God who couldn't hear me.

And for penance, I promised not to search for the truth. I would let it come to me.

And pretty soon I was asleep.

❈ " '*TOBY! TOBY! BURNING* bright . . . *In the foress of the night . . . What immortal hand or eye . . . Dare frame thy fearful symmetry?*' " a soft, familiar voice purred into my ear as two dark arms curled around my drowsing neck. "This whatchoo been doin' for community service, sittin' up here, reading shit to a dead man?"

"He's not dead," I said, waking up. "And it's not shit. Who let you in here?"

"Lady did, Toby. Got a note from Kickliter."

He held up a note in Kickliter's scrawl.

"K. told you I was here?"

"I axed him, an' he tole me." Juice rubbed his mask. "This the priess who spoke to us?"

I nodded.

"Got AIDS. I was *right*, Toby Sligh."

I took the Blake from him and told him he was.

"Poem's dope," Juice continued. "That shit about the 'Tyger'? I'm the Tyger," Juice boasted. "That *kid*, G., is *me*."

❈ WE DROVE JUICE'S shit-car to an inner-city playground just a couple blocks from where Juice's father lived. Juice wouldn't drive to the playground in the Porsche because he was convinced he was still being followed. The beeper Juice wore on his belt kept going off, and Juice would slap it quiet, then switch it on again. "Prob'ly my dad," Juice explained. "Sometime he calls me. When he wants crack. I ain't givin' it to him." Before we left, Juice took the cellular from Baby and dialed his mother's number over and over. There wasn't any answer, so he stuffed the phone in the glovebox. I heard a bag crinkle. Juice scratched his nuts. "Gonna try to stay with my aunt tonight, Toby. My auntie-in-law," Juice said. "Anquanna's mama."

"So your mother, or your father, is—"

"It's *complicated,* Toby."

I took his word for it: *families were.*

"When's your birthday?" Juice asked.

"September," I told him.

"Happy birthday early."

Juice produced a shopping bag.

In it were Ray-Bans, Nike Air Huaraches, baggy Converse trackpants, a silk Adidas tanktop, Reebok athletic socks, furry purple sweatbands, a fat gold chain, and a Knickerbockers cap. Also in the bag was some Oscar de la Renta. I squirted some on me, then I squirted some on Juice.

"All this stuff for me?"

The Buick smelled like a bordello.

"You shootin' with Juice, you gotta look fly. You already white, and you no Vanilla Ice, so we gotsta, like, *do* what we got-sta, like, *do* to make Toby Dick funky fresh on the playground!"

"Gifts make slaves."

"Said the whitey to the fly. And ya know, senior prom—that's on me, too, Tobias. In exchange for favors rendered."

"What favors?

"The other night."

"Oh, Jesus!"

"Don't play me! You good at hoops, Toby?"

I was trying on the new gear. I was totally naked. Juice looked at my equipment, then he mashed the brakes and screamed: "You got the smallest jimmy, like, I have ever *seen!*"

"I shoot okay, boyeee."

"Shoot *what?*"

"Shoot hoops. Where's my designer jockstrap?"

Juice nodded at my penis.

"Honey, you doan' need one," Juice said, and pulled away.

THE BASKETBALL COURTS were behind a baseball diamond in a city park littered with crack pipes and graffiti. The clothes Juice had bought me were fashionably baggy, and I slouched along like a hiphop Snuffalupagus, my body submerged in a swamp of pricy labels. Juice wore a loose-fitting Chicago Bulls outfit that hid the muscularity of his running back's body, and he wore a floppy hat in Mother Africa colors tilted down across his forehead, so you couldn't see his face. We looked like a P.C. crime-fighting duo. We were incognito, no doubt about it. And as we crossed the weedy outfield and hopped the peeling billboards that advertised bail bonds and Unitarian churches, Juice moved away from where the pickup games were raging and approached a rusty swing set opposite the courts. Somebody waved at him and Juice waved back; then he donned his Wayfarers and crashed on a swing, the metal chains groaning, and he asked me would I push him.

"This be my playground, Toby Sligh," Juice said. He cast a cool patch for my body to stand in. "You got a playground?"

I told him I had. But it had been purchased by a bunch of Scientologists who rode matching Schwinns and spoke in monosyllables and dressed like Kmart mannequins and frightened little children.

"That's America," Juice said. "We a shadow nation. Yesterday's playground is tomorrow's cult compound. Everything you see is on its way to somewhere else."

Juice's bulky body was hard to push at first, but it got lighter the higher it got. "I learned a lot here. How to scope, how to scrap, how to dress full a' flavor, and how to shoot hoops. But one thing I learned—somebody taught it to me—never just *walk* onto a basketball court. Check out the players. Scope out the competition." On the courts were a total of ten, fifteen fellas, shirts untucked and dripping, making fancy shots. Far away were two white men. They looked out of place. Something about them attracted my attention. "That nigger in the Hawks cap? His name is Parrish. And that kid in the Jordans? 'At's his brother Trixter. Those two can whoop anybody on the court. But you wouldn't know now, 'cause them boys be jess *messin'.*" I craned my head around as Juice's body swung toward me and saw the two black guys Juice was talking about. They were walking toward the white men who were playing one-on-one at the hoop near the parking lot, the farthest hoop away. "They hustlin' those crackers in a little two-on-two. Ten, twenty dollars. Gonna get they asses popped!" I was pushing Juice hard; I didn't realize how hard; I was trying to get a better look at the white guys. "My eardrums is bleeding! You pushin' too high!" Juice let his Air Icarus scud into the dirt, and then he staggered off. I got on and he pushed me. "Word up," Juice said, when I sat down on the swing. "Wanna have some fun? Finna set on it *backwards.*" I took his advice and sat facing him, then I leaned back in the swing until the world was upside down. "Just watch yo' head when you come down, Toby." He was pushing on my feet, and the inverted world was reeling. "It's a parallel universe!" Juice said, like a Martian. "Cars, trees, everything's wicked whack, *boyeee!*" "I feel like a kid!" "You *are* a kid, Tobias!" Juice yelled and pushed me. I was soaring upside down. "You ain't gettin' sick?" Juice asked. "Not yet!" My arms were extended, like an angel flying backwards. "Keep yo' eyes on the white boys on the basketball court. The one's gettin' hustled." I tried, but it was tough. They'd moved closer to us on the ceiling of concrete and were playing two-on-two against Parrish and Trixter. The guys were my dad's age. They were built like my father. It was funny; upside down, they even *looked* like my dad. "Catch that foul, Toby? That white boy fouled Trixter!" Parrish was helping Trixter up off the ground. One white player held the other one back; even upside down, the game was getting nasty. "They come to our courts, and then they play dirty!" Juice hocked some phlegm. He was pushing me slower. "Those two boys be comin' here last coupla days." The world was slowing down; it was coming into focus. "Come here and shoot hoops, just like they own the playground!" Trixter had fouled the white guy flagrantly, and the white guy was bleeding. He looked like my dad. "I'm feelin' sick, Leonard." "You want I should stop you?" I nodded sorta queasily; Juice caught my legs. Suddenly, as the world came skidding to a halt, my legs braced and scissored around Juice's waist, a parallel universe revealed itself to me, and I recognized my dad teamed up with Det. Thomas. Juice let me go, and I righted my body, and the trees and the concrete and the cars slid back to earth, and then I could see, not fifty yards from me, Thomas and my father in a game of two-on-two getting slaughtered by Parrish and Trixter, who were hot. "Boy looks like your father, don't he, Tobias?" "That boy *is* my father." "Unh-unh, the *other* one." Trixter fouled Thomas and left the guy reeling. "They been playin' here, you know, last coupla days. You see Parrish clock him? He yo' dad's friend?" "His name's Det. Thomas." When I said that, Juice cursed; then he sat laughing on the swing next to mine. "'Det. Thomas,' huh?" Juice couldn't stop laughing. "His name is Thomas, but he ain't no detective." Again, as I was watching, Trixter threw a subtle elbow that sent Thomas sprawling; my father helped him up. "They's gonna be a fight!" Thomas took a swing at Trixter; Trixter shoved Thomas; Dad and Parrish held them back. "He isn't a detective?" I asked. Juice was laughing. "That boy?" Juice said. *"He's the biggest punk in town!"*

✳ I WATCHED AS Dad led Det. Thomas off the courts into a
white Plymouth. The white Plymouth pulled away.

"What's your dad doin' with a drug dealer, Toby?"

"What am I doin' with . . ."

I let the sentence fizzle.

"Go and call the precinct downtown, you don't believe me.
You ever see his badge?"

It was true: I never had.

"And he owns the white Plymouth?"

"His *man* owns it, Toby. His man, Toby Sligh—he own everybody here."

Juice's arm swept out to include the whole neighborhood—a
girl on a manhole, her ass stopping traffic, skinny guys on
milkcrates smoking crack beneath the sun.

"Det. Thomas is a dealer?"

"He's the fuckin' competition."

"So he's just as bad as you are."

Juice spat into the dirt.

"Ain't hearin' that, Tobe. Ain't tryin' to hear that."

We watched the white Plymouth as it rounded a corner.

"Be cool, Tobias."

Juice held on to my arm. The Plymouth rolled toward us and
stopped suddenly.

"My dad is in there."

"Chilly chill, Toby Sligh."

"But Juice, that's my *father.*"

The white Plymouth peeled away.

I was shaking. I took off my shades and my cap. Parrish and
Trixter were loping toward us.

"*The Bruthas Kareem-Azov!*" Juice cried.

" 'Sup, Leon?"

Juice gave them fifty dollars.

"This is Tobe. Let's shoot some hoops."

ARTREMEASE GRAY, JUICE'S auntie-in-law, lived in a shotgun ten blocks from the park where we had played basketball with Parrish and Trixter. Her apartment had impressive-looking bars on all the windows and a coat of pink paint like a Candyland cottage. Across the street from her were the Paxton Place Projects, an enormous brick fortress that resembled the Pentagon and looked as forbidding and corroded and impregnable. Artremease Gray—a shy lady in her forties—sat on a glider flipping through *TV Guide,* children's blocks and blankets scattered underneath her feet. A cat was busy licking its butt in a corner, and when we approached, it got up and stalked away.

"Hi, Leonard," she said, as we passed through the gate.

She put down her *TV Guide* and let her nephew kiss her.

"Hi, Auntie," Juice mumbled. He said ahntie, not anty. "Is Anquanna here?"

"Well, I think you know she is."

Straightening her skirt, Artremease cleared her throat and worked on a crossword while Juice headed in. I introduced myself, and Aunt Artremease smiled. Inside I heard Anquanna and a child giggling.

"Is the prom tomorrow night?" Aunt Artremease asked me.

I told her it was.

"I'm going with Juice."

"Thought Juice was going with my daughter, Anquanna."

I laughed, and she smiled.

"But I know what you mean."

Inside, Anquanna was suddenly shouting, then Juice said something, then they quieted down.

"What do you think of my nephew, Tobias?" Aunt Artremease asked me, working on her crossword.

"He's probably my best friend," I said to her, honestly: Ian Lamb was somewhere a million miles away.

"Leonard's a good boy," Artremease agreed. "But he has this awful habit of getting folks in trouble. Look at Anquanna, what happened to her. . . ."

"What *did* happen to her?"

"You didn't see her face?"

Aunt Artremease set her crossword down on the glider, then moved slightly over, motioning for me to sit. A helicopter passed and Aunt Artremease watched it, then she turned toward me. Her eyes were in mine.

"You look like a good boy, Toby," she said. "Your last name is . . . ?"

"Sligh."

She bowed and laughed slightly. "You look more Toby than Sligh," she said wryly. Windowpanes chattered as a second copter passed. "Leonard means well. Remember that, Toby. But don't let him take you anywhere you shouldn't go to. His mom's a good woman, but his daddy is trouble. Eddy married my sister LaShonda, and he killed her . . ."

I tried to brace myself against Juice's family history.

"Those two had a boy who was bad as his daddy. Juice loved his brother, Eddy's first boy, Eddy, Jr.—"

"And where is he now?"

"Doesn't matter where he is. . . . But Leonard'll do anything to be just like him. Eddy, Jr., he went with a girl named Jackie Nivens, and he killed that poor girl like his daddy killed my sister. And if you've seen my daughter, my baby girl, Anquanna—"

"She's beautiful."

"*And* she got a beautiful soul. So when I saw her last week, those bruises on her face, I called Leonard's mama and I ask her, did he do it? She said Leonard couldn't. And you know? I believed her. You think he did it, Toby?"

I said I didn't know.

"I know he isn't like that. Leonard, he's a good boy. Still, you grow older, sometimes you get wild. His brother was the nicest boy until he started dealing. Does Leonard deal, Toby?"

I didn't say a word.

" 'Cause if he does, Toby, it'll just kill his mama. Valilian, like a fool, she married Juice's daddy when my sister,

LaShonda, he laid her in her grave; and Lily didn't have to, but she raised LaShonda's baby, she raised that Eddy, Jr. as if he was her own. Those boys was like brothers, and she raised 'em like sons. Then the drugs got Eddy, Jr. Cut him down dead. And now Leonard's daddy—he's the poorest kinda crackhead. So if Leonard is dealing . . . You under*stand,* Toby?"

I was staring at the children's toys discarded on the porch. Inside, I could hear Juice pleading with Anquanna.

"Drugs are poison, baby. They're absolute poison. The only things more dangerous than drugs," she said, "are lies. Would you tell me, Tobias, if Leonard was a dealer? I've been talking to his mama. That woman's broke in two."

A kid passed by, and he waved at Artremease. She waved back at him, and a smile hid his face.

"These projects," she said, nodding once across the street. "These bars on the window—they don't have to be. You listen to how Leonard Compton talks around you—so nigger, so stupid. Like he's ashamed of being bright! Only boy I ever seen brighter than Leonard was his brother, Eddy, Jr., and they got it from their daddy. Now look at those two! What a waste, Toby Sligh! What a waste of God's gifts! Is he dealing?"

I was silent.

"Is he *using?*"

I was silent.

"You can *tell* me, Toby Sligh."

But I didn't say a word. Another helicopter passed.

Artremease bowed and opened up her *TV Guide* and did her crossword puzzle, pointing at a missing word.

" 'Silence equals . . . ?' "

"*Death.*"

"I heard a' that, Toby. Who says that?"

"Dunno."

"It's the gay people do."

We sat there awhile on the glider, just gliding, watching police helicopters floating by. At last Artremease stood up and said, "Well . . . I'll get you a Pepsi," and she disappeared inside.

But she didn't come out. Juice did, with the Pepsi. And in his other hand he held the hand of his niece—his half brother's girl, whom Aunt Artremease was raising. It was Donna, the girl in the back of Peach's cab.

"*Jacaranda!*" she screamed, and ran straight toward me.

"It's like the Smurf *knows* you!" Juice cried and clapped his hands. "Go get her some Kisses!" he called to Anquanna.

"You get 'em yourself!" Anquanna called from inside.

"*Jacaranda!*" Donna shouted.

She was giggling in my arms.

And through the bars on the window, I could see Aunt Artremease. She was looking at me softly, helicopters in her eyes.

WE TOOK DONNA for a ride in Juice's shit-Buick. We were old pals already. Juice couldn't believe it.

"If I'd a' known you was, like, so *down* with the Smurf, I'd a' getchoo to sit for Anquanna an' me!"

When his beeper went off, Juice said, "That's my pops," and slapped the beeper quiet, and Donna slugged his shoulder.

"Easy there, Smurf!"

"Why is Donna called Smurf?"

"Because she so ugly!" Juice said and made a face.

Donna started laughing and I tickled her lightly. She wriggled in my arms and she shouted, "Jacaranda!"

"She don't even see purple trees, an' she say that! Donna, she's crazy! Sees purple trees everywhere!"

We were driving in circles round the Paxton Place Projects. Now and then Juice would toot the horn at folks he knew.

"Who's Donna's mother?"

"Bitch name-a' Nivens. Cunt killed herself. Donna be my brother's kid."

"Didn't know you had a brother."

"Jus' my half brother."

"Where is he?"

"Gone."

Juice's hand was trembling.

We passed a row of tenements beside the Paxton Projects. They were yellow. They were where Leonard Compton's father lived.

"You stay here a minute with Donna," Juice told me, and reached into the glovebox, and removed a plastic bag. Then he disappeared inside, walking slowly, like a prisoner; he disappeared like he'd been disappearing all his life.

"DONNA," I BEGAN. "Detective Toby's got some questions. Nod yes, like this, if the answer is yes. Go no, like this, if the answer is no. Do you understand, Donna?"

She was staring out the window.

"Donna? Donna *Comp*ton? Yes or no, kiddo?"

"No!"

"Is Det. Thomas a dealer?"

Donna Compton shook her head.

"Is Det. Thomas a detective?"

Donna Compton shook her head.

"Is Ian Lamb sleeping with my mother? Does he love me?"

Donna rolled her head in one great circular motion.

"Is Fr. Scarcross honest?"

Donna stared out the window.

"Is he gay, like me?"

Donna whirled around and grinned.

"Is your uncle my friend?"

Donna wouldn't look at me.

"Is he setting me up?"

Donna nodded her head.

"*Jacaranda!*" she screamed.

She was pointing out the window—at a Plymouth, a white one. It was cruising toward us.

I BOLTED FROM the car with Donna bobbing in my arms and bounded up the stairwell to Juice's dad's apartment. The stairs smelled like urine and unlaundered laundry, and two girls in a corner were playing jacks for penny candy. On the second floor I knocked on the first door I came to and a man with a gold tooth emerged and looked at me.

"Whatchoo want?"

"Edward Compton."

"He down at the end!"

The door slammed shut as I hurried down the hall.

From the second-floor balcony I spied the white Plymouth idling by the Buick like a sleepy barracuda. I got to Juice's father's door and banged on it loudly. There wasn't any answer, so I opened it and—

"*Toby!*"

Juice was on the sofa, sitting by his father. His father had a hypodermic sticking in his arm.

"The Plymouth, Juice!"

"Damn *it! Git outta* here, Toby!"

Donna was crying.

I stood where I was.

Juice's father was gray and impossibly thin. He looked more like a used pipe cleaner than a man. He wasn't very old, but his frame was devastated. He slumped to the floor with the needle in his skin.

"Fuck you, Toby!" Juice removed the dirty needle. He was crying so hard now that he could barely speak. *"Fuck you, Toby!"*

"I'm sorry," I told him. "The white Plymouth, and my father . . ."

I shut the door and walked away.

I GAVE DONNA to the girls playing jacks in the stairwell and asked them to watch her for just a little while. They seemed like nice kids and they calmed Donna down saying, "Hush, baby, hush," and they gave her a Starburst. I walked down the stairwell and out onto the street and toward the white Plymouth, which was parked beside the Buick. Det. Thomas got out. He was holding a briefcase. "Hello there, Toby," he said and stepped toward me.

"I want to see your badge."

He showed me his badge.

"Who are you?"

I was shaking. He put his badge away.

"I know about Compton."

"And I know about you."

"You don't know a thing."

He opened up his briefcase.

In it was an eight-by-ten black-and-white photo of me and Juice dealing underneath the water tower where the shots had gone off at the school the week before.

"*You* are an accessory."

"And you're full of shit."

"What if I show this to your father, Toby Sligh?"

"Leave my dad out of this."

"He's shown me things, Toby."

"What things?"

"Just . . . things. I know *things* about your father."

A police car passed. Det. Thomas tensed up. I thought of shouting out. Then I thought of Juice's father.

"Leonard Compton's the biggest crack dealer in the city."

"You're a bastard!"

I was crying. Det. Thomas looked embarrassed.

"Now we're gonna make a deal so I won't have to show you the other photographs that I've got in this briefcase."

"What kinda deal?"

"It's about the drugs, Toby. The drugs you and Juice stashed away at your mother's."

"How do you know we stashed the drugs at my mother's?"

"We just know, Toby. You can call it intuition."

The two little girls who'd been playing in the stairwell emerged holding Donna and set her down on the ground.

"What do you want?"

"I want to know where the drugs are."

"And if I don't tell you?"

"This goes to the D.A. This picture. With testimony from a P.E. teacher, a teacher who will testify. And the other kids they busted."

Donna, who saw me, started stumbling toward me. A car was tearing by and I caught her in my arms.

"Juice'll go to prison."

"But you won't, Toby Sligh."

"And my mother?"

"She doesn't have to know a thing about it. Just tell us where the drugs are and we'll go there and get them. She won't know what hit her. We're good at this, Tobe."

"You're so full of shit!"

Donna slapped my mouth.

"Watch your language, Toby," Det. Thomas said to me.

"I know you're a dealer," I said. "Juice told me!"

"Juice is a liar, and he'll take you down with him."

"What if I told you to go fuck yourself?"

"I wouldn't do that, Toby. I know things about your father."

"What things?"

"Just . . . things."

He took off his sunglasses. He was staring at me. His hand was in the briefcase.

"We have pictures. . . ."

"What pictures?"

"I said we have pictures. . . ."

"Of what?"

"Of your father . . . and your mother, Toby Sligh."

I could feel my heart pounding. I wanted to hit him. His hand was in the briefcase. Donna started crying.

"Would you maybe like to see them?"

I felt sick at my stomach.

"Would you like to see some pictures of your parents, Toby Sligh?"

I swallowed my fear as a cop car passed. Helicopters hovered. Det. Thomas was twitching.

"Excuse me," he said. He took some chocolate from his pocket. He ate it in great bites. His body stopped twitching.

"You keep your fucking pictures! I don't wanna see 'em!"

"Wise choice, Toby. The truth is always hard."

"When do you want the drugs?"

"I'll get them myself."

"You're not going near my mother!"

"That's the deal, Toby Sligh. You tell us where the drugs are, we get 'em, deal's done. Your mother is safe. *No more crosstown traffic.*"

"You're such a fucking liar!"

"I'm the truth, Toby Sligh."

"I saw what you did to Juice back in that alley!"

"I could do it to you."

I stepped away from him.

"I'll give you till midnight Monday, Toby Sligh."

And when he had gone I sat down on the curb with my head

in my hands, beside Donna: we were crying. When he finally came out, Juice stood over us, shaking.

"Shoulda never gone in there, Toby Sligh," he said to me.

ONCE AS A kid in my father's garage I was digging through a drawer when I found a tiny key. I knew that the key had to open up something, so I tried every lock in the shop I could find. I tried the big lock on my father's metal toolbox. I tried the smaller lock on a file cabinet. And then I found a strongbox in the back of a cabinet underneath hoses and corroded air filters. I took out the box, and I stuck the key in it, and I opened the box, and I found some glossy pictures. In them my parents were naked and smiling. I didn't understand that they had been making love. I looked the pictures over, then I put the box away. And for all I knew, the key was still there, in the same office drawer, and so was the box. I knew these were the pictures Det. Thomas had stolen. I didn't need a stranger to show them to me. I'd already seen my parents naked and smiling. They were in love. Det. Thomas made it dirty. And if there were other pictures, I didn't want to see.

JUICE DROPPED ME off in front of St. Osyth's. We didn't say a word. He got his Porsche and drove away. Donna waved at me through the window of Baby. I felt a little like I'd never see her again.

OUTSIDE 1111, SR. Cindy was waiting with my things in a bag, and she said, "Toby, go."

"Can I see Fr. Scarcross?"

"He's still in a coma."

I took my things and looked at her and turned and walked away.

We don't cry—Tim and I,
We are far too grand—
But we bolt the door tight
To prevent a friend—

Then we hide our brave face
Deep in our hand—
Not to cry—Tim and I—
We are far too grand—

Not to dream—he and me—
Do we condescend—
We just shut our brown eye
To see to the end—

Tim—see Cottages—
But, Oh, so high!
Then—we shake—Tim and I
And lest I—cry—

Tim—reads a little Hymn—
And we both pray—
Please, Sir, I and Tim—
Always lost the way!

SR. CINDY HAD put Eli's books in my bag, and I'd stumbled on a poem in a volume by Dickinson. I read it outside my mother's apartment. All her lights were off. She was sleeping or had gone. I put the book back in the bag where I'd found it and went to Mom's place and tapped on the door. I wanted to tell her about Det. Thomas. I wanted to see her. I wanted to talk. But when nobody answered I snuck around back to the crucified Corvair, got Juice's stash, and left.

AT THE SACRED heart rectory I found an old Jesuit and told him I'd left my books and school things in the chapel. He lent me a key and I entered the chapel and went to the altar and stood before the tabernacle. With the key I'd removed from the archbishop's towel, I opened up the tabernacle and hid the drugs in there. The stash contained cocaine and $87,000. There wasn't any gun. I looked at Jesus and I left.

BACK HOME, IN the driveway, I spied a soft light, a soft light spilling through the curtains of our house. The power was out, I could tell. It was candles. I prayed it was my parents. I prayed that they'd come home.

We must die—by and by—
Clergymen say—
Tim—shall—if I—do—
I—too—if he—

How shall we arrange it—
Tim—was—so—shy?
Take us simultaneous—Lord—
I—"Tim"—and—Me!

OUR HOUSE SMELLED of sulfur and smoldering wax as I opened the door and stepped into the foyer. On the carpet, surrounding a pair of crumpled jeans, were three candles anchored to three china plates. Beside them a note read: "Blow me out, Toby." I did as the note said and saw, down the hall, three more candles surrounding a shirt. I went over to them, knelt down before them, and blew them out, too. Again, I was in darkness. Then, at the entrance to my mom and dad's bedroom, I saw three more candles and a pair of underwear. I could hear somebody moving on my parents' big bed. A tape recorder played melancholy '50's music:

At last, I've awakened—
See what you've done?
All I can do
Is pack up and run—
Now I know the rules—
Find yourself another fool. . . .

And I knelt before the candles and blew them out, too. When I did, the music stopped. The house was in darkness. There were no more candles. I heard the boxsprings creak. "Toby," a voice said. I took a step forward. "Toby," it whispered. "Toby . . . Toby *Sligh* . . ." And almost as if I were moving underwater I felt a liquid hand hover underneath my waist and move to my fly and unbutton it slowly as ghost fingers peeled off my shirt like shedding skin. I stood in my underwear. The curtains were blooming. And someone was breathing in the darkness on the bed.

"Toby," the voice said. *"Come to me, Toby . . ."* I took off my underwear and moved toward the voice.

"Ian—"

"Toby . . . Don't talk. . . . *Come here—*"

I lay down beside him on the mattress. We were naked. He put his arms around me. He kissed my neck and chest.

"We've got to talk, Ian—"

"You feel so *good,* Toby. I've wanted to hold you like this for *so long. . . .*"

"Please, Ian—"

"Toby . . ."

His body was against me, on top of me, moving, in the darkness, in the night.

"I love you, Tobias. I've wanted to tell you—forever. *I love you.* I love you *so much. . . .*"

And there wasn't any noise. The night had gone quiet. There was only the sound of the wind in the palms. There was only the sound of our two bodies moving, skin against skin, and the wind in the fronds.

"Toby . . ."

"You lied to me, Ian—"

"Don't talk. . . ."

"You said you would meet me at Castiglione's and—"

"Shhh! *I love you. . . .*"

"You were dancing with my mother! I saw you! I saw you there, *kissing* her, Ian—"

"Come here, Tobias. . . ."

His face was on my face. His lips were on my lips. I was stiller than a stone.

"Kiss me. . . ."

His tongue danced across my dry lips. I was crying. He sighed and he kissed both my eyes.

> *Little Lamb*
> *Here I am;*
> *Come and lick*

My white neck;
Let me pull
Your soft Wool;
Let me kiss
Your soft face. . . .

Away in the night we could hear sirens singing. Our bodies lay together. Our skin was whispering.

"Don't cry, Tobias. I *love* you. *Believe* me. . . ."

"I want to believe you! And so many things! But I saw you with my mother—"

"We were just *playing*, Toby! Your mother's my *friend!* There's so much you don't *know*. . . ."

"Then tell me!"

"Not now . . . Do you *love* me, Tobias?" He was asking me questions; each came with a kiss. "Do you *love* me? Do you *need* me? *Can you live without me, Toby?* If I tell you the truth, will it tear us apart?"

"I have to know, Ian—"

"You *don't* have to know. It's *nice* in the darkness. *Isn't* it, Tobias?"

"This bed is my parents'—"

"We could always go to *my* house."

"That's not what I meant!"

"Just *kiss* me, Tobias . . ."

I opened my mouth and his tongue tasted mine. His body was inside me. I felt so *alive* . . .

"Please, Ian—"

"Toby . . ."

He was moving inside me. We were hard. We were close. The sheets were whispering.

"We've got to talk, Ian—"

"Toby, don't you *love* me?"

"Ian, I . . . love you! I do! You *know* I do!"

And I didn't surrender so much as give in to everything I'd

wanted from the day that we first met. His words, his hands, the nearness of our bodies, our tongues, our souls together—it was love, that was all. Everything was pure and all the pain had been suspended—all doubt, all sadness, all fear, all memory. There was no need to talk, no need to ask questions. Everything was answered in the riddle of our bodies joined together there against the very vastness of the night. And I think I knew then, before I could have known it, that this was the last time that I would ever love him—the last time that I would take his tongue inside my mouth, and hold it there, and taste it there, and taste his kiss, and the salt of our bodies; that this was the last time desire would rage inside the sad, sweet, corruptible, mad cages of our skin; that, in a night's time, Ian Lamb would desert me—his body, his soul, his love, and his lies.

"Ian!"

"Don't talk! . . . Say that you love me!"

"I love you!"

"I love you!"

"Ian—!"

"Toby Sligh—!"

"I—!"

But already it was over. We were sticky with each other. We lay tangled and untangling. . . .

So the leaving had begun.

IN THE MORNING, when I woke up, the house was full of light. I turned to wake Ian and I saw my mother standing in the doorway to the bedroom, watching Ian sleep. We were absolutely naked. My mother turned away. "Mom," I said, "wait." She walked out the bedroom door.

MONDAY MORNING IN chapel the Rev. Anthony McDuffy, S.J., made a special appearance before the senior class.

"There has been some speculation," McDuffy began, his face already a full florid blush, "that two unidentified students at Sacred Heart High will be attending tonight's senior prom as a couple. While the faculty council and myself have been unable to ascertain whether this is the truth or an elaborate hoax, let me say on behalf of the entire community that this sort of incident would seriously impair the dignity of tonight's ceremony, and that though we do not mean to chastise any seniors for what they feel may be their initial attempts to investigate a contemporary lifestyle option, we would seriously advise the concerned parties to refrain from any display of this nature, and to understand that the sternest disciplinary measures will be taken against any students attempting to make such an exploration at the expense of the dignity of Sacred Heart High. With that said, we would like to add that we are sure that this is merely another in a series of practical jokes that have become something of a tradition this time of year; in fact, we have informed the local media as such. And we hope that this incident, fabricated or otherwise, will not impede the senior class's ability to enjoy what should be a wonderful alcohol and drag—that is, alcohol and *drug*-free evening. And we would like to add that immediately following exams the senior class will be treated to a pizza-and-Pepsi party with the graduating class from our sister school, the Holy Dames Academy, in honor of your hard work, and a prom well earned."

Principal McDuffy received a standing ovation—complete with catcalls, dogbarks, and wolfwhistles. Ian, surprisingly, was the first to stand. Only Juice remained seated; he was staring at me.

✹ IN ETHICS, WHILE Zipser handed out the exams, I chewed
on my eraser and cast a glance at Juice. He was sitting
there, staring, his face in his hands. And he was talking to himself, as if he were his own confessor. When nobody was looking—no one except me—he took a pink pill from his pocket and
gulped it. Juice rested his head on his desk and sighed deeply.
Then he looked at me. I'll never forget it. I had to turn away. It
was the look of an accuser.

✹ *ESSAY QUESTION NO. 3:* Should homosexuals be permitted
in the military? Defend your opinion using historical
analogy, philosophical method, and personal experience.

✹ *HOMOSEXUALS SHOULD NOT be permitted in the military be-*
cause their inclusion would result in a weakening of
morale that would work to the detriment of the American armed
forces and inevitably to the detriment of society in general.

Ancient Greece condoned and even encouraged homosexual
behavior. Though the concept of Platonic love is arguably asex-
ual, Plato's ideal of masculine friendship characterized a culture
in which homosexual practice ran the gamut from the latent to
the blatant. Rome, patterning itself after the Greek model, en-
couraged homosexuality and other aberrations; and, like Greece,
Rome eventually collapsed. Though homosexuality would appear
to be an enduring cultural and historical phenomenon, the exam-
ples of ancient Greek and Roman societies suggest that such
practices, though common, are destructive.

John Stuart Mill's philosophy of utilitarianism provides a philosophical context by which we may justify the exclusion of homosexuals from military service. Because surveys like the Kinsey Report estimate that homosexuals constitute a mere 10 percent of the male population (and a lesser percentage of females), current military policy should reflect heterosexual predispositions; and so, if the majority of servicemen and -women feel uncomfortable showering, bunking, or receiving emergency blood transfusions from potentially homosexual comrades, Mill's theory would suggest that because a minority of gay soldiers will detrimentally affect the productivity of the straight majority, homosexuals must be excluded from military service.

To conclude with a personal experience, Dr. Zipser, I would just like to say that the first time I took my best friend's penis in my mouth occurred during a harmless and particularly heated wrestling match on the terrazzo floor of my best friend's mother's kitchen. Our bodies were naked except for Wesson oil, which we had distributed rather liberally on our persons to provide an essentially Lawrencian frisson, inspired as we were by recent close readings of Women in Love *in AP English class. Though my best friend is markedly stronger than I am, and though we undertook the match with no sexual intention, I would have been defeated had I not, in a clinch, lowered my mouth onto my opponent's genitalia. This maneuver was accompanied by an instantaneous diminishment in my best friend's ability to engage in combat and, not surprisingly, considering the tactic, an inverse expansion in the length of his penis. This experience has led me to conclude that if homosexuals were permitted in the military, entire battalions might find themselves preoccupied in acts of mutual oral gratification to the extent of the extinction of the war drive altogether. The ability to engage in combat would cease—an obvious advantage in the elimination of all war if one might only persuade the enemy to join in. But as enemies are even less likely to recognize gestures of affection than are the closest of friends, such practices could only weaken our ability to destroy those to and from whom we might give and receive pleasure.*

So, for all these reasons, I contend that homosexuals should be excluded from military service.

MY ESSAY HADN'T been on Zipser's desk five seconds when, lily-livered, I requested it back.

"Forget to put your name on each page?"

"That's it!"

I snatched the blue booklet, returned to my seat, and wielding a thick black indelible marker, obliterated entirely the penultimate paragraph, and inserted beside it, in the narrow, winding margin:

Having had no experience of homosexuality, I can only repeat what I have learned in school: that homosexuals are congenitally promiscuous; that homosexuals are responsible for the spread of AIDS; and that homosexuals are inclined to child molestation.

AFTER THE EXAM a busload of girls from the Holy Dames Academy arrived bearing pizza. They swarmed the cafeteria in a buzz of chatty energy, guys hovering around them on a hungry male periphery. They were beautiful girls despite their uniforms—madonna-blue potato sacks the nuns forced them to wear to hide their perky breasts in baggy clumps of sexless fabric. Most guys were in lust with them and absolutely helpless: the girls traveled in packs and talked with such rapidity that any approach by a male would have been unthinkable. Even girls who later on would make love to their boyfriends in the backseats of rental limos were impossibly aloof, as if they knew then (as most of them did) that the better part of desire is a disciplined denial. That was what I tended to admire about women: the premeditation, the calculation of their love. Everything for them was foreplay, the prelude to the kiss. For guys it was *hello*-there-and-welcome-to-my-orgasm.

In the middle of the swarm of cosmetics and chitchat stood Courtney Ciccone, Ian's escort for the evening. I had to admit she was a knockout of a girl. I couldn't be jealous: her beauty made me dizzy. She had frizzy raven's hair like a Vidal Sassoon Medusa, her tits were taut and ample under straining polyester, she walked with her nose a little lofty, like a princess, and she was always hugging everyone and calling them her darling. You could make out Courtney's voice above the general commotion, tinkling like a silver tine against a toasting glass, and wherever she moved, packs of boys staggered after—as if she were a lemming of unrequited love.

When she saw me she gave a shrill squeal—"Toby *Sligh!*"—and glided through the crowd to air-kiss my blushing cheek.

"How are you, *dar*ling!" she gushed. "Where is Ian? If Lamb Chop doesn't show up I'll just *have* to go with you! Oh, Toby, you're so *scrump*tious! Did anybody ever tell you? But you ought to get your hair cut like, ugh, what's his name? That guy on *210*, not Luke! Shoot, Dolores!" She appealed to her girlfriend, a wiry anorexic who was eating cheese pizza with the tips of her fingers, mozzarella tangled in her Lee press-on nails.

"Like, why are you going with Angelina Fishback?" Dolores, the anorexic, said and rolled her eyes. "She's such a toad, Toby!"

"*Dolores!*"

"Like, I'm sorry, but—"

"Dolores," Courtney whispered, "has a crush on you, Toby."

"Like, *ohmyGod*, Courtie! I can't believe you said that!"

They disappeared in a crisis of crocodile tears, and I felt two fleshy hands flutter down across my eyelids. The palms were moist and yeasty. They smelled like pepperoni. They smelled like stale anchovies. They smelled like pizza dough.

"Guess who, Toby?"

"It's the Domino's driver. And I'm not paying for all that fucking pizza!"

I turned around and smiled at Angelina Fishback. She was standing by a little girl who looked just like a dormouse.

"This is Grace Cage," Angelina informed me.

"I'm Toby."

"Hello, Toby," Grace squeaked, and walked away.

"Great personality, don'tcha think, huh? She's looking for my brother. And have you seen Sir Bubba?"

I pointed across the room to a cluster of jocks: Bubba sat among them, demolishing pizzas.

"He won't have any appetite for sushi tonight! But we will, Tobias! No Domino's for us! Where's Ian?"

"Dunno."

"I saw you with Courtie. Don't worry, I'm not jealous; I know she's just a *cunt*. Where's Juice?"

I looked around; I didn't know where Juice was.

"Look"—Angelina pointed—"over by the window."

Most of the girls from the Holy Dames Academy, and some of the guys, and all of the teachers had gathered by the windows that extended the length of the parking lot bordering the school cafeteria. Angelina, always a bloodhound for scandal, broke away and barreled elbow-first through the crowd. When I caught up to her, her nose was smooshed against the glass, and her eyes were glazed over like a gourmand of gossip.

"Juice has been arrested," she said, sotto voce.

I elbowed her aside to have a look for myself.

At the back of the lot, four police officers were surrounding Juice Compton, obscuring his Porsche. One of the cops broke away from the pack to search Baby's frontseat, and backseat, and trunk. The car alarm was shrieking like a wounded pterodactyl: even through the glass the noise of it assailed our ears.

"It's finally caught up with him," Angelina stated.

"What has?" I asked her.

"His dealing . . . Juice's *dealing*."

"He's a dealer?" I asked, trying hard to look retarded.

"Toby Sligh?" She stared at me. "Like, where have you *been?*"

When Kickliter and Fr. McDuffy arrived and the cops cleared away, we got a look at what had happened: the windshield of Baby was a web of smashed glass, as if someone had lobbed a cinder block through it; the paint had been scratched with a pocketful of nails; the tires were slashed; and the antenna had been snapped.

"Kee-*rist*," said Angelina, whistling like a sailor.

Courtney and Dolores were looking on in tears.

The officers pumped Juice's hand and drove away. They had filed their report.

And Juice hadn't been arrested.

WHEN I WENT to offer my condolences to Juice he reached into his pocket and produced a Polaroid of a stranger standing by the Porsche with a nightstick. It was Det. Thomas. The Porsche was intact. He was smiling in the photo. Juice tore it in two.

"See you at the Fishback crib at seven," Juice said. *"You better open up your eyes before the truth eats you alive."*

I WAS CRASHED out on the sofa where my father always slept when Lucinda telephoned from St. Osyth's. She said that Fr. Scarcross was out of his coma but that there was a chance he wouldn't make it through the evening. She said that she knew that I had the prom tonight, and that I had completed my community service hours, but if I wanted to, and if I thought I could handle it, she'd like me to be at Eli's bedside when he died.

"You're friends," Lucinda said. "He *considers* you a friend. You're just about the only friend that Fr. Ja's *got*."

I wanted to make it, I told her; I did. But I'd be in a limousine for most of the evening and couldn't get away even if I wanted to. Lucinda said she'd fetch me wherever I was so long as I promised to say goodbye to Scarcross. And she said, if I wanted, she'd lend me a beeper so I'd know the very second Fr. Scarcross needed me. "I don't give a shit where you are, Toby Sligh. I'll find you! Eli wants to say goodbye to you so badly."

"But—"

"Fuck the *buts,* you Jesuitical shithead! Eli is *dying,* don't you understand? You don't abandon somebody just because they're dying! Death is a part of the package tour, too! So get your penguin ass on over to St. Osyth's and I'll lend you a beeper. Is 'at a deal, Weeble-penis?"

I told her it was and she sighed and said, "Good. I knew, in the end, you would do the right thing."

Then, when I hung up, the phone rang again. This time it was Ian. He said, "I got the tuxes. You come by my house as soon as you can and we'll help each other dress and get our 'dates' for the prom."

"Your parents are there?"

"They're here. But they're *loaded.* Are you ready to waltz, Toby Sligh?"

"Am I *what?*"

"Are you ready to waltz with your boy at the prom?"

My mom had gone AWOL, Dad was missing (despite sightings), my best friend was in trouble on both sides of the law, I'd promised to waltz with a girl I would abandon, and to witness the death of a Jesuit priest. . . . *I just wanted to dance*—that was all I ever wanted—with the guy that I loved, with the guy who loved *me*. I didn't want drugs. I didn't want diseases. I didn't want death. I just wanted to waltz.

"Are you ready?" Ian said. "Are you *ready,* Toby Sligh?"

"I'm ready," I told him.

And I really was, too.

"IAN HAS GONE out to get a dozen eggs," Mrs. Lamb informed me when she opened the door. She was standing in the foyer holding gladiolas that were sprinkling drops of water on an Oriental rug. Behind her, in a living room as big as a warehouse, Lyle Lamb sat facing an enormous TV. I could only make out the back of his head, which was bald and polka-dotted with erupting corpuscles. Mrs. Lamb hauled me in and said, "Don't mind him. He's just a piece of furniture." The door closed behind us.

EDITH LAMB WAS pretty and superlatively tanned and held a slender glass filled with a cool pink concoction. She guzzled it in gulps, ice tinkling on her teeth, and let the gladiolas scatter nimbly at her feet as she dragged me through the kitchen, away from her husband.

"You must be Ian's friend! I've heard so much about you!" she said, springing suddenly and charmingly to life. "Ian, you know, tells me *all* about his friends! Are you the one going to Princeton in the fall or are you the one headed for the Naval Academy?"

When I told her I'd been accepted to a less prestigious college, her smile only broadened, and she lifted her glass.

"Oh, well! Just as long as you've been accepted *some*where! It's nice to be accepted! To college, I mean! Oh, excuse me," she said, and extended her hand, which was covered with psoriasis, and liverspots, and diamonds. "We haven't been·introduced— not formally, at least. I'm Edith, Edith Lamb . . . and *you* are?"

"Toby Sligh."

"Gosh," Ian's mom said, withdrawing her hand. "He never mentioned *you*."

And she gave a short snort.

Mrs. Lamb lunged forward and steered me by the elbow down several steps into a sunken sewing room. We were surrounded by endless folds of slick imported silk that fluttered around us like stationary clouds. Mrs. Lamb laughed and pulled me through the purling folds, then settled on a settee that was slippery with the fabric.

"We worried Ian wouldn't be, well, ya know, accepted. He was so very popular back in New Orl'uns. Of course, we're not originally *from* the Crescent City. That is, I am. But we've moved around a bit."

"Why's that?"

"Why's what?"

"Why've you moved around a bit?"

"Just business!" Edith answered.

The conversation halted. Far away, in the living room, we could hear her husband snoring.

"Ian was the most popular boy in his class. But when he lost his eye last Christmas, we moved."

"Because he lost his eye?"

Mrs. Lamb smiled at me.

"Business! Just business! . . . Would you like a Coca-Cola?"

When Mrs. Lamb left, I spied a Sacred Heart yearbook underneath some magazines on the coffee table. It dated from Ian's freshman year in New Orleans. Flipping to the index, I located Ian's entry: *IAN LAMB: Christian Youth Community, Debating Club, Dramatic Arts, Latin Honor Society, Junior Varsity Swim-*

ming; 12, 33, 47, 49, 56, 78, 90, 103, 147, 168, 169, 172, 177, 195, 220. The numbers at the end were the numbers of the pages on which Ian Lamb's photograph appeared. No other freshman had half as many photos. Even as a freshman, Ian had excelled.

"You looked so thirsty, I had to bring you two!" Mrs. Lamb said, handing me two frosty bottles. She'd also replenished her cool pink concoction and was sipping it idly when she sat up in her seat.

"There's Ian!" she exclaimed.

We could hear the Benz parking.

"Now you wait right here and I'll bring my jewel to you!"

MRS. LAMB RETURNED to the Silken Cloud Chamber with Ian in one hand and an egg crate in the other. She seated her son on the settee beside me and collapsed in a pile of silk on the floor.

"Edith, could you get me a beer?" a voice shouted from the booming echo chamber of the neighboring room. Edith put her finger to her lips and hitched her eyebrows: "If we ignore the monster, it will go away." In a matter of seconds, Lyle's snoring reached crescendo. Mrs. Lamb chuckled. Ian's Adam's apple bobbed.

"You must tell me every single detail of the prom!" Mrs. Lamb began, and opened up the crate of eggs. She tapped one briskly on the hard terrazzo floor, opened it, and drank the slimy contents of it raw. "I remember mine like it was yesterday, Tony!"

"It's Toby, Mom."

"What?" She waved away an unseen insect. "I went with your father. No! Not your father! Your father-to-be! We had just met then! The theme was *The Fugitive*, the television series.

They made us dance in legchains, shackled together! It may sound odd, but I found it romantic. And on the level of metaphor, talk about prophetic! Do you believe in prophecy, Tony?" she asked me.

She opened two more eggs and guzzled them whole.

"Mom's on a diet."

Edith Lamb licked her lips.

"Doctors say cholesterol's bad for the arteries!" Mrs. Lamb continued, talking over her son. "But I did thirty minutes with Jane Fonda this morning and my clunky old heart was purring like a Maserati!"

"I'll go get the tuxes," Ian said and stood to go. His mother caught him neatly by the shins as he went by.

"Aren't you going to tell your friend Tony what I'm making?"

Ian looked at his mother, and then he looked away.

"Guess what I'm making! Go ahead, Tony!"

Ian wouldn't look at me; his arms were at his sides.

"Draperies?"

Mrs. Lamb shook her head no.

"A wedding dress?"

Mrs. Lamb shook her head again.

"A tent for a harem of men?"

"*Bravo!*" Mrs. Lamb clapped; then she shook her head briskly. "Should I tell him, Ian? Should I tell your friend my secret?" She sat up with her hand curled around Ian's thigh.

"My mother," Ian said, "is making a parachute."

"That's right, Tony! That's *exactly* what I'm making!"

Ian left the room to go get the tuxedos and Edith grabbed her egg crate and settled down beside me.

"I am making a parachute, Tony—"

"It's Toby—"

"Because, more than anything, what I really want to do is to get into an airplane and hurl myself out of it and drift, just drift, with the whole world underneath me! Ian and Lyle, they don't have the courage! But I do, Tony! It's quite wonderful to fall!"

"When will it be finished?"

She drank another egg.

"Oh, any time now. *It's coming right along!* I started last Christmas—when Ian had his mishap. I never thought of jumping from a plane until then."

From the living room someone shouted, *"Bring me a beer!,"* then Ian entered holding two elegant tuxes.

"Oh, they're gorgeous!" Mrs. Lamb gushed. "Really, really gorgeous! And where did you get them?"

"From a catalogue."

She frowned.

"May I ask with what money?"

Ian spoke down to her curtly and swiftly.

"You know very well that I have my own money."

"It's true," Mrs. Lamb said. "Ian has a fund."

With a monumental effort Edith rose from the settee, bent down, and gave me a peck on the cheek.

"I'm sorry," she said, looking at me puzzled. "I thought you were Ian. I'm very sorry, Tony."

As Mrs. Lamb was leaving she cracked another egg and was just about to drink it when she stopped in her tracks.

"Gawd! Look at this!" she said and turned toward us. Egg white was dripping down the veins of her wrist and she held the broken shell like an abdicated crown. "It's an omen's what it is!" Edith slurred and staggered forward. "Look, boys! I've never seen anything like it!"

We rose from the settee, Ian set down the tuxes, and we approached Mrs. Lamb to see the omen in her hand. Within the broken crown of a single white eggshell, the contents of which she had very nearly swallowed, were two tiny yolks, two identical yolks, twin jaundiced eyes staring up at the world.

"Beware the number two!" Mrs. Lamb intoned.

"Mom," Ian offered, "is awfully superstitious."

"Beware things in twos!" Mrs. Lamb repeated, her voice burdened down by the weight of prophecy.

"It's only an egg, Mom," Ian Lamb stated, and snatched the broken crown from his mother, and gulped it.

Looking at her son as if he had just been sentenced, Mrs. Lamb kissed him and turned her back on him. "You poor boy. You unfortunate child," Edith Lamb said, and left the Parachute Room.

 "MOM'S A CRAZY drunk," Ian said later on, when we were getting dressed, in the mirror in his bedroom. "Dad's just a drunk. He isn't really crazy."

"I'm sorry," I said.

I wanted to help him.

Ian Lamb shrugged.

"Who cares? Let's get dressed."

"TOBY SLIGH?"

"What?"

"Have you ever seen my Mickey?"

We were lying naked in the backseat of his Benz. We were at the beach, and the windows were down. The night drifted in across our pale bodies. Ian's face was next to mine. The moon was blue and wet.

"Your what?"

"My Mickey . . . I've never shown you my Mickey?"

"I . . . I don't think so."

Ian said, "Well, *come on!*"

Ian got out and, without waiting for me, sprinted from the car to where the water met the shore. The beach was deserted. It was always deserted. No one would see us. It was our special spot. We'd go there on Friday and Saturday evenings when it started getting hot out. Our parents didn't know. We'd say we were going to the library to study, but we would meet each other, and we would drink beer, and we would park the Benz, and undress, and make love.

"Look," Ian said. He wrapped his arms around me. We were naked in the water. A stingray glided by. "Look at my eye in the moonlight," Ian said. He knelt in the water and he tilted back his head. "You see that little light? That little sliver of light? Where the moon hits my pupil? You see it, Toby Sligh?"

I bent over Ian and stared into his eye—I was looking at his good eye, not the artificial one.

"When the pupil is alive, it catches the light—and it makes a little sliver of moonlight, like that. Your eye has got it. Everybody's got it, Toby! Now take a good look at my artificial eye."

Ian turned his head and cupped his hands around my bottom. He drew me down toward him. He was holding me tight. As I leaned down to look, saltwater from my body sprinkled his face and ran in streams across his cheek. He looked like he was crying. His mouth opened slightly. His tongue touched his lips. And he laughed beneath the moon.

"Does my artificial eye have that same little sliver? Does the pupil in my artificial eye catch the light?"

Something was alive in his artificial eye—a glimmer of something, a glimmer in the night.

"Does my artificial eye catch the light, Toby Sligh? Does the pupil catch the light the way the *living* pupil does?"

To be honest, it did; and I told him it did. There, in the corner of his artificial eye, in the corner of his pupil a sickle of moonlight glimmered like an ember, stubborn, inextinguishable, breathing with blue fire, inexhaustible with life.

"That's my Mickey," Ian said, and plucked the glass eye from its socket. He held it up before me like a pebble from the moon. *"See?"* Ian said. He turned it slowly in the moonlight, then brought it down closer to my face, so I could see. "At the labo-

ratories where they make artificial eyes, they put a little sliver of
white in the pupil, just a little scratch, just a tiny little flaw, so it
has the same shimmer, so it's got the same sparkle, so it looks as
alive as any ordinary eye. But it isn't, Toby Sligh. It's just an il-
lusion. The glimmer's only paint. There isn't any life at all. The
falsest things, Toby, have a bit of truth in them. Just a little bit of
truth. To make the falseness seem real."

Then, as if his glass eye were an unimpressive seashell he'd
suddenly discovered on the floor of the Gulf, Ian, without looking, pitched it over his shoulder. Then he started coughing—Ian
never cried, he coughed. And he held me. Ian held me tighter
than he ever had.

"Swear you'll never leave me!"

"I swear I'll never leave you!"

"And that you'll never let me go!"

"I swear I'll never let you go!"

"Hold me tighter, Toby!"

"This tight?"

"Even tighter!"

"Like . . . *this?*"

"Like that! I swear to God I love you so!"

And we must have remained in that water for hours, the dying
tide receding around our naked bodies, because before we knew
it, we were kneeling in the open, our bodies together, listing underneath the moon. And I helped Ian up, and I led him to his
car, and I drove him to his house, and I tried but couldn't wake
him. And in front of his mother and father's house I dressed him
and looked once again at his desecrated face—the eyelid collapsing around the empty socket that fluttered and twitched in
the throes of some dream, the envelope of skin where the false
eye had been in a desperate pucker, like a kiss-hungry mouth. I
covered him and left him asleep in the driveway, and I walked
for an hour through the night to my car. When I got home I swept
the sand off my body, and I crept inside the house, and I looked
at my parents. They lay sleeping in the static of the television

screen, on the floor, in their bathrobes, tangled up in each other. Their bodies looked slightly submerged underwater, as mine and Ian's had been before the tide had drawn away. Their bodies, as always, looked complete with each other. I wondered if Ian's and mine had looked that way.

"WE NEVER GO to the beach anymore."

We stood in our tuxedos in the mirror in Ian's room.

"We'll go there tonight," Ian said, "after the prom."

He came around behind me and kissed me on the neck.

"You'll dance with me, Ian? You really will? You promise?"

"I promise," Ian said, and he stepped out of the mirror.

"BUT I WANT to know one thing," I said to Ian Lamb as we sat in the frontseat of his folks' Mercedes-Benz, in our tuxes, in our closets, and waiting to come out. "Why did my mother move out of the house?"

Ian looked at me, and he looked at his hands, and he wiped a clot of mucus from his eye, and he coughed.

"Maybe you should wait until after the prom, Toby."

"I want to know now."

Ian trembled a little. "Why do you want to—"

"You *promised* me, Ian."

"After we waltz."

"*I want to know now.*"

I could tell Ian Lamb was thinking of something. His face was like a clock without hands keeping time. He started to speak, and then his voice failed him. When the words finally came, most of them were in pieces.

"Go to your mother's," Ian said, softly. "Don't let her see you. Just go there, Toby Sligh. If you want to know the truth, it's there, waiting for you."

Ian drew his lower lip between his teeth and bit it.

"Ian . . . Do you love me?"

His lower lip was bleeding. I got out of the Mercedes. He was watching me go.

"Ian . . . *Do you love me?*"

"I love you," Ian said. But he wasn't looking at me. He was looking in the mirror.

"Could you stop by St. Osyth's?" I said, before I left. I explained about the beeper and that Scarcross was dying. When I said Scarcross was dying, Ian flinched like he'd been hit, and his hand drifted up as if to ward away a blow. "Just call the social worker, Lucinda, from the lobby, explain who you are, and she'll bring the beeper down."

"If the beeper goes off while we're waltzing, Toby Sligh, will you go and see Scarcross?"

"I promised I would."

"You don't have the courage," Ian said, and drove away. "You'll never have that kind of courage, Toby Sligh."

 "THE FALSEST THINGS, Toby, have a bit of truth in them. Just a little bit of truth. To make the falseness seem real."

AS I DROVE to my mother's I remembered the photos my father had shown me the night Mom went away. Who'd taken the pictures of the two of them together? And the ones where they were naked—who had taken those?

TWO SLEDGEHAMMERS—THE kind on the baking soda boxes—lay crossed before the threshold of my mother's apartment. They were coated with a fine white powdering of dust, like the sugary stuff on Danish wedding cookies. I would have walked through the frontdoor if it had been there; it lay on its back, completely off its hinges, and my mother's bridal slippers lay akimbo atop it as if they'd flown off from the force of her kick. In the minuscule bedroom in Mom's efficiency her wedding dress squatted on a mattress stripped of bedding like a prehistoric moth pinned and mounted by the past. By the headboard, a hammer-sized hole in the plaster allowed a ray of sunlight to laser-beam through. The portraits of Ian had fallen off the wall, and the purple shag carpeting was dirty with plaster. In the kitchen, a bucket of Popeyes Chicken and a pyramid of beer cans formed an altar on the stove. The wall in the kitchen had been half obliterated, plaster and rubble made a jigsaw on the tile, and through a man-shaped silhouette in the devastated wall I could make out my mother on the hood of Christ's Chevy catching some rays in the dwindling light. Evening was approaching, but the sun was still out, and even though all I could see were Mom's feet astride a loaded shotgun metronoming time, I knew, as before, Mom was absolutely naked, and that the boy who was once an uninvited castaway was now little more than a rude conquistador.

The raffle Cadillac commandeered by Fr. Diaz arrived and dropped Dad off with wine and roses in his hands, and I wondered whether I should warn my dad about my mother as he stumbled up the driveway to the free-fire zone. Sure enough, a shotgun shell shattered his Chianti; and as the blast died away I mounted the trellis and took to the roof to view the carnage from above. Dad crouched behind a willow tree, quaking in his tux. *"How do I know,"* my mother slurred, *"that it'sh you!"* *"It's Timothy!"* he shouted. *"Who else would get this close?"* My mother let off another startling warning shot—she was making my poor father earn his transgression. Dad wound his way to her, bobbing in and out of bushes like a lovesick civilian infatuated with a sniper. I couldn't see Mom; she was holed up in the house. She didn't want to talk; she let her shotgun do the talking. Dad, who was bawling throughout the ordeal, whose red roses lay like fallen buddies behind him, was slowly removing every piece of his tuxedo, and tossing each high in the air, like a skeet, so Mom could take aim while he gained his advantage: just one step, two steps closer to his love. *"Jesus, it's our wedding night!"* my father caterwauled, crouched behind a willow tree in Cuddle Puppy boxers. And Mom let out a blast that slashed through the willows till Dad ripped off his boxers and naked as God made him charged kamikaze through the doorless frontdoor. Then: all was silence. All except the sound of kissing. This was their ceasefire. *Peace, at last, had broken out. . . .*

As I lay belly down, chin in the raingutter, eyes like Kilroy's peeking out at the world, I saw the most amazing thing that I had ever seen—my mother and father waltzing naked in the yard. They didn't waltz like champions; they didn't waltz like amateurs; they didn't waltz like anyone: they waltzed like a couple. Happy and drunken and shameless in love, they took their sweet time and never once stopped kissing. I was sure Dad was glad he had braved my mother's buckshot. All of the terror of combat had gone; everything, from then on, would be blissful armistice. So when Diaz returned (in formal wedding vestments), and Dad put on his tux, and Mom put on her wedding gown, and the three of them stood in the moonlight together, and Diaz said some things, and my parents said some things, and the two of them swapped rings, and then hugs, and then kisses, I climbed down from the roof just as quiet as I could and drove across town to pick up Angelina. . . .

Funny, they always used to *call* me a bastard, but I thought that they were being, um, *figurative.*

THE FISHBACKS LIVED in a split-level ranch house in the city's newest and most prestigious neighborhood. From the outside, their residence was tasteful and impressive. The grass was luxuriant, the oak trees were noble, even the lawn jockey seemed glad to be alive. Ivan Fishback's Ferrari—entirely paid for—posed in the driveway like a testament to money. Dr. Fishback never drove it, Angelina confided. He would polish it and sit in it and take pictures of it, but it never once budged. It was only a symbol. A clear plastic sheet imperceptible to the eye had been stretched between branches above the parked Ferrari to ensure that errant sparrows didn't foul its perfect paintjob, and a white plastic tarp tucked away in the trunk robed the idle beauty during inclement weather. Parked on the side of the house was a Lincoln with a Sacred Heart Mothers' Club bumper sticker on it. This was what the Fishback family used to get around in; it was their only car, apart from the Ferrari. And Angelina said they would get in awful fights about who got to drive it when her dad came home from work. Affluent families always made a habit of using one and only one car to get around in, as if this were their concession to a middle-class existence, as if to say, "See, we've got our hardships too!"

Mrs. Fishback, a muffin-sized woman in a muumuu, was disposing of a stack of grease-stained schiacciata boxes behind the Continental when I pulled up in the driveway. Tied to her wrist was a bunch of balloons that looked capable of launching her small body into orbit. She removed a pin from a bun in her hair and with a dozen quick pricks reduced the toy balloons to shreds. When she had disposed of the soiled schiacciata boxes, she lifted her head and saw me waiting in the drive. "Toby!" she cried. She was overjoyed to see me. She loved everybody. She was *that* kind of mom. "Where have you been?" I got out of the car. She hugged the daylights from me. "And what happened to your tux?" Removing a handkerchief from the bosom of her muumuu, she began to dab messy clumps of tar from my lapel.

"You come inside and I'll get a damp washcloth and tidy you up," she said, lugging me toward the house. "You did have an accident, didn't you, Toby?" I was thinking that the accident my parents had was me. "You're coming inside and you're having some schiacciata! Gosh, you look like you been dragged by a truck! If you say another word, I'll tan your silly tuckus! Ivan! It's the boy who broke Angelina's *hea-art!*"

FROM THE OUTSIDE, like I said, the Fishback home was impressive. But on the inside, well, it was an absolute dump. The wallpaper was discolored, paintings hung crooked, couches were tattered and covered with trash, a warehouse of unused Sharper Image gadgets cluttered the rug, which reeked of dog urine, and a platoon of outrageously well-groomed poodles converged on our ankles like canine piranha. "Mitzi! Tasha! Pinky! Fifi! Sissy! Kiki! Give Mommy *room!*" Mrs. Fishback squealed as we bustled down the hall. Dr. Fishback was sitting on a stool in the kitchen eating schiacciata and guzzling buttermilk. He extended his hand without looking at me: "Ivan Fishback," he said. I took it and shook it. "Scooch over, Ivan!" Mrs. Fishback shouted, and punched her husband's shoulder. Dr. Fishback scooched over. "Have some schiacciata." He shoved the plate toward me. I sat on a stool and started scarfing up the stuff. "This guy is hungry," Dr. Fishback observed.

"Then get him some more, you big lazy lummox!" Dr. Fishback rose from his stool with a groan; he was shaggy and ungainly, like a housebroken woolly mammoth. "Imagine showing up for the senior prom such a slob! Doesn't your mother take care of you, son?" Mrs. Fishback was stationed beside me on a barstool stabbing at tarballs on my tux with a washcloth. "Here, have some buttermilk," Dr. Fishback said. He poured me a big glass and force-fed me more schiacciata. "Wanna live to be a hundred? Drink lotsa buttermilk. Tastes like clotted urine. But it's the key to fucking health." "Don't just sit there!" Mrs. Fishback screamed. "Go get the camera! We gotta take pictures!" "Pictures?" I said. "What about Angelina?" "Oh, she's still here." Dr. Fishback yawned. "She's crying in the bedroom. She thought you stood her up. My daughter is in love. I'll go get her. . . . *Angelina!*"

I PICTURED ANGELINA in the bathroom mirror, cursing guys and regulating her breathing and swabbing fresh scars of mascara from her cheeks. I was a shit for being late for the prom. Angelina was a pal; she didn't deserve this. And I'd be a double-shit sometime around midnight when I'd abandon her, as planned, to dance with Ian Lamb. I never should have waltzed with her that night in the library. You waltz with somebody, they always fall in love—girls especially; girls are love-happy; girls fall in love just like guys get erections: all the time, constantly, for everything they see. I would have to tell her right away about Ian. I owed Angelina my honesty, at least. But when at last I saw her on the elbow of her father, striding in measured steps down the lighted hall, in a zinger of a dress like an emerald gumdrop, her bosomy body like a bauble in the rough, I felt my courage falter: Why'd she have to be so *pretty?* And I took the corsage her mother handed to me, and I pinned it to her breast, and we posed for photographs, and I said I was sorry, "Angelina, my parents—," and Dr. Fishback coughed and pressed some car keys in my hand. "Take the Ferrari! Go ahead! Just *take* it! But you bring it and my daughter back in one whole piece, *capisce?*"

✵ "LOOK AT THE odometer," Angelina was saying as we
pulled away in Ivan Fishback's Ferrari. Angelina's pudgy
fingers patted the upholstery; the odometer read: 000000. "You
don't understand what my father's *done*, Toby. This car, this Ferrari *has never been driven*. When he bought it, he bought it direct
from the factory. Then he had it flown by helicopter to Venezia. It
arrived in the U.S. in the hull of a cruise ship, like some pam-
pered poor relation escaping a war. And Daddy hired movers to
deliver it here, and with a custom-made winch they installed it in
our driveway. Since then, it hasn't *moved*. It hasn't *budged*, Tobias. It's the only pure thing in my dad's entire world. And now
you, a stranger, are popping its cherry! If I were superstitious, I
would turn around now. I would turn around and drive back
home and watch Schwarzenegger movies with my dad and eat
schiacciata. . . . Nothing bad's gonna happen tonight, is it,
Toby?"

We were on our way to the Japanese restaurant. The place
was named Namida. Namida means tears.

"I mean, *you aren't in love with Ian Lamb, are you?* It occurred to me tonight when we were watching television. Sacred
Heart was on the news. It was Principal McDuffy. He was talking to reporters about the rumor going round that a same-sex
couple would attend tonight's prom. And I thought about you,
and the days you were out. And I thought about Ian, and the
days he was out. Then when all the couples came, Ian Lamb arrived late. Courtney didn't care; she was flirting with Juice. And
Ian had two corsages—one for him and one for you. And your
tuxes, even now, they're exactly *alike!* And I thought about how
both your folks were in Barbados. And I thought about how
you've both been out of school a lot. And all the girls in my
class—you know, it's like a lottery. Who's gonna get stuck with a
flamer for a date. So tell me I'm just being paranoid, Toby. Tell
me you and Ian Lamb are really just good friends. 'Cause I don't
wanna go as somebody's fag-hag girlfriend. I care about you,
Toby—but I care about me, too. I'm not the most beautiful girl

in the world, but I have my good qualities—my charm, my joie de vivre. And we've been such good pals. And you know, this would just ruin it. I don't care what you are. . . . *Remember the library?*"

I told her I remembered. I did remember, too: the way we had waltzed across the crunching bug bodies, the cataracts of moonlight, the novels we rescued.

"When I saw the news tonight, I thought, *Shit, it's Tobe and Ian!* And when Ian came late, and he wouldn't talk to Courtney, and he wouldn't talk to anyone, a chill went down my spine. And when you didn't show, and no one answered at your house, I knew that I was right, and I knew I was a fool. So tell me, Toby Sligh, that it's my imagination! Tell me it's *me* you want to dance with at the prom! Because, if it isn't, you can take me home right now, in my father's Ferrari, before I get crushed. You can take me home now and I'll forgive you, Toby Sligh. You can take me home now and I'll forgive everything."

We were parked beside a limo. The chauffeur was dozing. The limousine was longer than Pinocchio's nose.

"You're the one, Angelina," I said to her, and kissed her. I was thinking of my parents. "You're the only one I want."

She looked at me awhile—a dark, probing look. Then she turned away and said, "Would you get my door for me?"

I got it. She stepped out, leaning on my arm.

"Ya know, I always thought my dad would open that door for me."

✺ *"IRASSHAI!"* A SUSHI chef called out to Angelina as a skittish woman in a blue silk kimono led us past the bar to our party in back. Angelina, who had studied Japanese on the sly ever since she'd seen Kurosawa's *Rashomon,* spoke in soothing tones to the jittery hostess, who nodded at Angelina through a strained smile. In a beautiful room at the rear of Namida our party sat huddled around a low table. Anquanna wore a ravishing Pierre Cardin gown—black, chic, and strapless; she had fallen asleep. Juice sat beside her in a James Bond tuxedo playing Jinai Seijin, "The Goddess of Saintly Love," a black market Japanese video game that emitted gross gastrointestinal noises and which Juice had commandeered from Namida's owner's son. Across from him, Bubba was using a chopstick to dig at a plantar's wart bedded in his heel. Leaning against him was his date, Grace Cage, dressed in a gown that looked like a greasy lunch bag and holding up a piece of raw fish between her chopsticks as if it were a lump of contaminated flesh. Across from Grace, Courtney Ciccone sat gazing at a compact, enamored of herself; she wore a scarlet dress that plumped her breasts up like tomatoes, and I wondered what her feet were doing underneath the table. Opposite Courtney, back to me, sat Ian. He was placing pink petals of ginger on his eyes. When Ian turned around he looked like Little Orphan Annie. He couldn't even see me. Angelina screamed.

"What did you order?"

"Sashimi," Ian told her.

"Sashimi? I wanted you to start things off with sushi!"

Juice snorted, "Girl, I ain't eatin' no *bait!*"

"We thought we'd begin with something *easy,*" Courtney added.

"Sashimi?" Angelina said. "Sashimi's *raw fish!*"

"Well, we didn't know that," Ian said. "Hello, Toby."

"Hello, Ian," I said.

Angelina looked at us.

Grace Cage whispered, "People *die* eating sushi. Fish have parasites."

Bubba said, "They any good?"

"Excuse me," Angelina said, bowing to the hostess. She went over to her brother and she slugged him in the stomach.

"Ow!" Bubba shouted, upsetting the table.

A cup of green tea splashed Anquanna's sleeping lap.

"*Sushizume!*" cried the waitress.

Anquanna sprang to life.

"Bubba Fishback, shit, I finna whip yo' white bootie!"

"Wha'd I do?"

"Down, Anquanna!"

"Help me, Toby!"

"*Angelina!*"

IT WAS DECIDED, after a brief deliberation, and after Angelina had calmed Anquanna down, that we would get bottles of sake to go. Juice bribed the waitress—who was happy to get rid of us—and soon we were piled in the stretch limousine, which was redolent of rice wine and cloying corsages. In no time at all we were thoroughly shit-faced—all but Grace Cage, who sipped her green tea, whose sobriety was part of a loftier mission.

"Anquanna?" Juice whispered.

"What is it, Leon?"

She was running her fingernail down her cousin's wrist.

"Check it out," Juice said.

Anquanna leaned over.

Juice showed her something in his pocket, and she flinched.

"What is it?" Courtney asked. "Like, can I see it?"

Anquanna was fuming; she wouldn't look at anybody.

"*Secrets!*" Courtney sang. "*Everybody's got secrets!*"

Grace Cage held a copy of the Bible in her lap.

"Have you heard about the gay couple going to prom?" Grace Cage began.

"Who hasn't?" we all answered.

"Who is it, do you think?" Grace Cage asked Angelina.

"It's Toby and Ian," Juice said.

We all laughed.

"They find out what happened to your Porsche today, Juice?"

Anquanna looked at Bubba.

"What happened to his Porsche?"

"Somebody," Bubba said, "put a brick through the window."

"And they slashed its pretty tires," Courtney chimed in.

Anquanna looked at Juice; then she swore and looked away.
"I cannot believe you didn't tell me this, baby."

"I was fixing to tell you."

Everybody got quiet.

"If my mama knew, boy—"

"Your mama won't know."

Anquanna was seething; she was glaring out the window.

"What did you do?" Grace Cage asked Juice.

Grace was leaning into Bubba; Juice was studying his
knuckles.

"You must have done something to make somebody so hate-
ful. Have you talked to the Lord?" Grace asked.

"I lost His number."

Anquanna shook her head. "Then you better find it, boyee!"
I ain't gettin' caught in the crossfire this time!"

"What crossfire?" Grace asked.

Anquanna only cursed. I watched as her hand wandered up
to her face, to the place on her cheek where her bruises had
been.

Courtney touched Anquanna.

"Like, what crossfire?"

Anquanna whirled around and slapped Juice's padded chest.

"Leonard Compton's wearing a bulletproof vess!" Anquanna
announced. There was a dull, leaden thud.

Juice bowed his head.

"Open up and show 'em!"

Juice picked his teeth.

"Go ahead, you coward!"

When Juice didn't move, Anquanna reached over and unbuttoned the studs above Juice's cummerbund. A gray sheath of sturdy material emerged. Juice buttoned his shirt and wouldn't look at anybody.

"Please take me home," Grace Cage said to Bubba.

"Why are people after you?" Angelina asked Juice.

"He deals," Anquanna said. "Juice Compton is a dealer."

Everybody knew it, but now it had been said.

"Better watch your back tonight!" Anquanna warned the party. "Juice Compton is a dealer—he got gangsters after him!"

"And why don't you shut your fucking mouth now, Anquanna?"

"It ain't gonna help yo' ass talkin' dirty now!"

Anquanna started crying; everybody was embarrassed. Ian Lamb was looking out the window of the limo.

"Juice had a half brother."

"Shut up, Anquanna!"

"*Nobody's tellin' me to shut my mouth now!* Juice had a brother, half brother name a' Eddy! Folks called him E-Eye 'cause he only got one eye! You know how he lost it?"

Courtney said, "Let's change the subject."

"No way, Li'l Miss Teen Bitch! Not a chance! . . . Juice's brother lost his eye, and a whole lot more because—"

"Anquanna Gray, I am *warning* you, baby. . . ."

"Whatchoo got to warn me about, Mr. Big Stuff?" Juice was curling in on himself like a snail. "You're the one wearing the bulletproof vess! You're the one's got the automatic in his pocket! You're the one's puttin' your friends on the line! You put me on the line dealin' product for you! Maybe you can't see the bruises on my cheek, but I got 'em in here! I got 'em inside! They held me down, Juice! They held me down and hit me! We all deserve better! We entitled to the truth!"

Juice said to Anquanna, "You've had too much sake."

Anquanna just laughed: "Yeah, I had too much of *you!*"

"This is a downer," Courtney Ciccone pouted.

I said, "I think we've all had a bit too much to drink."

Ian turned from the window.

"How'd your brother lose his eye?"

Juice turned on Ian.

"And how'd you lose yours, Ian?"

"Everything's so ugly," moaned Courtney Ciccone. "Let's try to be *happy!*"

Grace Cage cleared her throat: "I'm not so sure that I like the idea that I'm riding in a limo with somebody with a gun."

Juice took an automatic pistol from his pocket and looked at it and rolled down the window and pitched it.

"That's better," Anquanna said. "What about the blow?"

Juice pitched a nickel bag of cocaine out the window.

"Now the vess!" Anquanna said. "Get rid of that vess! And then we can go to the prom like normal people!"

Blushing, Juice removed his ruffled cummerbund, unbuttoned his shirt, and drew out the leaden vest. He rolled down the limousine's window and pitched it. Then he buttoned up, and he kissed Anquanna's hand.

"That's how I like you!" Anquanna said, nodding. "I just wanna live normal, tha'ss all I want!"

Grace Cage was looking from Ian to me.

"You two really going to the prom as a couple?"

Angelina, Courtney, and everybody laughed.

Ian asked, "And would we go to hell if we did?"

"There's only one way to find out," Grace Cage told him.

A SECRET CLOSELY guarded by the Senior Prom Committee was the annual theme: Stranded on a Desert Island. Ten tons of sand, several potty-trained macaws, and coolers of non-alcoholic margaritas had passed undetected by the likes of Angelina into the ballroom of the Downtown Hyatt Regency. But as our limousine drew up to the luxury hotel—a Dunsinane forest of palm trees filing past us—we didn't need to see the firetrucks or local news crews to know that something more than the theme had been spoiled.

"*Bomb scare?* There's really been a bomb scare?" Courtney squealed as we turned on the TV in the backseat of the limo. There we were, captured by our pixilated eye, our limousine idling on a screen within a screen. We could see a reporter sidewinding toward us. We would watch ourselves live on the news as we became it.

"SPENCER CALLOWAY REPORTING *live* at the Downtown Hyatt Regency, where a bomb threat from an anonymous phone caller has thrown an abrupt hitch in the Sacred Heart prom festivities.

"Though school officials have persistently denied rumors that two students of the same sex would attend tonight's private function as a couple, today local gay rights and anti–gay rights activists *converged* upon the Hyatt to voice support and concern for what may prove to be the educational dilemma of the future."

Here the coverage switched to earlier footage of lethargic demonstrators waving placards at each other. When the camera cut back, Calloway was next to Juice, whose head was sticking out of the limousine window. We had the option of watching Juice's face on the screen or staring at his butt as he leaned out of the limo.

"We're now talking *live* to Sacred Heart senior and local All-State running back Leonard 'Juice' Compton. Juice . . . do you mind if I call you Juice?"

"Go for it, Spence."

Juice wagged his ass at us.

"We understand that the Sacred Heart prom will be relocated tonight to an undisclosed locale. But do you have *any* idea who might have been responsible for the *terrible* bomb scare that *has rocked* this small community?"

"Some gay basher ain't got nothin' else to do."

"And *Juice,* is there any *truth* to the rumor that a *same-sex* couple will attend tonight's prom?"

"Don't look at me, Calloway. I like the *ladies.* You the one's dressed by *International Male.*"

Then Juice looked at the camera and said, "I love ya, Mama. I'm sorry what I done. I'm still yo' baby. . . . *Come dance with me tonight!*"

Inside, Anquanna pinched Juice's rump.

"Just when I think Leonard Compton's a monster," Anquanna said, "he goes and says something sweet."

"Gotta go now, Spence!" Juice told an outraged Calloway, and he winked at the camera. *"My boyfriend's goosin' me!"*

✳ THE PROM HAD been relocated to Sacred Heart High—an "undisclosed locale" any moron might have figured out—and moving vans arrived bearing beer kegs full of beach sand, which were rolled out and strewn around the school cafeteria to give it an impromptu "desert island" look. The cafeteria was surrounded by squad cars and security guards—squad cars in the event of any gay-related violence, and private security as a visible deterrent to members of the press who might conveniently forget that the Sacred Heart prom remained a private affair. Nevertheless, in a city our size—which was barely a city, and too mean to be a town—scandals like these brought the media running: camera crews were drinking coffee somewhere in the bushes, boom mikes masqueraded as telephone poles, and frenzied helicopters from rival TV stations were circling in the moonlight like sublunar sharks. Juice seemed to know a good deal of the security: they were on loan from an import-export magnate (read: mafioso) who was a big alum. They were all duded up in identical tuxes with Sicilian flags emblazoned on their satin cummerbunds. Most of them, however, were decidedly not Sicilian; most of them were black and built like brick shithouses. They were the muscle behind the local hero, a hero whose traffic included stripjoints and crackpipes, ponies and greyhounds and dirty syringes, bingo and porno and underage escorts who came, if you were lucky, with complimentary condoms. Two guards, twins—Lonnie and Johnnie—had played ball for Sacred Heart, and Juice introduced us. He pointed to their names high above the lunch counter, to the records they had set for tackles and sacks. When their boss came around—a wheezy padrone with red licorice trailing from his lips like a fuse—the duo said, "Juice, you better not let Twizzler see you," and Juice disappeared to empty beer kegs full of beach sand.

Anquanna and Courtney and Grace and Angelina retired to a table at the back of the hall and were sitting with their feet up sipping Crystal Pepsi. In front of the curtain on the stage where all our plays were, a four-piece outfit of Bob Marley wannabes were setting up kettledrums, guitars and amplifiers. Teachers dressed nicer than they ever had occasion to were milling around with their eyes peeled for queers, and I spied Ian Lamb in a big pack of jocks. I went over. When I did, everybody got quiet. There was soft sporadic laughter. All the guys were in cahoots.

"Ian," I said, "could I talk to you a second?"

I thought I heard whispers; everyone was staring at me.

"What is it, Toby?" Ian said, not moving.

He was standing in the middle of a circle of jerks.

"I need to talk to you."

"So go ahead and talk."

Guys on either side of Ian Lamb started laughing.

Someone said, "Can we tell him?"

"He wouldn't get the joke!"

"But he'd get *something else!*"

"And he'd *like* it!"

They all roared.

"It's about my *parents.*"

Ian stared at the floor.

"Who cares about your parents?"

Everyone was looking at me.

"Is something going on?" I asked Ian.

No one spoke.

Ian cracked his knuckles. "Go dance with Angelina."

"Excuse me?"

"You heard me. Go dance with your fat girl."

The circle of guys around Ian grew tighter. I was outside the circle. Reggae music started playing.

"We have to talk, Ian."

Somebody started laughing.

"Talk then, you faggot," Ian said.

They all laughed.

Someone gave Ian some liquor, and he drank it.

"I'm going now, Ian."

"Suit yourself, buddy."

Courtney came over.

"Hi, Ian!"

She kissed him.

"Cute tuxedo, Toby!" Courtney said.

Somebody whistled.

"Just how'd you get those *tar* stains?"

I turned around and left.

ANGELINA FOUND ME crying buckets in a corner. She was standing with her shoes off. "Redemption Song" was playing.

"I wanna know what's going on," Angelina began.

"I'd really like to tell you, but I don't know myself!"

"Something's going on and it's been going on all evening!"

"You're just being paranoid—"

"I trusted you, Toby!"

Angelina broke away and stamped out onto the dancefloor. She wrapped her arms around herself and danced alone awhile. People were watching, but Angelina didn't care. She closed her eyes and swayed and sang along to the music:

> *Emancipate yourselves from mental slavery;*
> *None but ourselves can free our minds. . . .*

When I saw her on the floor I stabbed the tears from my eyes. Everyone was staring, but I went out and I joined her.

"May I cut in?"

Angelina stopped dancing.

"Lemme ask my partner," she said, stepping back. She consulted with her shadow, who was watching from the dancefloor. "Are you big enough to dance with the truth, Toby Sligh? My partner wants to know if you can dance with the truth."

I nodded.

"All right. But she gets very jealous. She should. She's my partner. Be careful, Toby Sligh."

> *Won't you help me sing*
> *These songs of freedom?*
> *'Cause all I ever have—*
> *Redemption songs,*
> *Redemption songs.*

✳ We were boogying together to the tang of kettledrums
when Angelina caught me in a newlywed clinch and
pointed to a couple making love behind a palm tree.

"Don't even have the decency to do it with the lights off," Angelina scolded.

"Who?"

"Courtney and Ian—"

I gulped and my heart catapulted to my throat as I stood on
the dancefloor watching Courtney mauling Ian.

"She's practically got her fucking hand down his jockstrap.
And Ian doesn't look like a very good kisser. And Courtney, she
must have a tongue like a *plunger!* . . . You all right, Toby?"

"I feel kinda funny—"

I was stumbling toward Ian. I was shouting.

"Ian! *I*—"

✳ "YOU FAINTED, TOBY Sligh," Angelina sighed.
We were lying outside on the grass beside the chapel.

"I dragged you outside. Me and Bubba, we dragged you. Ian
didn't help you. You fainted at his feet."

Chaperons were standing beside the chapel, watching. Angelina waved. They turned and walked away.

"I haven't been sleeping. I haven't been eating. I keep *fainting lately," I said.

She sat up. "I know why you fainted," Angelina began. "I
know the real reason." Her brassy voice was breaking.

"Please, Angelina—"

"You think I'm a fool."

"It's not what you—"

"Toby, I've known all along!"

Angelina stood up and straightened her gown and looked at
me and blinked and disappeared into the night. Through the

strobe-lit windows I could see all the couples laughing and kissing and dancing with each other. Courtney and Ian were in the
middle of it all, orbited by couples no less beautiful than they
were. I looked at the two of them with envy and regret—after
what I had done, I had no right to feel betrayed. And I had to admit it: they made a handsome couple. You could almost imagine
the kids they would squirt. Me and Angelina, we were misfits-
in-the-making—faggot and fat girl, equipped to face the world
with little more than heartache and lowered expectations. How
could I have ever thought that Ian Lamb could love me? Look at
the way he was dancing with that girl! He had danced with my
mother like that, and with me. He would move through life, he
would move through partners never knowing how to love, only
knowing how to lie.

"Excuse me?" a voice said.

It came from behind me—a voice at once familiar and oddly
unfamiliar.

"I couldn't help noticing that scene with your girlfriend, and
I wondered, young man, if you were still *in*terested in your complimentary Polaroid senior prom portrait?"

As I turned, a brilliant burst of light scorched my eyes and
put me in mind of Alfred Hitchcock's *Rear Window*—of the cli-
max, where Jimmy Stewart, to escape being strangled, dazzles
his assailant with bursts of flash photography. As the image
ebbed away in the template of my retina, the vision of my father
wearing thick nerd glasses blossomed before me like a '70's Bad
Dream. He was holding a camera, a vintage Polaroid. Only thing
was, it *wasn't* my father. It was his double—Det. Thomas, undercover.

"Good evening, Toby Sligh! Welcome to the prom! I hope you
haven't forgotten our gentlemen's agreement!"

The Polaroid camera was whirring in his hands. Thomas
handed me a snapshot of my miserable self.

"You're a dark angel," I said. "Go away. The day that I met
you was the day that I died."

"I'm not a dark angel! *I'm an angel of light!*" Det. Thomas said, and set off another flashbulb.

"I'm going inside," I said and stood up. "And you can take your camera and shove it up your ass."

"You shouldn't talk that way to a figure of authority," Det. Thomas lectured. "Show some respect!"

"Respect this," I said. I displayed my middle finger. "I know who you're here with, and I know it's not the cops." Det. Thomas's eyes went narrow in the darkness. "And you'd better be careful or I'll tell the police about the Polaroid you planted in the Porsche you trashed today. And I'll tell them what you did to Leonard Compton in that alley. And I'll tell them the truth—that you're the biggest punk in town!"

Thomas whirled around: there was movement in the bushes. A cameraman emerged, and excused himself, and left.

"Do you think I'm afraid of the cops, Toby Sligh? Don't you think if I were, Juice would have given them that picture? Do you think if I were frightened I would leave a trail of clues as long as a list of Leonard Compton's drug connections? Don't you know the Mafia owns the police? Don't you realize the Mafia owns your buddy Juice? They own everybody here, but they don't own me. And I can do anything because I'm well con-nected. I'm down with the cops, and I'm down with the mob, and I'm down with your folks—I'm down with everybody. You know as well as I do that this is bigger, Toby. This is not about the prom. *This is about us.*"

"Who's us?"

"Me, you, your father, your mother."

"You go near my parents tonight and I'll kill you!"

"That's not our happy Toby! *Big Smile,* Toby Sligh!"

A flashbulb exploded and a hand fell on my wrist—it be-longed to Leonard Compton.

"What's that cocksucker want?"

Det. Thomas was vanishing behind a podocarpus, camera around his shoulder. Juice started after him.

"Let him go, Leonard!"

"That boy wants trouble."

"He doesn't want nothing."

"That boy wants your *soul*. You gonna trust me, Toby?"

I looked at him: "What?"

"Are . . . you . . . gonna . . . trust me?"

I nodded at him.

"Sure. I gotta trust someone."

"I know ya do, G."

LEONARD COMPTON ASKED me what I'd done with his stash and I said that I'd hidden it in the chapel tabernacle. I handed him the archbishop's little gold key, and with only a paper clip—just like in the movies—we busted into the chapel while everyone was dancing and waded toward the altar through the underwater light.

"THIS WHAT I do with narcotics, Toby Sligh."

He took the cocaine—about a cup of it—and mixed it in the chalice with a splash of red wine. Then he took the drug money—$87,000—and tore it in four pieces, just like the Eucharist.

"This is my body," Juice said, to nobody, and tossed the money high above the altar, like confetti. "This is my blood," Juice said, and drank the wine, which was syrupy with cocaine, a poppy-red narcotic porridge.

"Don't, Juice!" I yelled and knocked the chalice from his fingers.

The poppy-red porridge stained the marble altar floor.

"God's just opium, Tobe. He can't hurt me."

And with the rest of the coke, and a half carafe of wine, he made another coketail, and he chugalugged it down.

❈ "AREN'T YOU GONNA die?" I said to Leonard Compton, walking toward the strobelights, his lips bleeding red. "Aren't you gonna have, like, a heart attack or something?"

"Never felt better." Juice belched. "Let's dance! But when the Castoria kicks in—I'll be squirtin' for a week!"

❈ AT THE DOUBLE doors leading back into the cafeteria Grace Cage was standing by a girl with choppy hair. They spoke in low tones, leaning up against each other, and when I walked by they looked up at me and laughed.

"Pay no attention," Juice said. "Hold your head up! You gotta hold your head up, Toby Sligh, and be proud!"

"Proud a' what, Juice?"

"You know what, Toby Sligh! Everybody else does. . . . There's Lamb. *Talk to him.*"

❈ IAN WAS SITTING at a table in the shadows with his back to the wall and his cummerbund undone. In his right hand he held the hospital beeper Lucinda had given him to pass on to me. Courtney Ciccone was seated by the dancefloor surrounded by girls; they were looking at us. Wherever I turned, and whomever I turned to, teachers, students—everybody was staring.

"What's going on, Ian?"

He wouldn't look up.

"You might want this beeper."

He slid it over to me.

"Saw Scarcross," Ian said. "You're right. Guy's dying."

"He's not the only one," I said and sat across from him.

"Everybody knows," Ian said.

"About what?"

"About you and me. Or about *you,* at least."

"What do they know?"

"That you're in love with me, Toby."

"I'm in love with someone else. And I don't think that you're him."

"Who am I?"

"You fucking tell me, Ian Lamb. A liar. Somebody I thought that I loved."

"You're crying. Don't be sad."

"Fuck you."

"Oh, Toby. You're such a little boy—"

I got up and walked away.

"Toby!" a voice cried.

Everybody was staring.

"Toby! Toby Sligh! *Don't walk away from me!*"

With my back to Ian Lamb—and staring at a clock that said a quarter to twelve, and surrounded by faces—I felt Ian's voice like a wire at my spine, tugging me backward, a dead fish on a line.

"I want to talk to you. Out*side,* Toby Sligh. Would you let me talk to you?"

I turned and followed him outside.

WE WALKED ACROSS the campus of Sacred Heart High, spotlights intercepting helicopters in the sky, steeldrums from the senior prom sounding vaguely tribal, pine trees and buildings and television news crews lit by the wilting blue light of the moon. We had never been more publicly in need of privacy: every gesture we made was now officially on display. Word had leaked out to several hump-busting journalists, and already camera crews were trailing at a distance in the hope that this lead wouldn't prove to be false, that these two disheveled boys with their hands in their pockets were discussing matters less mundane than cars and beer and girls.

I didn't have anything left to say to Ian, and I refused to award him the trophy of my tears. But still, all the same, I couldn't stop looking at him—at those lips I had kissed I didn't know how many times, at those eyes, those mismatched eyes, that had inspired my devotion. It struck me as ironic that the boy who had kissed me not three days before in a jam-packed coffee shop was passing up the chance to go flamingly public in a way that would make modern media history. If only he had stopped, turned to me, and said, *"Toby,"* and taken my face in his hands and French-kissed me—what a picture for the front page of the daily newspaper, or the local gay weekly, or *The Florida Catholic!* But even these fantasies tasted sour now. Ian was a liar. He could keep his goddamn distance. We would talk, that was all. What were kisses now were words.

"I NEVER LOVED you, Toby Sligh. I never *really* loved you. And you didn't really think that I'd have the strength to *do* it?" Ian Lamb began, in an inaudible voice. "I only lied to you because you wanted me to. I can't even be sure at this moment that I'm gay."

We had come to the track. We were walking circles round it. Above us, helicopters swarmed in the sky.

"I knew it tonight. When I saw Fr. Scarcross. When I saw his body, Toby. I'll never be gay."

"You'll never be gay 'cause you're straight, Ian Lamb? Or you'll never be gay because you're frightened of AIDS?"

"I'll never be gay because it's all so *complicated*," Ian Lamb said. "All the pain, all the lies . . . You lied to Angelina. Have you seen the way she looks at you? How have my lies been any different from yours?"

"It's true, we're both bastards," I agreed and looked away.

"But of course," Ian said, "you're a *different* kind of bastard. . . . *Did you like your parents' wedding?* It almost never happened. I talked your mother into it; she didn't want to do it. Your mom used to be in love with somebody else. But now she loves your father. At least she thinks she does—"

"Did you sleep with her, Ian?" I asked.

He was silent.

"Did you sleep with my mother?"

Ian Lamb kept walking.

"I used to be in love with somebody, Toby Sligh. You'll never guess who."

A helicopter chattered by.

"Are you HIV-positive?" I asked Ian, finally. "Did you infect my mother? Have you infected me?"

Somewhere across town my folks were making love. If my mother had the virus, then my father . . .

"Toby Sligh—?"

"It's just like the Mickey in your motherfucking eye!"

"Don't talk that way, Toby."

He was walking with his head down.

"You know I would love you in a perfect world, kiddo. You know I do love you. It's all just so—"

"Gay."

Above us, a helicopter made a pass at us. The grass on the
football field divided like a dress.

"I'd kiss you right here if I could, Toby Sligh."

"Don't start that shit again."

"I would. You know I love you."

We were standing somewhere on the fifty-yard line. I could
swear, in the night, I heard the ghost of Leonard Compton running with a parachute strapped to his back.

"You'll never know how much I really love you, Toby Sligh.
You'll never believe me, after tonight. I'm not the one to blame if
your parents never married. I'm not the one to blame if you fell
in love with me. I'm innocent, Toby. *I'm my own victim.* I'm not
betraying you. *I'm betraying myself.*"

I thought of everybody laughing at me back inside.

"But I'm the one they think has a crush on *you,* Ian."

"It wasn't my fault that you fainted at my feet. You gave yourself away."

"And you helped." I turned on him. "What did you say when
people asked about me? 'Is it true Toby Sligh invited you to the
prom?' 'Yeah, poor faggot, I couldn't break his heart. Even
bought him a tux, just to cushion the blow. I can't help it if
everybody falls in love with me—girls, guys, even best friends'
mothers.' Just what kind of special strain of liar are you, Ian?
How can you tell me after six months together, after everything
we've said, after everything we've done, that tonight is nothing
more than a goddamn complication, and that you never loved
me? You even *cried* to me! You held me on the beach with your
arms wrapped around me and you made me swear forever that
I'd never let you go, and now you say you'd love me if the world
was fucking *perfect?* Well, the world's *not* fucking perfect! It gets
less perfect by the minute! I'm a bastard, we're faggots, my parents just got married, and right now there's a Jesuit dying across
town because people like you can't face up to who they are! *I'm
here, Ian Lamb! Toby Sligh is right here!* And when we say goodbye we'll never have this love again! You wanna come out? We've

got fucking helicopters! We've got the Mafia, the media! They're prob'ly phoning CNN! *The biggest fucking lie you've told all evening is that you never loved me! Why else would you be crying? . . .* If you love me, let's do it! *Right now, Ian Lamb!*"

Ian stopped crying. The chapel bell struck midnight. He handed me something in a brown paper bag.

"All right. Let's do it. Let's waltz, like we said."

"You mean it?"

He sniffled. He wrapped his arms around me. Flashbulbs exploded. Helicopters dived.

"I know it's not a perfect world. I wish it were, Toby. . . . But the bag. Don't open it till after we've waltzed."

ALL THE LIGHTS in the cafeteria were out—except for a mirrored ball that cast swirling shadows—and the security guards were outside shooting craps, and the cops were eating crullers behind Jai Alai programs, and the media—who must have bribed security well, unless organized crime owned the local TV stations and got distribution rights to the most select footage—had emerged from the bushes like so many roaches and stood with their lenses propped up against the glass trying hard to sneak a peek at potential fag couples through the whirling mirrored shadows and unfurling fog machines. Midnight had arrived, and it was time for the waltz, and everything was secrecy and saturnalian shadow, and even the helicopters seemed suspended in midair, caught up in the question marks of arching silver searchlights.

An enterprising anchor who'd seen Ian and me embracing in the moonlight on the fifty-yard line shouted out behind us as we threaded our way back through camera wires and empty kegs toward the prom, "Would you two fellas care to formally declare your love for each other on the twelve o'clock news?"

"We have a prom to get to," I said, not looking back, and slapping Ian's ass to a flurry of flashbulbs.

"I'll meet you inside," Ian said at the backdoor leading to the curtained stage that bordered the dancefloor. "I'll find Courtney, you find Angelina, and in the middle of the waltz we'll switcharoo, okay?"

"I'm trusting you, Ian," I said, looking at him.

"You can trust me," he said. "There's no turning back now."

And he kissed his index finger and he put it to his lip, and he told the world, *"Shhhh!"*—as if the world had guessed our secret—and then he put the finger he had kissed against my lip and said, "I'll see you, Toby," and he disappeared inside.

WHEN IAN LAMB left, I took the bag from my pocket—the bag Ian had given me on the fifty-yard line. It was the same paper bag in which I'd hidden Ian's rose—the pink rose I'd stolen the day I first saw Scarcross. Now the bag was weathered and softer than leather. It felt like an animal's pelt in my hands. But I wouldn't look inside it until we had waltzed. I had promised Ian Lamb, and I would keep my promise.

As I bundled up the bag and stuck it in my pocket, I heard a voice searching for mine in the dark. I was standing in the stairwell leading to the stagedoor; I took a step down, and my eyes scanned the shadows. "Toby," the voice cried. I took a step forward. "Toby!" the voice repeated. *"Toby . . . Toby Sligh!"* Behind me, a hand brushed the nape of my neck. I turned to see Anquanna. She was hugging herself.

"Where you been, boy? I was looking all over!"

"For me?"

"For my Leonard . . . You the next best thing."

"Juice isn't inside?"

"He ran away, Toby!"

"Where'd he run away to?"

"You didn't see what happened?"

Anquanna sat down on the steps to the stagedoor, squeezed her body once, and sighed apocalyptically. Inside, they were waltzing. The music had started. I could picture Ian dancing. Anquanna offered me a joint.

"No, thanks," I said curtly.

"Have a seat, Toby! You been with Ian Lamb or you been with my baby?"

"With Ian," I said.

"That's okay. I believe you. I know Juice ain't *like* that. . . . So you didn't see what happened?"

I told her I hadn't and watched her nurse her joint; she sucked it in slow drags and shivered in the heat.

"Juice's mama, Valilian, Valilian Compton—I dunno, she musta seen Juice on the news, 'cause a little while ago she arrived at the prom in a housecoat my mama she give her for her birthday, and Juice and me, you know, we dancing on the dancefloor, we was having a good time, just holdin' one another, and Mrs. Compton see us, and I say, 'Juice, yo' mama,' and she walks across the dancefloor in her bunny rabbit slippers. Juice, he just stands there, he stand there like a baby, his arms open wide and his mama walkin' to him. And he grinnin' like a kid; he wasn't lookin' at Valilian; that boy be so happy that he couldn't see straight. And, Toby—I never will forget it, Toby Sligh—Mrs. Compton, she stops about twenty feet from him, and she take a long look, and then she draw a breath. And Juice, he goes to her and he says in this voice, so everyone can hear him, so everyone can hear, 'You wanna dance, girl? You wanna dance with your baby?' And Valilian, you could see her lower lip workin', she cryin' to herself, and her mouth is sealed tight. And she goes up to Leonard and spits in his eye: *'Dealer,'* she say. *'You killed your brother Eddy.'* And then she slapped his face. And she just walks away."

Inside the cafeteria, the first waltz had ended—the first of three waltzes. Ian would be waiting.

"So where is Juice now?"

"He disappeared, Toby—I tol' you! No one's seen him! And who's gonna dance with *me?*"

"I'd dance with you," I said, "but—"

"What? Angelina? Girl's gone, Toby. She went home with her brother."

WE PASSED THROUGH the stagedoor, past a struck set—a rack of clouds were lying in a pile on the floor, the sun had snapped in half, and a tree was upside down—and it was pitch black, with shadows whorling in the darkness, and An-quanna squeezed my arm and she whispered, *"What was that?"*

We stopped and we listened. We saw a figure moving.

"Maybe it's Juice!" Anquanna said, and took a step.

Out on the dancefloor, beyond the closed curtains, the second waltz of the evening had officially begun. There was just one more, the last waltz of the evening; then the lights would flood up and everybody would go home.

"C'mon, Anquanna—!"

"Gotta see if it's Juice! Never thought my Leonard might be hiding back *here!*"

"But the *last waltz*, Anquanna—!"

"I'll dance with you, Toby! Don't leave me here alone and—Shhh! Somebody's movin'!"

It was true: in a corner of the stage beside the curtains, before a grand piano that was slightly out of tune, a figure sat hunchbacked on a squat piano bench, a shadow in the darkness, staring at the two of us. It was sitting very still; it gave off an acrid odor. All we could hear was raspy breathing in the dark. Then there was a rolling noise of levers and pulleys, the figure on the piano bench bolted upright, and the curtains separating the stage from the dancefloor opened on a teeming sea of senior prom faces. McDuffy took the stage with a microphone in hand and pointed at the figure huddled on the crooked bench— a woman, a nun, a collection of wrinkles, a come-undone mummy: she looked older than the world.

"IT HAS BEEN a tradition," McDuffy began, beaming at the audience beneath a single spotlight, "to let Sr. Aloysius of the Holy Dames Academy perform the final waltz at the senior prom. Alumni down the ages have remembered her fondly, and have said that of all their high school memories, Sr. Aloysius's final waltz at the prom has remained a special highlight and a treasured memory. I would like to congratulate all of you for weathering what has proved to be a truly trying ceremony; and I would ask you, for a moment, to step back from all the chaos and to celebrate this waltz in the spirit God intended it— a spirit of faith, and of truth, and of honor, and of family, and community, and dignity, and love. And with that said, bow your heads and ask God's blessing." McDuffy spoke Latin; everybody crossed themselves. "And now, without further ado—the last waltz, as performed by our very own Sr. Aloysius!"

The single white spotlight directed at McDuffy diverted its beam and landed on the seated nun. She seemed composed of dust and other less substantial stuff, but she was sturdy and graceful in an ageless white habit, like a girl who'd never jettisoned her First Communion dress. There was a disarming serenity about her, and her face was bright and mocking, and her long fingers fine as she sifted through leaves of desiccated sheet music as if she'd never seen the waltz she'd played for countless years. She took a sip of soda, winked at me and at Anquanna, then coughed, and made the sign of the cross, and struck a chord. Then she stopped, and smacked her lips, and she wrinkled up her nose; and she stood at her piano bench and announced to everybody:

"I would like to dedicate 'the last waltz' to Father Eli Scarcross who is dying tonight at the AIDS ward at St. Osyth's. Eli is the most remarkable man I have ever met, and when he is gone I will miss his presence dearly. Eli has God's love if he has nobody else's. And he has mine. This last waltz is for him."

Only then did she begin. She didn't wait for anybody. So Anquanna and I had to hurry to the floor.

The last waltz—
And I'm with you—
Can it be true?
Last waltz—
The party's end
And two hearts blend. . . .

WALTZING WITH ANQUANNA was like waltzing with a shadow—her svelte figure felt insubstantial to the touch, and no doubt Juice's substitute felt insubstantial too. She had longed to waltz with Juice; I had longed to waltz with Ian; and Ian was waltzing with Courtney Ciccone in a corner of the floor where all the pretty couples were—while Juice had disappeared with his pride into the night, as had Angelina, who longed to waltz with me. Certainly Bubba, who had vanished with his sister, hadn't thought twice about abandoning Grace Cage. On the purlieu of the dance floor the modest Mormon dormouse sat talking to her girlfriend with the choppy hair. They wore doomed but persevering pioneers' expressions, and occasionally the pair would press their foreheads together as if they were conspiring against the whole human race in that way that girls who're never asked to dance tend to do. Then they would smile at all the silly waltzers, and once they even stood up. But they sat back down again.

> *Heaven—*
> *This night was heaven—*
> *For at last I have met you—*
> *Oh! how can I forget you?*

Sr. Aloysius—whose voice was angelic in spite of, or perhaps because of, her age—had taken an obscure melody by Chopin and given it just the sort of wistful little twist that could send a room of young lovers twirling through the ceiling. Anquanna wasn't really a very good dancer, and neither was I—we were *hopeless* together—but Sr. Aloysius invested the waltz with such sadness, such pathos, such willowy yearning that we pressed against each other to stem the melancholy the otherwise hopelessly hopeful words implied:

> *Once more,*
> *Let me repeat—*
> *You're oh! so sweet . . .*
> *Once more,*
> *Remember this—*
> *A goodnight kiss*
> *Means love.*

The waltz would have sounded twice as heavenly with Ian: we would have borne each other up into the empyrean. After all, it was our waltz; it was written for us; it meted out the alpha and omega of our love. I could still close my eyes—as I'd done with my mother, as I'd done with Angelina—and imagine it was him. I could imagine his body brushing up against mine as it had so many times in so many darker waltzes; I could imagine his words as he murmured in my ear: "It's *me*, Toby Sligh. . . . It's *Ian Lamb*, Toby. . . . *I love you so much*. . . . *Never ever let me go!*"; I could imagine the Mickey in his artificial eye, the breeding pool of all the lies he'd spread to seem more truthful. Would it sparkle in the shadow of the mirrored glitterball that projected chilling chiaroscuro phantoms of us all? Would it engender all our skeletons beneath the shadowlight as if the lies that we had told were taking shape before our eyes? How many waltzers—straight or gay—were dishonest? And how many waltzers—true or false—had the virus? And how many would get it? And how many would spread it? And how many would be spared it? And how many would die? A dozen years from then, at a ghostly class reunion, would the waltzers who were living underpopulate the dead? And which side would I be on? And Ian? And Courtney? And Juice? And Anquanna? And Bubba? And Grace? Or would we all be ravaged by an enemy more common: heartbreak—which was deadlier, and easier to catch. How many couples turning circles round each other had betrayed a tender confidence or sacrificed a heart? How many guys (apart from Ian and yours truly) longed to dance with other guys assembled there that night? And how many girls longed to dance with other girls? Or guys with *other* girls? Or girls with *other* guys? Heartbreak didn't give a damn for sexual preference; heartbreak was an equal opportunity destroyer. And if the crosseyed kid who overshot the Teflon arrows could set aside his bow to rearrange these moving targets, how many miserably mismatched waltzers would find themselves coupled with the ones they'd always wanted? Somebody, somewhere, should have shouted out:

"STOP!"

Everyone was executing bad steps gracefully. So I closed my eyes, and leaned my cheek against Anquanna's (feeling as battered as her, in my way); and dreamed about Ian, and about a perfect world, and about the love that stood a chance until the

last waltz ended; and Anquanna said, "*Shhh!* You ain't as bad
as *all that!*"; while Sr. Aloysius spread her tender tendrils
through the night:

> *In my dreams, love,*
> *I'll be dancing*
> *The last waltz with you,*
> *The last waltz with . . .*

"*YOU CARE TO DANCE?*" Ian Lamb interrupted.

He was standing by Anquanna, his hand outstretched to
mine.

"Anquanna, do you mind?" Ian asked my partner.

"Go for it, fellas," she said and stepped aside.

A hush like a brushfire rustled through the crowd as other
couples cleared the floor and Ian drew me to him. It wasn't a
dream; this time I wasn't dreaming: Ian's body was real, and his
smile was real, and his face was fresh and shaven as he pressed
it next to mine. Sr. Aloysius slowed the waltz's presto tempo so
Ian and I could make a full turn round the floor. And nobody
was screaming. Nobody was complaining. Everybody stepped
back and let us have our final waltz. And I thought to myself, as
I held my boy to me, If I'd known it was this easy, if I'd known it
was this simple, if I'd known it was this painless I'd have done it
long ago! Ian danced beautifully; he glided like a swan—and I
could feel my mother gliding somewhere underneath his skin. I
had never been more conscious of the beating of my heart; it
was like an undiscovered ocean opening in my veins. And I
looked at Ian's face, his lovely face, still not believing: Had God
really given me this angel for my own? Was this person, this
courageous young man, really mine? If he had lied to me before,

he had made good on his promise: we were waltzing together at
the Sacred Heart prom! Here we were, at last, in front of everygoddamnbody, glorious and graceful and unabashed in love! We
were even more naked than my parents had been when I spied
them from the rooftop several hours before; we were even more
naked because we'd cast aside the clothes we had worn for so
long and had now forsworn forever. Why wasn't there a riot?
There were riots in my blood. I could feel Ian's soft balls pressing into mine. And our souls were together; they had never been
closer—they were twirling in midair to Sr. Aloysius' waltz. And
I wanted to kiss him. I needed to kiss him. We needed to kiss
more than anything then: but as I looked into his eyes, at his
glittering Mickey, and I looked at his lips, and I finally parted
mine, a laugh escaped his throat, a dry bitter laugh, a laugh like
a pebble skipping down a dirty hillside, while behind it, an
avalanche of jollity began, little laughs and bigger laughs and
rollicking boulders of crushing, mocking sound, and the lights
flooded up and security burst in and Ian jerked his head back
and clapped me on the shoulder, and I stepped away and saw,
separating on the dancefloor, fifty other couples just like Ian
and me, fifty other guys dancing with their secret boyfriends,
fifty sets of lovers who had tumbled from their closets. And their
girlfriends were applauding, and their teachers were applauding, and the media and Mafia, they were applauding, and the
curtains on the stage had swallowed Sr. Aloysius, and I watched
Courtney run and give her loverboy a kiss, and only then did I
realize it had all been prearranged, a practical joke to dispel the
ugly rumors: through the course of the evening all the guys and
their girlfriends had agreed to stage a big faggot waltz for a fi-
nale—as a joke for the media, who were starving for scandal, as
a gag for the faculty, for being such good sports, as a cover for
each other, to cover up the awful truth: that only through a joke
could they turn themselves away from the punchline that would
hover in their shadows all their lives. The only party unamused
by all this was Anquanna. She stood with her hands on her hips

and said: "Jesus! Bunch a' mean motherfuckers, ain't they, Toby Sligh?" And then music, ghost music, swelled to life behind the curtains, a waltz the likes of which no one had ever heard before. And with all the lights on, Grace Cage and her girlfriend with the choppy hair started waltzing in a corner. They waltzed very poorly. They kept tripping on each other. Their breasts were pressed together. Then they stopped and French-kissed. No one said a word. Everybody was quiet. Then the ghost music stopped. But Grace & Co. kept dancing. Lonnie and Johnnie, the former football players, the guards on loan from the mafioso chieftain, finally had to pull the tender couple apart. By then they were screaming. It was triumphant screaming. They were screaming the words I had wanted to scream: "I love you. . . . Forever! . . . *I'll never let you go!*" And they were taken outside, and the media were on them, and already the squad-cars had switched their sirens on, and Principal McDuffy took the stage with a microphone and shouted at the audience, *"Everybody is dismissed!"*

Ian and I stood at opposite corners of the Sacred Heart High cafeteria that night. We were looking at each other across a gulf of faces.

I could see Ian Lamb, but he couldn't see me.

PRINCIPAL MCDUFFY DIDN'T have any trouble convincing everybody at the prom to go home. I sat in the center of the dancefloor watching them file outside, couple by couple. Occasionally the press would pull a guy and girl aside and ask their opinion of the lesbian lovers. "Everybody thought it would be fags," they confided. "We had no idea it was gonna be dykes!" Courtney Ciccone left, crying hysterically. I wanted to smack her. Why should *she* cry? She wasn't the one who'd be taken downtown and questioned about offenses that weren't even on the books. She wasn't the one who would have to explain to her parents why she preferred pussy to dick. And she wasn't the one who had posed as a Mormon to shake bloodhounds off the scent of her sexuality. You could hand it to Grace—she was one clever cookie. She had blinded everybody with their own hypocrisy.

THE LIMOUSINE DRIVER was nowhere to be found, leaving Anquanna and me stranded on our desert island.

"Had to call my cousin," Anquanna reported. "Peaches said my mama Artremease has disappeared, so she's gonna dress my niece and they're gonna pick us up. Peaches drives a cab."

"I know."

"*How you know?*"

I was sitting on the dancefloor and I showed no sign of moving.

"How you know, Toby?"

"Some things I just *know.*"

Anquanna looked at me; you could tell she was troubled.

"I'll be waiting outside. Peaches comes, we'll toot the horn. You comin' with, Toby?"

Everybody had left.

"Dunno." I exhaled. "Nowhere to go to."

"You spend the night at my place," Anquanna suggested. "Then, when Juice gets in, you two, you know, can *talk.* I'm sorry about Ian," she said, apologetic.

I smiled.

"You love him?"

I nodded. "Uh-huh."

Anquanna bent down in her Pierre Cardin gown, swept the bangs off my forehead, and kissed my frigid cheek.

"You love somebody no matter what they do, and then you just keep lovin' till there's nothing left of you. Good night, Toby

Sligh," Anquanna said and stood to go. "Why you gay boys gotta be so *tasty?* Now, you come when my cousin honks the horn."

LIKE A LITTLE kid abandoned by his family at the beach, I sat amid the ruins of other people's castles waiting for my parents to come and rescue me. Outside a number of security guards were talking to the press, who hadn't left yet. In fact, as predicted, CNN had arrived and were setting up lights in the lot outside the building. This made Twizzler, the mafioso, nervous. He stood nearby slicing licorice with a switchblade, chewing it, and staring at me menacingly. So I improvised a kingdom out of beachsand on the dancefloor, playing patty-cake-patty-cake and getting really filthy. "Hey, fella," Twizzler muttered. "Ain't you got a lift?" "I'm a orphan," I replied, and tried to wipe my hands clean. But the sand—funny stuff, a sort of artificial pow-der—got up my nose, and then I started sneezing. In fact, I sneezed so badly I couldn't catch my breath, and my heart was pumping wildly as Twizzler helped me up. With his switchblade in one hand and licorice in the other, he led me toward the stage, where someone plunked out "Heart and Soul." It was the musically retarded two-knuckled version, and Twizzler's grip closed like a vise around my wrist, and I was saying, "Hey, *hey!* You can lemme go now, *hey!*" when Leonard Compton stuck his bloody nose between the curtains and whispered to Twizzler, "Let him go—Tobe's with me."

WE SAT IN two clumps on the cluttered-up stage like Vladimir and Estragon having met Godot. Outside we heard reporters, police and security. Somewhere beyond the curtain, someone was sweeping up. I could almost picture Twizzler manhandling a broomstick, masticating licorice, and scowling at the world. If Juice hadn't been there, would Twizzler have done more than carve licorice with that switchblade of his? I wouldn't think about it; I was safe, for the moment. My pride alone was damaged; and I was with Juice. He lay down on the stage and stretched out his legs, and I lay down beside him and stretched out my legs. Then we lay together, breathing softly in the dark, our bodies barely touching, side by side, in the night.

"Most of them kegs are filled with cocaine, Toby."

"I think I kinda sorta went and figured that one out."

"Somebody accidentally dumped some on the floor," Juice continued, sneezing. "My boss was really pissed."

"Your boss?"

"Fella Twizzler. The guy that I work for. His boss—"

Juice's beeper went off and he hit it.

"What's it all worth?"

"Couple hundred million dollars."

"Why'd they bring it here?"

"Because the ports was crawling. And who's gonna raid, like, a senior *prom*, Toby? We called in the bomb scare. I arranged the whole thing."

"Z'at why your mother slapped you?"

"She slapped me 'cause she loves me."

I slapped him.

"Thanks, Toby," he said.

He slapped me back.

"You should stop dealing," I said. "It's fuckin' stupid."

"And you should stop fucking Ian Lamb up the ass."

"I haven't fucked Ian up the ass!" I protested.

Juice rolled over.

"Has he fucked *you* up the ass?"

I was quiet.

"Who's stupid? Who's *stupid*, Toby Sligh?"

Juice reached over and draped an arm across me. Reaching over, I draped an arm across him.

"You're talking less black."

"And you're talking less faggot."

"I talk like a faggot?"

"Sometimes you do, yeah."

Juice raised his head and I slid my arm beneath it; I raised my head and he slid *his* arm beneath.

"Juice, who's E-Eye?"

His body twitched a little.

"Who's E-Eye, Leonard?"

I could feel him looking at me.

"Who told you 'bout E-Eye?"

"Nobody told me. . . . Anquanna talked about him in the limousine, remember?"

Outside, in the night, thunder boomed across the sky. We could hear it, like God rearranging furniture.

"E-Eye was my half brother," Leonard Compton said.

"What happened?"

"He died."

"And what did he die of?"

"Crack," Juice whispered. "Smoking crack, like my father."

"Why'd they call him E-Eye?"

" 'Cause Eddy lost his eye."

"And how'd he lose his eye?"

"Someone shot him with a gun."

"Who did?"

"I did. We was just kids. We was playin' with a BB gun. I pointed it and—"

Thunder.

"That was my fault," Juice said. "And everything. My mama even said so. She told me so tonight."

"What was he like?"

"What do you care, Tobias?"

"I just wanna know."

Juice moved in closer to me.

"E-Eye was smart. He was smart and he was funny."

"So why'd he do crack?"

"Because he got a taste. Would you like a taste, Toby? I got some in my pocket."

"No, thanks," I told him.

"You just saved your own life. . . ."

"You really loved your brother?"

Juice nodded in my shoulder.

"Did he overdose on crack?"

"E-Eye . . . he got killed."

"How'd he get—?"

"Um, he was teaching me, Toby."

"Teaching you what?"

"Teaching me how to *score*. I asked him to teach me—E-Eye was a teacher—and he stole a bunch of crack, and somebody gunned him down. He was crossing a street, he was running toward me, and I was calling to him . . . and it burst right through his chest."

"What did?"

"The bullets. The *bullets* did, Toby. He was running toward me. And they shot him through the back."

Outside, in the night, we could hear sirens calling. We could hear rain falling on the corrugated roof.

"So you deal even after your brother got murdered?"

"I have my reasons, Toby Sligh," Leonard Compton said.

"Who killed your brother?"

"Cunt Twizzler works for."

"How do you know?"

" 'Cause he's owned the streets for years."

"How can you deal?"

"I got my reasons, Toby. You can't bite the hand that bleeds you, not unless you're sly. How'd Ian lose his eye?"

"You know, he never told me."

"Guess he got his reasons too," Juice said, and slapped me. "Or else he doesn't love you."

"Ian Lamb loves me."

"If you love someone . . ."

"Yeah?"

"Then you tell . . ."

"What?"

"Everything."

Juice's beeper sounded and he slapped it again. Then he sat up and his hand fell on my ankle.

"Juice," I said, sniffling. "I wanna ask you something. Why do you like me?"

I was looking up at him.

"Sit up, Toby."

He poked me in the ribs.

"Sit up, Tobias, and ask me that again."

"Why do you like me?" I repeated, in a whisper. "Of all the people in our class, why'd you choose me for a friend?"

Juice wrapped his arms around his knees and pressed against me. I wrapped my arms around my knees and pressed against him.

"I like you, Toby Sligh," Leonard Compton began, his mouth in the darkness breathing breath into mine, "I like you, Toby Sligh, 'cause you're such a goddamn baby, and because you believe all the bullshit everybody tell you, and because you'd follow Freddy Krueger into Toys 'Я' Us. I like you, Toby Sligh, 'cause you're so fuckin' *white*. Everything you do is white— folks can always see it comin'! You're a fag and people know it! You're a kid and people know it! And when it comes to other people, Toby White Boy don't know *shit!* You're the baby sea tortoise in Biology movies, at night, in the moonlight, busting outta its shell—and the birds a' prey are circling, and the cameras are rolling, and I just wanna help your little bootie along. 'Cause if you make it to the water, and the waves don't getchoo, and the sharks don't getchoo, you're gonna swim a thousand miles. You're gonna swim a thousand miles and you're gonna find your *island*. That's why I like you, Toby Sligh," Juice said.

"How come you like *me?*" Juice asked, after a while, when he had let me think about the things that he had said.

"I like you, Leonard Compton, 'cause you helped me with that statue."

"What statue?" Leonard said. Then he grinned. "Oh, *that*."

On the dancefloor, somewhere beyond the drawn curtains, security guards and janitors were breaking down chairs. Twizzler the gangster had finished sweeping up—the empty kegs of cocaine were probably full again. Of course, with all those cameras, the mafia were helpless. They couldn't move their shipment till the media cleared out.

"How much money will you make tonight, Juice?"

"Already been paid: a hundred thousand."

"So why'd you tear up all that cash in the chapel?"

"That was funny money. The coke was fake too."

"Then why does Thomas want it?"

"Thomas *wants* something, boyee?"

"I meant to—"

"Tobias?"

I was looking at my hands.

"I promised I'd tell him where your drugs were stashed, Juice. I promised I would help him hand you over to the cops."

"When did you promise?"

"By midnight tonight."

"It's *past* midnight, Toby."

Juice's beeper started beeping.

"Those drugs weren't real. That money wasn't real. Det. Thomas isn't real. *And he wants something else.*"

"What does he want?"

Juice switched off his beeper.

"I dunno, Tobe. You'll just have to wait and see."

Outside, in the night, we could hear helicopters. They charged the cafeteria and chattered away.

"But that stuff in the kegs—that stuff is real, right?"

"Is it ever, Tobias. Colombia's finest."

"And they'll turn it into crack."

Juice didn't say a word.

"And the crack'll be used by people like your brother."

Juice popped his knuckles and sighed a feeble sigh.

"It should make you sick to be a dealer, Leonard Compton."

"Maybe I should go and get a job at Burger King."

Juice's beeper beeped, and he slapped it off again.

"Who's beepin', Juice?"

"Just my fuckin' father."

"What does he want?"

"What else? He wants a hit."

"Who's Det. Thomas?"

"A punk, like I tol' you."

"I saw what he did to you back in that alley."

"You saw that?" Juice said.

I nodded.

"Uh huh . . . Why'd you let him do that?"

"Two against one."

"You were bigger than both of 'em."

"G., I ain't *that* big."

Juice started shivering softly in the darkness. I was shivering, too. We pressed up against each other.

"Thomas has a picture of you and me dealing."

"Can't prove nothing with a picture, Toby Sligh."

"He showed it to me outside your dad's apartment."

"When was that, Toby?"

Juice had stopped breathing.

"I was outside in your Buick. Thomas pulled up in the Plymouth. I left Donna playing jacks with some girls in the stairwell. When I got back down, Det. Thomas was there. He had a briefcase with some pictures. They were pictures of my parents."

"Did he see where my daddy lived?"

"What?"

Juice was nervous.

"Do you think he saw the apartment you came out of, Toby Sligh?"

"Dunno," I told him. "He was waiting outside. He might have. He might have seen me coming out of—"

"Shit!"

Juice was sitting up now, shaking in the darkness. I huddled up against him.

"What's the matter, Juice?"

"I don't want my father getting caught up in this bullshit!" His beeper went off, and he slapped the thing again. "My father's got problems *enough*, Toby Sligh."

"Do you think Det. Thomas—"

"He's capable of anything."

"What's he want from me?"

"How should I know, Toby?"

"He told me those kids at Anquanna's school were busted."

"That's a bold-faced lie," Juice said. "Nobody was."

"But they beat up Anquanna."

"She blames me for that."

"She has a right to blame you."

"I know it," Juice said.

"Our lives are complicated, Leonard Compton," I concluded.

Juice was very quiet; then his laughter blew the roof.

"That's just the kinda stupid thing Toby Sligh would say! That's just the kinda lame-ass comment Toby Sligh would make at a moment like this! You're one big dumb motherfucker, ain'tchoo, Toby?" Juice hooted, and caught me in a headlock, and pinned me.

"Lemme up!" I shouted.

"You're Jacob! I'm the angel!"

"Since when'd you get religion?"

We were breathing in the dark.

"I guess we'd better go," Juice said.

We were lying there. We were both just lying there. We were lying there.

"Uh-huh," I said. "I guess we'd better go."

I was looking at Juice; we were looking at each other.

"Juice?"

"Uh-huh?"

"Have you ever?"

"Uh-huh?"

"Have you ever, umm—"

"What?"

"Have you ever . . . Never mind."

Juice wasn't moving. It had stopped raining. We could hear raindrops dripdripdripping off the roof.

"Have you ever, uh—"

"Yeah?"

"Have you ever, like—"

"What?"

"Have you ever, um—"

"Toby . . ."

And I put my lips to his.

Juice started coughing. His hand was on my shoulder. I tried again to kiss him, but he turned his face away.

"I think we better go now."

"Uh-huh."

"We're just friends."

"My best friend," I told him.

And I helped him off the floor.

WE WERE SITTING in the cab of the white limousine that was owned by the mob and which the driver had abandoned. It was hidden behind punk trees, and Juice had the keys, and we saw a raincloud in the shape of a hand passing over Sa-

cred Heart as we left our alma mater. Juice was very quiet as we
headed crosstown. He pulled onto the interstate, driving too
smoothly. I'd stashed Ian's yearbook in the backseat of the limo
and when I went to look through it, there were pages ripped out.
I flipped to the index and double-checked quickly: they were
the pages on which Ian's photo had appeared. I abandoned the
yearbook and stared at the night, and Leonard Compton looked
at me and handed me the cellular.

"Dial 911."

"What?"

"Dial it, Toby."

I dialed 911 and Juice said, "Give it here."

"THIS IS LEONARD Compton," Leonard Compton announced to the little voice chirping at him on the other
end. "Am I being tape-recorded?" The little voice chirped yes.
"Well, that's good. 'Cause I'll only say this once. I'm driving on
the interstate in an unmarked limo owned by Santo Rondi; he's
a druglord, and my boss. Tonight we got a avalanche of cocaine
from Bogotá and it's sitting in about a couple dozen empty beer
kegs in the Sacred Heart cafeteria, where they just had prom.
For the last four years I have worked for Santo Rondi and have
sold bogus drugs to different suckers in the area. The narcotics
I received for distribution from Rondi have been given to my
guidance counselor, Mr. Jerry Kickliter, who has kept them in a
safe deposit box in his office. I have made in excess of three
hundred thousand dollars selling phony product to students and
friends—money I intend to return, *after expenses.* I was recently
threatened by one of Rondi's stooges—a white guy who goes by
the alias of 'Thomas'—for pushing bogus product at my cousin's
public school. And I was given an additional hundred thousand
dollars for planning the storage of the Bogotá shipment at the

senior prom at Sacred Heart High. My confession and my ef-
forts to get Santo Rondi arraigned have been part of a special
community service project designed under the supervision of
my counselor, Jerry Kickliter. Mr. Kickliter has advised me to
request the intervention of the Witness Protection Program provided by the FBI and will appear with my mama and my auntie
Artremease at the downtown police precinct at six o'clock this
morning, after and on the condition of Santo Rondi's arrest. If
Rondi is not arrested, I will not make my appearance and Mr.
Kickliter will deny everything I have just said. Rondi's the
motherfucker whose punks killed my brother and if you guys
don't bust him I sure as fuck will! I haven't worked four years
just to go to the prom, *even though it was a good time, wasn't it,
Tobias?* So this is Leonard Compton, informer, signing off. See
you in the dawn's early light, motherfuckers."

"You forgot to say 'Peace.' "

"Oh yeah," Juice added: *"Peace."*

Juice's beeper went off.

"Better go check on my father."

A WHITE PLYMOUTH was parked in front of Juice's dad's
apartment. The headlights were on and they glowed like
the eyes of an alligator gliding through a storm in the night.
Leonard took an automatic from the glove compartment and
looked at me once and stuffed it down his cummerbund.

"What are we gonna do?" I asked Leonard Compton.

We had parked the limousine on the side of the building.

"We ain't gonna do a damn *thing*, Toby Sligh. You're gonna
stay here while I check on my father."

"What if Det. Thomas is up there with a *gun?"*

Juice checked his automatic to make sure it was loaded.

"Think I like to play with automatics, Toby Sligh?"

"What if Thomas comes for me while you're up there with
your father?"

"There's another automatic hidden underneath the dash."

Juice produced it, loaded it, and handed it to me.

"I get sick to my stomach holding something like this."

"Would you feel any better holding a wreath?"

The rain started falling and Juice switched off his beeper—
the noise of it was something we had sort of gotten used to.

Juice said, "Should've known from the moment you told me.
Should've known that that bastard would come after my daddy."

Juice gave me the keys to the limousine. Then we switched
positions. I was in the driver's seat.

"You stay here, Toby. You keep the engine running. If I'm not
out with my pops *in five minutes,* or if you hear *gunshots,* you
call the police."

Juice had his hand on the door to the limo and was about to
step out when he stopped and looked at me.

"Hey, G., it's me. It's your old buddy, Leonard. . . . *I been
your friend, ain't I?*"

I nodded; he smiled.

"You follow in after me, Toby? *I'll shoot you.* I'll put a bullet
through you 'fore yo' ass is in the *door.*"

AFTER FIVE MINUTES I honked the horn twice, left the limousine idling, and zigzagged through the storm. I had
called the cops, like Juice had requested, but unlike he'd requested, I wouldn't wait for them. As I approached the stairwell
where I had left Donna, my knees buckled. But I got back up
again. And I couldn't help thinking about Leonard Compton
running with that parachute strapped to his back as I crept up
the stairs, and I stepped down the hallway, and I stopped at
Leonard's father's door and pressed my ear against it. I could

make out two voices—Det. Thomas's and Juice's. And then I heard a third. It belonged to Juice's father.

"You know where she lives!"

"I ain't got no idea."

"I'll shoot the old man!"

"Do I care if I live?"

"Where's Toby Sligh!"

"G., how should I know?"

"You tell me where she lives or—"

"Do I care? Think I care?"

I knocked on the door.

"Leonard! It's Toby!"

The voices went quiet. I unpocketed the gun.

"Leonard! It's Toby! I'm coming in, Leonard!"

I turned the knob slowly and entered the apartment.

DET. THOMAS WAS sitting on the couch with Leonard's father, the barrel of a pistol pressed to Leonard's father's forehead. Leonard's father sat with a phone in his lap and was dialing Juice's beeper number over and over. "I have to call Leonard," Juice's father was saying. "I have to call Leonard . . . he's *such* a clever boy."

"Take the gun from Toby," Det. Thomas ordered. Juice took my automatic and tossed it in a corner. "Hello," Juice's father said, smiling up at me. He was shaking and a crackpipe stuffed with crack lay before him. Juice stood beneath a naked lightbulb in a corner. "Do I care if I live?" Juice's father was saying. *"Do I care if I live? Do I care? Think I care?"*

"Maybe you can tell me where Compton's stash is hidden," Det. Thomas began, and tapped his finger on the trigger.

"Tell him what happened, Toby Sligh," Juice said.

"Juice ate it. It was phony. And the money was bogus. There's a hundred thousand dollars in the limo, if you want it."

"That's not what I *want*, Toby Sligh," Thomas said. *"Tell me where your mother is."*

Mr. Compton started speaking: *"Valilian Compton, you're a beautiful woman. . . . Will you dance with me, Valilian? Will you marry me?"*

"The drugs aren't there! I told you, Juice ate 'em!"

"That wasn't the deal—"

"But the drugs aren't there!"

"Tell me where your mother is," Thomas said evenly. "Tell me where your mother is or I'll blow this old man's brains out."

"Do I care? Think I care?" Juice's father was saying. *"Do I care? Think I care?"*

He was reaching for the crackpipe.

"I told you you never should've come here, Toby."

We could hear sirens.

Thomas smiled, "Those for me?"

With the gun to his forehead, Edward Compton lit the crack-pipe, sucked it till it sparkled, and collapsed back on the couch.

"We can call him Leonard. How's that sound, Valilian? He has his mama's looks, but he's got his daddy's brains!"

"Did you phone the police? Tell the truth, Toby Sligh."

Thomas aimed the gun at me; I nodded.

"Naughty, naughty."

"You got all A's? Let me see your report card! Eddy, don't be jealous! You had your share of glory!"

"Compton is right. You never should have come here. And now we're gonna make another deal, Toby Sligh."

Thomas rose from the couch. He aimed the gun at Juice's fa-ther. He was moving toward a catwalk beyond an open window. "I'm gonna count ten, and you'll tell me where your mom is. If you don't"—he yanked the phone cord—"Leonard Compton's father dies. And if you end up giving me a bogus address, I'll find your father, Toby, and I'll shoot him. Understand? One—"

Juice said, "He's a coward, Toby Sligh."

"Two—"

"*Jesus, Juice!*"

The sirens were approaching.

"Three—"

"Don't, Toby! He's a coward and a liar!"

"Four!"

Thomas drew a bead on Juice's father's head.

"Five."

"*I'll call Leonard. . . . he's such a clever child.*"

"Six."

"*Look at E-Eye! E-Eye's lyin' on the ground!*"

"Seven!"

"*You're too good! You're too good for me, Valilian!*"

"Eight!"

"*Do I care? Think I care if I live?*"

"Nine!"

"*Someday, Leonard, you will make us very happy!*"

"Ten! It's your last chance!"

And I gave him Mom's address.

AS SOON AS I had, Thomas leapt from the window and Juice's father crumpled in a pile on the floor. He was fighting for air, and clutching his chest, and Leonard screamed and lifted him and held him aloft in his trembling arms. Outside it was storming and I got the automatic and the sirens that were singing in the night had passed us by. "Go to your mother, Toby Sligh! *Warn your mother!*" And I left Leonard standing there, cradling the body, rocking his father in his arms: "*God, I'm sorry!*"

✳ AS I HURTLED down the stairwell I heard shots exploding, and when I got to the limo the windows were shattered and the engine was on fire and the tires were destroyed. I rescued Juice's money—Thomas hadn't touched it—and stuffed it and the automatic down my cummerbund. On the cellular phone I got through to 911, then I fished Peaches' telephone number from my wallet and rapid-fire dialed her and begged her to hurry. *"Keep your pants on, Tiger, I'm right around the corner!"* She arrived at the same time the paramedics did. "Toby!" she hollered. "Take a look at that limo! Who the ambulance for?" "It's for Leonard Compton's father." "You know Leonard's daddy?" she asked. I nodded. "Here," I said. I gave her the $100,000. "This money's dirty," Peaches said, and wouldn't touch it. "My mom is in danger! I need your taxi, Peaches!" Peaches was looking at the burning limousine. *"I'm Leonard Compton's friend! You gotta believe me!"*

She shouted out the window at the paramedic driver: "Apartment 2B! Hurry up! Someone's dying!" Then she jumped from the taxi and handed me the keys and said, "Be careful, white boy," and she hustled for the stairwell. In the rearview mirror I saw her turn around: "Toby! Come back! *I forgot something, Toby!*"

But Peaches was too late; Toby Sligh was gone already.

✳ I TOOK THE expressway that cut across town and threw the gun and Juice's money in the blanket-strewn backseat. I thought I heard a noise like an animal crying, a faint dreamy noise. But I was just imagining.

> *Wont't you help to sing*
> *These songs of freedom?*
> *'Cause they're all I've ever had—*
> *Redemption songs. . . .*

The storm was beginning to cataract now as I passed a jacaranda bleeding on a median. It was a beautiful tree, top-heavy with flowers, and the blossoms made a carpet of violet on the highway. I was thinking of my mother, and my father, and Ian; I was thinking of Juice with his father in his arms; I was thinking of Angelina dancing in the library; I was thinking of Grace and her anonymous friend; and I was thinking of Eli alone, at St. Osyth's, and the promise I had made, and the things that we had said. I listened to the rain and pulled the beeper from my pocket—the beeper St. Osyth's had given to me. Only then did I see that someone had switched it off—that it had been switched off, in fact, the whole evening. So I switched it back on and shoved it in my pocket, and almost immediately it began to beep; and as I left the expressway and arrived at my mother's, I turned down the stereo and drew from my pocket the weathered brown bag Ian Lamb had given to me. In it was a rose and an artificial eye. The petals were withered. The eye had been smashed.

Full fadom five thy father lies,
Of his bones are coral made:
These are pearls that were his eyes:
Nothing of him that doth fade,
But doth suffer a sea-change
Into something rich and strange,
Sea-nymphs hourly rings his knell:
Ding dong.
Hark now I hear him—ding-dong bell. . . .

✸ AS I WALKED up the drive to my mother's apartment, past the white Plymouth, which was sideways in the yard, I did not pay attention to the Polaroid photographs strewn on the ground, and in the bushes, and in the trees; I did not pay attention to the photos of the three of them taken together seventeen years before; I did not pay attention to the picture of my parents kissing either cheek of a young Det. Thomas; I didn't pay attention to the picture of my mother sandwiched in between their naked bodies in bed; I didn't pay attention to the picture of my father, younger and handsomer and wrestling with Thomas in the frontyard of a house I had never seen till then; I didn't pay attention to the picture of my mother standing on the shoulders of Thomas and my father with her hands on her hips, at an unknown beach; I didn't pay attention to the photo of my mother kissing my father in the backseat of a Chevy; and I didn't pay attention to the photo of my mother kissing Det. Thomas in the same backseat; and I didn't pay attention to the picture of my mother, now slightly pregnant and staring at the camera while a thumb, swollen with whorls, obtruded on the photo and hinted at more than the photographer's identity. I only paid attention (Ian's bag in my pocket, the gun and drug money abandoned in the cab) to the pictures of Ian woven through the weeping willow, yearbook photos threaded onto slender willow branches—a younger Ian, probably no more than fourteen, standing in a swimsuit beside a man who looked like Scarcross, a younger, haler Scarcross with a staff and gorgeous robes. I only paid attention to a sound like a machine, as if God were wandering the world devouring metal. Jimi Hendrix was playing on the white Plymouth's radio, the volume cranked and booming out across the cringing night:

> *You jump in front of my car*
> *When you know all the time*
> *That 90 miles an hour, girl,*
> *Is the speed I drive.*
> *You say it's all right,*

You don't mind a little pain;
You say you just want me to
Take you for a drive! . . .

My mother was crying on the side of the house, her head in her hands, as I approached unseen. Her wedding dress was muddy in a puddle at her feet, and her shotgun lay broken and empty of shells. At the threshold to the door I spied the loaded pistol Thomas had held to Leonard Compton's father's forehead: it too lay open and empty of bullets—as if, out of honor, all guns had been relinquished. The efficiency was empty, except for cardboard boxes which lay packed and neatly stacked beside the doorless frontdoor. As I passed through the apartment, the pounding sound of metal clashed with Jimi Hendrix in the deafening night:

You're just like
Crosstown traffic!
So hard to get through to you!
Crosstown traffic!
I don't need to run over you!
Crosstown traffic!
All you do is slow me down!
I'm tryin' to get on the other side of town. . . .

Then, through a hole in the devastated plaster, I spotted my father opposite Thomas, naked from the waist up, crouching with a sledgehammer, reducing Christ's Chevy to a twisted heap of metal as Thomas, also shirtless, matched my father blow for blow. Dad would look at Thomas and obliterate a windshield; Thomas would respond by walloping a taillight. They circled each other like the cats in the storm, like the toms I had seen the day I got ill, with no intent to kill, just orbiting each other, engaged in a violent and meaningless dance, taking out their anger on the abject Chevrolet which received their rain of blows with tortured shouts of mangled metal. Their bare feet shuffled unharmed through shards of glass, their white eyes were livid

with something like love, the night was thick and dank as sweat
sweltered off their bodies, and they could hear my mother in between their hammer blows while Jimi Hendrix sang to the siren-
less night:

> *I'm not the only soul*
> *Who's accused of hit and run;*
> *Tire tracks all across your back—*
> *I can see you've had your fun;*
> *But, darling, can't you see*
> *My signals turn from green to red?*
> *And with you I can see a traffic jam*
> *Way up ahead! It's just like . . .*

When at last Mom emerged from the side of the house, she was
holding the gun I had stashed in Christ's Corvair. Mom gripped
the handle. She was fingering the trigger. And she saw me and
shouted, *"Get the hell out of here!"* When Det. Thomas saw me
he abandoned his hammer, and my father dropped his: and they
landed on each other. They were rolling in the glass beside the
crucified Chevy, their tumbling bodies indistinct and glistening
with blood; and my mother was watching them, trying to decide
when to shoot, if to shoot, who to shoot, what to shoot. Then
Thomas did something and my dad stopped moving, and Thomas
rose above my father and looked at Mom and me. "You're mine!"
Thomas roared. *"I've waited too long! I love both of you! You're
mine! And I'm sorry. . . ."* And his face pale and weeping, his
body drained and trembling, the muscles of his chest and torso
fluttering with tics, Thomas swayed a little in the heat, as if faint,
as if something were devouring him from the inside, and he shut
his twitching eyes, and he lifted his chin, and with barely the
strength left to raise the sledgehammer, he raised it; and my
mother dropped the gun and said, *"I can't!"* So I picked up the
firearm and pointed it at Thomas, who stood with the hammer
poised above my father's head. *"You can't, Toby Sligh! You
wouldn't if you knew! We shared your mother, Toby! We'll always*

share your mother! I'm the one who's searched for her for seven-
teen years! I'm the one who's dreamed about the son he never had!
I'm the one who's lived a life of loneliness and lies! Aren't I enti-
tled to the truth? Don't I have a right to answers? Unless—! Un-
less—!" Thomas swayed and drew a breath. And just as he was
about to bring the sledgehammer down, my father paralytic in a
scattering of glass, we all heard a voice, a tiny voice cry,
"Jacaranda!" and we turned to see Donna, Peaches' stowaway
cousin, stumbling toward us, a lost look in her eyes. In one hand
she held a gun, in the other she held money; and she left a trail of
bills in her sleepy, awkward wake. *"Jacaranda!"* she shouted,
and aimed the gun at no one, and I grabbed the weapon from her,
and I took her by the hand. "C'mon, Donna," I told her. "Let's get
outta here. . . ." And as we turned our backs I thought I heard a
branch breaking—a sharp protracted crack, like a shattering
limb—and I turned to see Thomas collapse across my father. He
was having convulsions, and my dad had awakened, and he and
my mother steadied Thomas in their arms. "Your uncle's diabetic," my mother explained. "Uncle Thomas, Toby—he's hypo-
glycemic. There's some O.J. in the icebox. Would you put some
sugar in it?" And when I returned I knelt down between them
and lifted the juice to Thomas' lips, and my father held the body
of his brother in his arms, and Donna was afraid and looked
away; but I didn't. When Det. Thomas at last came to, he pressed
his ringfinger to my father's gory chest, and he brushed away the
bangs from my forehead with his free hand, and drew an upside-
down cross, and whispered, *"L-I-E."* I didn't know if my uncle
was my uncle or my father. In fact, I didn't care. Everybody was
alive. And as we drove in Peaches' cab to St. Osyth's Hospital,
Donna in the frontseat laughing at my beeping beeper, and as I
helped the brothers stagger in the E.R. arm in arm, my mother
already heading for the interstate, I thought to myself, *I have two*
fathers: one who loves, and one who lies. I've got one of each kind.

✸ I PARKED PEACHES' cab beside a jacaranda dripping purple petals in the pinwheeling rain. The petals tumbled
down and made a quilt across the windshield. Donna pressed
her hands against the cumbersome glass.

It was three in the morning. High above, in St. Osyth's, a light
burned brightly, and figures cast shadows. The beeper kept
beeping. I could hear somebody moving. Then a voice unraveled in the hollow of my ear:

> *Full fadom five thy father lies,*
> *Of his lies is Toby made;*
> *These are pearls that were my eyes:*
> *Nothing of Eli that doth fade,*
> *But doth suffer a sea-change*
> *Into something rich and strange.*
> *Ian hourly rings his knell:*
> *Ding-dong.*
> *Hark! now I hear him—ding-dong, bell.*

The rain stopped. Donna got out to gather flowers. Ian's face
blossomed in the rearview mirror. It was ashen. His left eye was
gutted and weeping. His hands folded down across my face, like
tattered wings.

"*Toby, forgive me, for I have sinned. . . . It has been four years
since my last confession, and these are my sins . . .*"

✸ "*I MET ELI SCARCROSS at school in New Orleans. I was fourteen when he fucked me up the ass. I didn't have to let him,
but I let him, Toby Sligh. We were in* The Tempest. *We didn't tell
a soul. . . .*

"*Three years later he was too sick to teach. We were in love,
but he had to go away. When I tested positive for the HIV virus, I
put a pair of sewing scissors in my left eye. I spent that Christmas*

at a psychiatric clinic. When I got better my family moved to Florida. . . .

"How did I know Fr. Scarcross would follow me? How did I know he would come here to die? When he spoke to us in chapel, I knew I had to see him. Love is an infection. It never leaves your blood.

"But I couldn't face him, Toby. I couldn't face his body. The way it looked that day in chapel was too much. This was the body I had touched, Toby Sligh. This was the body I had let touch me. Looking at it, I felt like I was looking at myself. I was looking at what happens when love and lies collide. . . .

"And so I made a plan—I'm deadly clever, Toby—I would use you as an earpiece for my lonely dying God. He would speak to you the final words he would have spoken to me had I found the strength to listen, which I knew I never would. And, to be fair, I would help you with your mother—who had slept with two brothers, and who had married neither, and who, very soon, would be forced to choose again. . . ."

"Did you sleep with my mother?"

"No, Toby Sligh."

"Have you given me the virus?"

"If I have, will you forgive me? I forgave Elijah. I gave him your rose. Forgiveness is the only act greater than love."

His hands smelled faintly of flowers and rain. Ian's fingers opened, and I saw a purple lesion.

"I can't leave till you forgive me, Toby Sligh. I know that you love me, but you have to let me go. You were so lonely, like I was before Eli. Eli was my lover. Eli was my lie. . . ."

"Did he know he had the virus?"

"No. I don't think so. He wasn't sick then. . . . And I forgive him all the same."

I looked at the rose and the artificial eye that lay scattered and shattered in the weathered brown bag.

"I'm going to New Orleans. I'm never coming back. You have to kiss me, Toby. You have to let me go. . . ."

Outside, Donna's arms were full of purple petals. The rain had started up again. She was laughing at it.

"He was Prospero. . . . I was Ariel. . . . It started with a kiss. . . . It always starts with a kiss. . . . Forgive me, Toby Sligh . . . Forgive us all, Toby. . . . Forgive Fr. Scarcross for sleeping with a child. . . . Forgive your parents for the secrets of their past. . . . Forgive Juice for dealing the drugs that killed his brother. . . . Forgive Angelina for being your friend. . . . Forgive us our sins. . . . Forgive our trespasses. . . . We're lonely, like God is. . . . We're liars, Toby Sligh—"

"I'm not a liar, Ian," I said.

He was quiet. Outside, Donna Compton was laughing in the rain.

"That's the only lie I've ever heard you tell, Toby Sligh," Ian Lamb said, and pressed his mouth against my ear. *"Kiss me, Tobias. Say that you love me. . . . Say that you forgive me. . . . Release me, Toby Sligh. . . ."*

I looked at his face in the rearview mirror. Lifting my lips, I kissed his reflection.

"Goodbye, Toby Angel," Ian said, and got out.

And then I knew I loved him because I set him free.

SEATED IN A CIRCLE around Elijah Scarcross were Jerry Kickliter, Lucinda Delaney, Sr. Cynthia Rose, and Sr. Aloysius. Fr. Scarcross was breathing in great bursting breaths, like an ancient sea animal surfacing for air.

Kickliter stood, and Sr. Aloysius stood, and Lucinda said, "Toby, come say goodbye to Eli." With Donna in my arms I approached the dying man and knelt down beside him and said, "Hello, Elijah."

I felt somebody wrap a light coat around my shoulders. I was shivering, I guess. Donna giggled at the ceiling.

"What's it look like on the other side, Eli?" I whispered to Scarcross, and listened to his rattling breathing. "Do children who lie go to paradise, Father? Or is there only room for the ones who tell the truth? I'm sorry I didn't come sooner, like I promised. I would have come sooner, but . . ." I reached for his hand. "Would you hear my confession if I told it, Fr. Scarcross? Is it even worth telling? Would anybody hear?"

Donna laughed aloud and scattered petals on the bed. Eli started nodding and his chest began to heave. Then he stopped and his hand shot up, and Donna caught it like a bird, and he said, *"Ariel."* He was still. Donna laughed. Somebody said, "It's over." And Sr. Aloysius crossed herself and left the room.

In the bed beside Eli's, Magda was crying. Her voice was unwinding like a siren in the night. From the window, through the rain, which was starting up again, I could see Ian Lamb hitchhiking on the roadside, and Peaches' yellow taxi parked beside the jacaranda, and then a Ferrari, an immaculate Ferrari, pulled up into the parking lot and idled with its brights on.

"See ya, Fr. Scarcross," I said and bent to kiss him. "You can have my forgiveness, if God will have mine."

IN THE PARKING lot Angelina sat on the Ferrari with a copy of *Don Quixote* smearing in her lap. In the backseat, her brother Bubba Fishback was snoring. It was four in the morning. The rain was pissing down.

"I saw it on television," Angelina began. "Who would have thought Grace Cage and her girlfriend? . . . I'm sorry I thought you were gay, Toby Sligh."

"I *am* gay," I told her.

Angelina said, "I know."

✸ IN THE BIGGEST drug bust in local media history, Santo Rondi and his men were rounded up and arrested. Juice was acquitted, became a local hero, and received an award for community service, which meant he had to give a speech on graduation night. Because Juice was enrolled in the Witness Protection Program, his speech was recorded on a video cassette and projected on a gigantic television screen above the craning heads of friends and family. My father was there. Mom was still AWOL. Juice's dad was in rehab. Det. Thomas was in jail. And Valilian Compton sat among federal agents in the front row of the civic hall, nodding at the screen.

Juice said, "I wanna dedicate this to my father, and to my late brother E-Eye, and to my mom, and Toby Sligh. And I would also like to dedicate this speech to Jerry Kickliter, the best high school counselor a crack dealer ever had. And I would also like to thank Sacred Heart High School for teaching me what it means to take part in your community. Whatever else you heard about the Jesuits, forget it. They a righteous bunch of fellas. And they got it going *on.* . . . Now I'd like to begin this graduation address by telling you the story of two boys and a statue. And how they knocked it over. And how they picked it up again. It may sound made-up, but it's a true story. Like all the best stories, *it only sounds like a lie.* . . ."

✸ TOWARD THE END of summer I helped Juice play hooky from the Witness Protection Program in which he was enrolled. We shook off the agents and played Scrabble with my father and rented Bruce Lee movies and drank Magnum malt liquor. Then, when we were sober, we drove to Dr. Wu's, where Wu had been waiting for over three months to give us the results of our HIV tests.

We went in.

"You're negative," Dr. Wu announced.

We kissed her.

"But you should get tested again."

 "MY MOTHER WAS moving out of the house, and she took me out of school that afternoon to help her. . . ."

ONE NIGHT, THE week before I headed off for college, at the end of a summer of insufferable heat, when my father and I slept blanketless in our beds in only our underwear, with all the windows open, I felt a clammy hand applying pressure on my thigh, and I woke to see her seated like a shadow at my bedside, her slender arms folded, a suitcase at her feet.

"Hi, Toby," Mom said.

Her bangs were in her eyes. I brushed them away. We could hear my father snoring.

"You back?" I asked.

"I guess."

She sort of sniffled. Outside, a cat was moaning. Mom was shaking in the heat.

"Where have you been?"

"Away," my mother whispered.

"Where is away?"

"*Anywhere . . .* is away."

Mom rose up and floated over to a window. The curtains bloomed about her and moonlight flooded in. Her skin looked blue and incredibly fluid. She sat back down. She was looking in my eyes.

"Toby," she began, "you know I love your father—"

"*Is* he my father?"

She took my hands in hers.

"I guess he is, Toby. I guess he's your father. He loves you like a father."

I listened in the dark.

"Tell me—"

"*I made some mistakes when I was younger.*"

"Tell me the truth."

She wove her fingers into mine.

"I kinda I fell in love with your uncle and your father. We did things, Toby. We did things—together. And when I got pregnant I was mad at everybody. Mad at those two, and mad at myself, and mad at my parents—who didn't give a shit. I remember I stole my mom's wedding dress and the Chevy Corvair your dad and uncle used to cruise in. I drove here, Toby. I drove to this city. And I said, 'Whoever finds me, that's the one I want—' "

"Who found you?"

"Your dad did. A week before I had you. He wanted us to marry, but I didn't see the point. I told him to go, but he wouldn't go, Toby. And then you came along. And he's been with us ever since."

Somewhere across the house we could hear my father snoring. My mother wove her fingers through my fingers in the dark.

"So imagine how I felt when your uncle shows up after seventeen years—just imagine, Toby Sligh! He said he was a cop, but I knew he was a liar. He wanted me back. I could see it in his eyes. He said he had pictures of you and Leonard Compton. He said you two were dealing crack cocaine across the city—"

"That's a lie."

"I know it is. But your father, he believed him. Juice had tried to sell us marijuana, after all. And when your uncle promised to bust Leonard Compton and extricate you, I knew it was a ploy. He wanted me, Toby. *And I still had feelings for him.* And when your father tried to help him—"

"You ran away. Again."

"I said, 'Whoever finds me, that's the one who loves me.' And this time I'll get married. This time 'I'll thee wed.' And you know who found me, Toby? You know who found your mother? The boy who loved my baby . . . Ian Lamb did."

"Ian never loved me!"

I was suddenly bawling.

"Of course he loves you, Toby!"

I was crying in her arms.

"It's okay. *Shhh!* It's okay, Toby Sligh. It's okay to be gay. And it's okay to love somebody. But just because you're gay, and just because you love somebody, don't expect anybody but yourself to understand. *First you gotta figure yourself out, kiddo.* That's why I went away. And that's why I'm back again. Stand up," my mother said.

I stood up in the darkness. I was crying in my underwear. Mom snapped back the elastic.

"Where's your father?"

"Snoring."

"Does he need me?"

"Do you love him?"

She nodded. "Uh-huh."

"All right, then. *Follow me. . . .*"

I led her to the bedroom where Dad lay on the mattress, his arms above his head like a kid on a rollercoaster relishing the biggest and most delicious dip.

"You sure you wanna do this?" I said to my mother, in the darkness, in the bedroom, underneath my father's breathing. "If you love Det. Thomas, if you love my uncle more, you could always steal away and I wouldn't tell a soul. You can trust me, Ma. It would be, you know, *our secret.* I've lied for you before; I can lie for you again. Faggots, you know, we're *excellent* liars. It's, like, our second nature. We got it in our *blood.*"

"No more lies, Toby Sligh," my mother said, and kissed me on the forehead, and crept in bed beside him. Already my father was coming alive, like Lazarus, like a patient arising out of ether. "Close the door behind you," Mom whispered. And I did. And I heard my father speaking. And I heard the boxsprings sing.

BEFORE I WENT to bed I opened up my mother's suitcase, and I sat there in the moonlight, and I looked at all the pictures.

They were Kodak Instamatics of Mom and of Ian, in New Orleans, on a streetcar, in a steamboat, in a bar. They were pals, I could tell. They were sitting having coffee. They were buying gladiolas. They were by the Mississippi. And Ian Lamb's eyes were dark and scarred with circles, his dimpled chin forever averted from the camera. But in one, just one photo, Ian Lamb was looking at me, and holding up a rose, and smiling through his fear. *Here,* his eyes said, his smile said, his flower said, *I don't know if it's love, I can't say that it's true, but it's yours, Toby Sligh. Will you take it?*

And I took it.

And I dreamt of him that night. And I dreamt of Fr. Scarcross. And I dreamt of Angelina. And of Juice. And of my parents. We were waltzing. Really waltzing. All together, we were waltzing. It was true, every bit of it. . . .

And for now, the lies were over.